TRACKING A KILLER

"So why are you pursuing this story now that Derek is dead?" Daisy asked.

"None of the rumors I've followed about the show being canceled, about why he changed co-hosts, have panned out. I thought that was a bit suspicious. If there was a scandal, that type of thing always resurfaces . . . or something else happens. I'd like to be the first reporter to break the story. Since Derek was from Willow Creek, since his chef show began in Lancaster, since he died here, I think it's a good place to start."

Daisy summed it up. "So what you're saying is that Derek's bad professional history led to his murder."

"I believe it's an exceptional possibility." Clementine ate the remainder of her scone. Wiping crumbs from her mouth, she declared, "This is delicious. If Derek didn't give you a good review, then either something had spoiled his palate . . . or his peace of mind."

Daisy knew either of those reasons could lead to murder . . .

Books by Karen Rose Smith

Caprice DeLuca Mysteries
STAGED TO DEATH

DEADLY DÉCOR

GILT BY ASSOCIATION

DRAPE EXPECTATIONS

SILENCE OF THE LAMPS

SHADES OF WRATH

SLAY BELLS RING

CUT TO THE CHAISE

Daisy's Tea Garden Mysteries
MURDER WITH LEMON TEA CAKES

MURDER WITH CINNAMON SCONES

MURDER WITH CUCUMBER SANDWICHES

Published by Kensington Publishing Corporation

Murder
with Cucumber
Sandwiches

KAREN ROSE SMITH

KENSINGTON PUBLISHING CORP.
www.kensingtonbooks.com

KENSINGTON BOOKS are published by

Kensington Publishing Corp.
119 West 40th Street
New York, NY 10018

All Kensington titles, imprints, and distributed lines are available at special quantity discounts for bulk purchases for sales promotions, premiums, fund-raising, educational, or institutional use. Special book excerpts or customized printings can also be created to fit specific needs. For details, write or phone the office of the Kensington sales manager: Kensington Publishing Corp., 119 West 40th Street, New York, NY 10018, attn: Sales Department; phone 1-800-221-2647.

ISBN-13: 978-1-61773-964-4
ISBN-10: 1-61773-964-2

First printing: June 2019

10   9   8   7   6   5   4   3   2   1

Printed in the United States of America

Electronic edition:

ISBN-13: 978-1-61773-965-1 (e-book)
ISBN-10: 1-61773-965-0 (e-book)

*To Delynn Royer, fellow writer, good friend,
and first reader on my mystery projects.*

*If she doesn't spot whodunit,
I've accomplished my writing goal!
Thank you, Delynn, for your ongoing support.*

ACKNOWLEDGMENTS

I would like to thank Officer Greg Berry, my law enforcement consultant, who so patiently answers all my questions. His input is invaluable.

Chapter One

"I can't believe how he trashed that tea room," Foster Cranshaw said, studying Daisy Swanson's office computer screen on a Monday morning in mid-March.

Sitting at the desktop computer, Daisy worried her lower lip. Daisy's Tea Garden hadn't opened yet for daily business. She and her aunt Iris, who was her partner in the tea garden, had switched on the computer and googled Derek Schumacher. Soon, he'd be giving his professional opinion on Daisy's Tea Garden's offerings.

Foster was one of Daisy's assistants and her social media expert to boot. She'd become fond of him, in part, because he was dating her daughter Violet who was on spring break from college. She would be coming into the tea garden tomorrow to help out. When Foster had arrived for his morning shift, he'd brought up Derek Schumacher's blog to check on the critic's latest reviews.

"He's reviewing several tea rooms," Aunt Iris reminded them. "He can't give *everybody* a good review."

"He can if the food is good," Foster muttered,

pushing his rimless glasses up higher on the bridge of his nose.

Although her aunt was repeating a practical line, Daisy could see Iris was worried, too, by the way she brushed her ash-brown curls up over her brow. She did that when she was anxious.

"Maybe he can't give everybody a good review," Daisy murmured, "but he doesn't have to be this harsh." She read his review aloud. "'Virginia has many elegant tea rooms. The Flowered Tea Cup isn't one of them.'" Daisy's voice rose as she continued. "'The bread on their sandwiches was as dry as the sand in the Mojave Desert.'"

Daisy clicked on a link for another review. "He says that Carla's Tea and Concessions served strawberry jam that stuck to his teeth like glue. Why did I *ever* agree to let him come here to taste our food and tea?" When she shook her head in exasperation, her blond low ponytail swished over her shoulder.

Foster straightened and backed away from the computer. "You accepted his request because publicity is good for any tea room."

"Not bad publicity," Iris warned Foster. "If he determines our food isn't tasty, it could hurt our business."

Daisy turned her head and peered through the glass windows of her office across the hall to the kitchen. Then her glance swerved to the doorway that led into the main tea room.

Daisy and her aunt had purchased this Victorian when Daisy had returned to Willow Creek, Pennsylvania—deep in Lancaster County—about a year after her husband died. When she'd made the decision to return to her hometown instead of remaining in Florida, she'd known she and her two daughters had needed a change . . . and a fresh start. Her aunt Iris had always been a tea aficionado. Daisy's degree in nutrition and her love of cooking had made partnering with her aunt an easy decision. Ever since Daisy's childhood, her aunt had been a stalwart supporter of any project she'd taken on.

The pale green Victorian with its white trim, ginger-bread edging, and covered porch had once housed a bakery. Converting it to a tea garden, with an apartment up above where her kitchen manager Tessa Miller lived, hadn't been too difficult. Two main front rooms on the first floor hosted their customers. They could be served or buy tea and goodies to-go in the main room, where the walls were the palest green to promote calm just as tea did. The room was furnished with oak, glass-top tables. The second room facing the street was a spillover area. With its walls the palest yellow and its bay window, that room was used when they were extremely busy or when they took reservations and served afternoon tea by appointment. Weather permitting, they also served tea, baked goods, soups, and salads on the side patio. In mid-March, with the first hint of spring in the air, their tourist business was picking up again.

Foster broke into Daisy's musings. "Derek Schumacher as a chef wasn't this nasty when he had his TV show. He traveled to popular restaurants and brought home cooks from the area to the restaurant to cook. The best cook won kitchen appliances. No one really knows why he left the show and began critiquing food instead of cooking it. His reputation as a chef had really taken off. He even had his own line of cookware on one of the home shopping channels."

Daisy continued to read a few reviews of other tea

rooms Schumacher had visited. She pointed to a line of text on the screen. "In this review, he said the tea room's pound cake was as heavy as lead."

"Maybe he thinks because he's a food critic he *has* to be critical," Foster decided.

"That does not make me feel any better," Daisy said.

Foster pointed to a number at the bottom of the screen. "Just look at how many views his blog gets. That's why advertisers line up to market their products on his website."

Daisy blew out a breath. "Maybe he has that many hits because of his controversial way of reviewing. It's hard to believe his TV show became so popular. It had its beginnings in a studio in Lancaster. He lives in Willow Creek, you know. It's his home base."

"Maybe that means he'll be kinder to us," Iris suggested.

"Or harder on us so his audience doesn't think he's playing favorites," Foster explained. "I understand that Derek and his brother Bradley are opposites."

"Bradley Schumacher?" Daisy repeated. *Where* had she heard that name?

"His brother is the principal of the high school," Foster elaborated. "Everybody there thinks he's terrific— a great role model."

Now Daisy remembered. She'd seen Bradley Schumacher's name on the program when Vi had graduated. Her daughter Jazzi, who was a sophomore, had mentioned his name lately in regard to the talent show the school would be putting on. Jazzi had been texting with Vi about it for weeks, discussing what to sing, what to wear, and how to keep the jitters at bay.

"I can't quite picture Bradley Schumacher," Daisy

said. Fortunately, Jazzi was a good student and hadn't had any association with the principal. Vi's senior year at the school had passed quickly without incident. Her older daughter had been focused on getting accepted at Lehigh University.

Foster shrugged. "He looks like an average guy . . . not too tall, not too short, brown hair and glasses."

"I believe Jazzi said he stops in at the practices for the talent show." Changing the subject and trying to divert her attention away from Derek Schumacher's visit the following week, Daisy said to Foster, "I hope Vi will be able to get home for Jazzi's show Easter weekend. How are her end-of-the-semester projects going?" She knew Violet talked to Foster about school projects more than she talked about them at home.

"She's on schedule with her research papers. It depends on how much progress she makes until then . . . although she is determined to come home for Easter."

"I certainly understand that, and I know Jazzi will too. But she'll be disappointed if Vi doesn't make it home."

Violet and Foster both were in their first year of college, although Foster was a year ahead of Vi. He was attending nearby Millersville University. At twenty, he had a mature head on his shoulders, was paying room and board to his dad to earn independence, and took as many hours to work as Daisy could schedule him at the tea garden. He'd also set up websites for a few other businesses in Willow Creek. He was definitely a self-starter with a huge dose of ingenuity.

Suddenly, Tessa appeared in the doorway. Entering the office, she said, "Good morning, everyone." She hung her sweater coat on the wooden coat rack in the corner.

Iris headed toward the door. "I'd better put the blueberry scones in the case. Foster, do you want to pull the salads out of the walk-in?"

Daisy rose from the computer. "I'll put the soup on. I'm planning chicken noodle for today."

When merely Daisy and Tessa remained in the office, Tessa asked her, "So what were you all doing in here?"

"Checking Derek Schumacher's reviews. That was a mistake. He can actually be vicious. What if he gives us one of those miserable reviews?"

"He won't," Tessa assured her.

"How can you be so sure?"

"Because we're going to make each item we serve him perfect, tasty, and the best we know how." Tessa hung her arm around Daisy's shoulders. "Right?"

Daisy had to laugh. Tessa had been her cheerleader in school too. They'd been best friends when they'd skipped a grade, and they still were now. Having Tessa as her kitchen manager had made opening the tea garden an even more special endeavor.

After Daisy had put the soup on and her servers had arrived, she baked lemon tea cakes until Iris called her to the counter to help three women who wanted to take along Daisy's special blend of tea. Customers came and went all morning along with two buses full of tourists. Daisy didn't even think about lunch as she worked beside Iris and her servers to maintain steady service.

To Daisy's surprise, her mother entered the tea garden around three o'clock. Her mom and dad owned and ran Gallagher's Garden Corner, a nursery that serviced Willow Creek and the surrounding area. Rose Gallagher was as involved in the business as her husband Sean. It was unusual for her to be out and about instead of at the nursery on an early spring afternoon.

As her mother hurried to the counter, her ash-blond hair permed tightly around her head hardly moved. As usual she wore a bright pink lipstick. She was dressed in a knit pantsuit because casual clothes were what she wore for a day at the nursery. The steel blue color of it matched her eyes. Daisy's eyes were more like her dad's—sky blue—and she hoped they held the twinkle that his did. Right now, however, she forgot about her father and focused on her mom, who wasn't smiling.

The tea room had quieted for the moment as it often did midafternoon unless they were serving tea by appointment.

"It's good to see you, Mom, but this is a surprise."

"No doubt it is," her mother said, looking tense.

"Is something wrong? Did Dad get hurt carrying a tree ball?" Daisy worried that as her father aged, he wouldn't be able to keep up with the physical demands of the nursery.

"Nothing like that," her mother snapped.

Daisy and her mother had clashed more than once since Daisy had returned to Willow Creek. There were lots of reasons for that. The main one—her mom's critical attitude. That's why Daisy and her aunt Iris had always been close. Although sisters, Iris's personality and Daisy's mother's were very different.

The latest clash concerned the man Daisy was

dating—Jonas Groft. He was a former detective and now the owner of Woods, a store that sold hand-crafted furniture, some of which Jonas made himself. Rose didn't believe Jonas had the ambition he should have, or that he was thinking seriously about having a family to care for. Daisy had made the mistake of telling her mother that she and Jonas were taking their relationship very slowly. However, they'd been dating steadily since January when Daisy had become involved in her second murder investigation. She and Jonas were both happy with the way things stood, and she didn't want her mother interfering. But Rose Gallagher's interference was a given.

"I didn't come to have a cup of tea or chat," her mother explained. "I came to see your aunt. Where is Iris?"

Daisy knew sisters argued. She and her own sister certainly did. Vi and Jazzi did sometimes, yet there was always an underlying bond. Since she'd returned to Willow Creek, Daisy hadn't felt that bond between her mother and her aunt Iris.

"She's in the kitchen," Daisy said. "I'll let her know you're here. The two of you can use my office if you need to talk."

"We certainly do." Her mother marched into Daisy's office as if she owned it.

Daisy entered the kitchen and crossed to her aunt, who was running the mixer. Iris's ash-brown curls were bound in a hairnet. At five-foot-six, she was about three inches taller than her sister. But the laugh lines, rather than worry lines, around her eyes and her ready smile set her apart.

Unable to hear above the sounds of the running

mixer, Daisy placed a hand on her aunt's shoulder to get her attention.

Iris glanced around and turned off the machine.

"Mom's here to see you. Do you know what it's about?"

"I have no idea," Iris responded with a shake of her head. "I guess she can't wait until I finish mixing up this scone batter?"

"I'll handle the scones. Go ahead and see what she wants. She's in our office."

Iris headed that way. After Daisy finished mixing the scone batter, Eva Connor, Daisy's dishwasher and Girl Friday, said she'd scoop them out if Daisy wanted to join her mom and her aunt. Daisy let Eva take over the scones as she hurried to the office.

Daisy stopped outside the closed door because her mother's voice was raised. But through the glass window, Daisy could see the anger in her mother's eyes.

"You should never have encouraged Sean to go on a fishing trip. He's leaving on Thursday." Rose's cheeks were dotted with color, and she looked more upset than Daisy had seen her in a while.

"You can survive, Rose," Iris said. "Sean told me he has plenty of help coming in."

"This is our busiest season at the nursery. Sure, we have help, but they don't run things, and I can't run everything without Sean."

"Can't you give the people you hire more responsibility? Sean said even his temp employees would work more hours."

Rose's face, already with high color, reddened more. "You just don't understand what running a business is like."

Iris crossed her arms over her chest. "I think I do. Daisy's Tea Garden is a business."

"Maybe so, but it's very different from the nursery. I can understand Sean needing an escape for a day or two. But a whole week?"

"He's only going upstate," Iris pointed out. "It's not as if he'll be that far away."

"Well, he's not going to drive back here to take care of a special order or to clear the network if the computer goes down."

Daisy was about to enter the office to intervene, but she stopped when her aunt said, "Maybe you should give Sean freedom to do what he wants. Maybe you'd both be happier that way."

Daisy expected an explosion . . . but it didn't come. Instead, her mother pushed the office door open and said to Daisy, "I'll see you this weekend."

Daisy was going to try to follow her and catch her, to find out why she was really upset. But her mother gave her no chance to do that. Rose rushed through the tea room, swiftly passing Jonas as he strode in.

He was over six feet, lean and perceptive. A scar marred his cheek but only made his face more interesting. With silver at the temples of his black hair, he represented a picture of what a detective on TV or in the movies might look like. But his years as a detective in Philadelphia had been very real rather than pretend. He, too, had come to Willow Creek for a fresh start.

When Jonas arched a questioning brow at Daisy, she felt world-tilting attraction for him that could take over her dreams and desires if she let it. His green eyes sometimes seemed to see straight through to her heart, and she was hard pressed to deny her growing feelings for him.

He must have seen her frustration or maybe her fatigue from a full day of waiting on customers. On the other hand, perhaps he recognized her worry about the food critic and the argument between Aunt Iris and her mother. He came up to Daisy and asked, "Would you like to take a break? You can come to my workshop and see the reclaimed wood island I just finished."

Could she? "I should talk to Aunt Iris first. She might be upset. She and Mom had a disagreement."

"If she is upset, she might need to calm down a bit before she wants to talk."

Jonas was probably right. "Do I need my jacket?"

"Haven't you been out since you came in this morning? It's warm for March."

"No. I didn't take time for lunch either."

"Do you want to take along soup? I don't think you'll need your jacket."

She pulled the bow from the tie of her apron at her back waist. She liked the Tea Garden's aprons with their huge daisies and DAISY'S TEA GARDEN printed on the front. But she'd rather just walk around in her normal clothes—a pair of navy slacks and a pale blue, boat-neck top. "I'll just tell Aunt Iris I'm leaving."

Five minutes later, they were walking to Jonas's shop, which was located behind his store. "I told Aunt Iris we'd talk when I get back. She'll have time to gather her thoughts, and I'll be fortified with fresh air and soup."

Jonas raised the bag she'd handed him. "This feels heavier than soup for one."

"That's because it's soup for two with pecan tarts thrown in."

He smiled. "You just want to make sure I eat healthy snacks."

"I do. Sometimes I think you're addicted to fast food."

He cut her an amused sideways glance. "Not addicted. It's just more convenient than cooking. But I know *you* don't fall into that trap."

"It would be easy to order pizza every night," Daisy admitted. "But I've always wanted to teach Violet and Jazzi the right way to eat. Maybe it's the dietician in me."

"Dietician?" Jonas asked. "Have you mentioned that before?"

Daisy took in a huge breath of fresh spring air. "I guess I haven't. It's no secret. It just never came up."

"Where did you work?"

"I was a dietician at a hospital. I also gave workshops on nutrition and saw patients that general practitioners diagnosed with diabetes. Nutrition has always been important to me, and I've taught Violet and Jazzi why."

"I guess we'll just have to spend more time together so I can learn details about you."

"Same here," she said. It had taken Jonas a while to tell her his background and why he'd come to Willow Creek.

Jonas held the door open to his shop so Daisy could precede him inside. They both waved to Elijah, an Amish craftsman, who also built furniture for Woods.

Jonas guided Daisy through the showroom and out a back door that led to his workshop area and office. It always smelled like fresh-sawed wood back here. Jonas had an excellent ventilation system, so only a touch of the scent of stain was evident. Since his office in the far corner was small, he motioned to a card table with two folding chairs in the work area. They'd shared lunch here many times over the past few months.

As Jonas pulled two bottles of water from the small fridge, Daisy unpacked the soup containers. "It's chicken soup today," she said.

"One of my favorites."

"They're *all* one of your favorites," she joked.

Their gazes met as he sat across from her, and Daisy felt that fluttering in her stomach that wasn't from hunger for lunch.

Jonas Groft was an enigma to her sometimes. He could be reserved, yet he could also be compassionate and a good communicator. She imagined his years as a detective made him wary and not too trusting. Also, what had happened between him and his partner had been a trust issue that seemed like betrayal. Unwise for partners, they'd been having an affair. Without telling Jonas, Brenda had had her IUD removed and had gotten pregnant. They'd argued and gone to their shift, lots of tension between them. While investigating a murder suspect that night, they'd been ambushed. Brenda had been killed and Jonas injured.

When he'd told Daisy about it, she'd seen how fresh the trauma still was even though he didn't want to believe that. However, lately he'd been more open with her, smiled more, seemed to take joy in their dates. Kissing Jonas was one of the utmost pleasures in her life.

Opening his soup container, he asked, "Do you want to tell me why your mom was in such a tizzy when she left?"

"I'm not exactly sure, but it seems my dad is planning a fishing trip. My mom doesn't want him to go, but

Aunt Iris encouraged him to go. Aunt Iris thinks my mom needs to give him some space. I don't know why that is, and that worries me a little."

When Jonas didn't say anything but dipped his spoon into his soup, Daisy asked, "Do you have an opinion about it?"

"It's probably not a good idea for me to give an opinion."

"I want you to be honest with me," Daisy prompted. "What do you think?"

Jonas seemed to go into detective mode. "Does your father often go away like this?"

"No, hardly ever. He fished when Cammie and I were kids, but he usually did that on family outings when we went camping."

Jonas tasted the soup and gave her a wink and a smile. After he savored his spoonful of chicken, broth, carrots, and peas, he asked, "So going away without your mother isn't usual?"

Opening her own container of soup, Daisy just stared at it a moment. "No, and leaving her to handle the business alone during a busy time of year isn't usual either."

Jonas dipped his spoon into the bowl again. "Then I'd say your father's probably going away to think about something. Maybe he just needs quiet time to make decisions."

When Daisy considered that conclusion, her mind took flight. What if her dad had health problems he hadn't revealed? What if the nursery was in financial trouble?

Knowing Daisy and her dad were close, Jonas held up his hand like a stop sign. "Don't think of everything that could be wrong. The reason for this trip could be simple—your dad needs a break. Wait until he tells you what's going on. Then if you have to worry, there will be plenty of time to do it."

Daisy just gazed at Jonas's face, at the lines that said he'd experienced life in hard ways. She liked the way his black hair fell over his brow in a slight wave, and that he didn't care if it was perfectly styled. She liked the way his green eyes got all deep and mysterious when he was thinking about kissing her. They were that way now.

She laid her spoon on the table. Jonas got up and walked around the table to her chair. He held out his hand and she took it, standing. Then he kissed her, and she felt her knees wobble and her heart race.

When they came up for air, he said, "I just couldn't wait to do that."

"I'm glad you couldn't."

He fingered the strand of her blond hair at the end of her ponytail. Then he cleared his throat. "Let's finish that soup and then I'll show you the reclaimed wood island."

They were both trying to maintain control of their relationship and everything else that was happening between them.

But sometimes control was highly overrated.

Chapter Two

On Tuesday evening, Daisy dug her fingers into the bowl of ground ham and pork to form meatballs. After she rounded one, she placed it on the cookie sheet where she'd already formed three rows. Jonas was coming over for supper tonight. He liked ham balls over rice with sweet and sour sauce, and so did Jazzi. It was a meal Daisy could make in an hour, which was an advantage after a busy day at the tea garden. She'd invited Vi and Foster, but they were driving to Harrisburg for dinner with Foster's friends.

Daisy expected Jonas any minute. She smiled when she thought about him . . . when she thought about *them*. She was careful when thinking about what could be in store with their future, but being with Jonas filled a void in her life. With him, she felt as if she were more than a mother, more than a business owner, more than a widow.

Daisy glanced through the dining area—where a floor-to-ceiling fireplace was a focal point—into the living room where Jazzi was stretched out on the sofa. A huge wagon wheel chandelier lit the area. Jazzi had earbuds in her ears, a notebook and pen in her hand, and Pepper—their black tuxedo cat—stretched across her lap on the blue, green, and cream plaid sofa. Marjoram, a tortoiseshell kitty with unique markings, kept them both company by lying on the blue, green, and rust-braided rugs woven by a local Amish woman.

Jazzi's phone sat charging on the dock on the kitchen counter. Daisy had just shifted the tray of ham balls into the oven and closed the oven door, when her daughter's phone played a favorite pop tune. Jazzi obviously didn't hear it, and Daisy glanced at it to see who was calling.

Portia Smith Harding's face stared back at her from the screen. Portia was Jazzi's birth mother. Quickly disengaging the phone from its charger, she hurried into Jazzi and tapped her on the shoulder. "It's Portia." She spoke loudly enough that Jazzi could hear her even with her earbuds in.

Jazzi pulled the neon green buds from her ears and eagerly took the phone, accepting the call. *Thanks, Mom*, she mouthed before she answered.

Daisy would have liked to have stayed and listened in, but of course, she couldn't do that. She could only hope Jazzi would fill her in on the phone call afterward. Up until now, Jazzi had been open about what she thought and felt concerning Portia. Daisy hoped that would continue.

In the next few minutes, Daisy started Carolina rice on her stovetop. After she'd turned down the heat to let it cook for twenty minutes, she took a saucepan from the cupboard. It was probably a little early to make the sweet and sour sauce, but it could simmer. Should she text Jonas to see if he was on his way?

She convinced herself that wasn't necessary. She

could keep everything warm if he was late. The rice might be a little mushy, the green beans overcooked, but it would all be edible.

She'd mixed the sauce and let it thicken, when the low buzz of Jazzi's voice in the living room ended. She was smiling as she came into the kitchen and approached Daisy, who was standing at the counter and reaching for a bowl in an upper knotty pine cupboard.

"Good conversation?" Daisy asked.

"Exceptional." Jazzi's brown eyes sparkled, and her voice held a bit of excitement.

"Do you want to tell me about it?"

"I sure do because this could affect you too."

Daisy's pulse raced, but she told herself to calm down. It could simply be that Portia was coming for another visit. "Do you want to sit at the island to talk? I could make us tea."

"Let's sit. But no tea."

Daisy had to smile at that. Tea was her passion, as well as her aunt Iris's. Jazzi appreciated it now and then but not daily.

The aroma of the ham balls and the tangy sweetness of the sauce wafted through the first floor. She waited for Jazzi to tell her what was going on. From experience, she knew that pushing her daughter didn't coax out information any faster. Patience was always best when dealing with Vi and Jazzi . . . with Jonas, too, for that matter.

Jazzi seemed to be bubbling with happiness over whatever Portia had told her. She released a tortoise-shell clip that was holding her straight black hair on top of her head. Then she pulled her hair up, collecting each strand, and fastened it again. "Portia's going away with her husband soon. He has a business trip, and he's taking her along."

"That sounds nice," Daisy commented. "Where are they going?"

"His meetings are in New York State. They're staying at some kind of big resort."

"That sounds like it would be a vacation for her."

Jazzi's eyes flashed with happiness. "It might be, but there's something even more important about it."

"What's that?" Daisy asked the question nonchalantly as if the answer didn't matter at all.

"Portia's going to tell Colton about me. She's counting on alone time with him, and she'll have a chance to explain everything. Isn't that wonderful?"

Would that be wonderful? Daisy wondered.

Portia hadn't yet told her husband about Jazzi. In fact, when Jazzi's biological mother had visited Willow Creek for the weekend, she'd told him she was visiting friends. Lies never worked in a relationship, especially not in a marriage. Daisy knew Portia had been under stress ever since she'd met Jazzi this past fall because she had to keep her daughter a secret.

What to say to Jazzi so she could keep a bit of perspective. "You have your hopes up about this, don't you?"

Jazzi flounced from the stool at the island and practically danced around the kitchen. "How can I not? This will be great. Everybody will know about me. I'll have a half brother and half sister."

Daisy did not want to rain on Jazzi's parade. However, her job as a mom was to make sure her daughter could see all sides.

She motioned for Jazzi to sit again and Jazzi reluctantly did. Daisy began with, "First of all, Portia could back down from doing this if she gets scared, if her husband's too busy, if she doesn't feel the time is right."

"At least she's considering it, and if not on the trip, then soon. I'm sure of it."

"You need to think about something else too," Daisy said.

Now Jazzi looked wary. "What?"

"It depends on how Portia's husband takes the news. That's going to determine your relationship with her."

Seeming actually puzzled, Jazzi shook her head. "I don't understand. Once he knows, he knows. Then we can do everything out in the open—the phone calls, video conferencing, and visits."

To just be hopeful for Jazzi or to give her a dose of reality? "But what if he doesn't want her to visit? What if he doesn't want to accept the fact that she had a child, gave you up for adoption, and never told him about any of it?"

Jazzi's face fell, but then she looked angry. "I won't believe that. I think that's what *you* want to happen. That way, you don't have to deal with Portia. You can still be my mom." Jazzi paused, then added rebelliously, "But you'll never be my biological mom."

Daisy froze . . . hurt. That's what she got for trying to help Jazzi stay realistic.

When Pepper moseyed into the kitchen and meowed, Jazzi took the opportunity to push her stool back and stand. "I'm going upstairs to work on homework. You can call me when dinner's ready."

"Jazzi, wait."

"There's nothing more to talk about, Mom. What I want and what you want are two different things. I'll just be glad when Portia's trip is over and you can see that I'm right."

Contrary to what Jazzi thought, Daisy hoped her daughter *would* be right.

On Monday morning, Cora Sue's bottle-red hair was pulled high on her head in a topknot, and it wiggled a little as she licked her index finger. Bubbly any day of the week, today she appeared to be filled with enthusiasm with Daisy's menu that she was going to serve for afternoon tea service.

Cora Sue popped the last bit of the small sandwich into her mouth. "These pimento and cucumber sandwiches on pumpernickel are delicious. If our service is a hit today, I think you should repeat these sandwiches tomorrow together with the cheesy cauliflower soup. The food critic will think he's died and gone to heaven."

Foster, who had tasted the sandwiches with Cora Sue, nodded. "Definitely. That pimento spread's a winner. Do you think you should add fresh arugula?"

Daisy looked at Cora Sue, and her server gave a nod. "We could try it with and without today and see what your customers say."

Foster bobbed his head again. "That's a great idea."

Foster wore an apron with the daisy on the front just as the rest of the servers. He didn't complain about it either. With his black slacks and white shirt open at the collar, she suspected he was a draw with some of her younger customers. She knew he was certainly a draw with her daughter.

Thinking of Violet again made her smile. She'd gone back to Lehigh yesterday, her break over. Daisy couldn't wait until her older daughter was home for the summer. They could have long chats on summer evenings as they weeded the vegetable garden, take hikes like they used to take on weekends, and barbecue burgers and chicken outside with Jonas.

That was daydreaming, and she shouldn't indulge in it.

She said to Cora Sue and Foster, "Any spare minute you have this morning, help Aunt Iris and Tessa in the kitchen. We have a full house for tea service, and we still have to produce baked goods to fill the case. The morning crowd almost wiped us out."

"I'll handle filling the case and standing at the counter to handle new customers," Foster assured her.

It wasn't unusual to have a lull after the first morning rush. They used it to catch their breath and do whatever was necessary to fill the case for their lunchtime clients.

After Cora Sue and Foster went to the kitchen, Daisy made a quick inventory of the case. When the bell above the door dinged, she looked up and saw Russ Windom coming toward her. Russ was a retired teacher with gray hair that started high on his forehead, bushy white brows, and titanium black glasses. He came in most mornings for baked goods and a cup of tea. A widower with time on his hands, he enjoyed chatting with everyone. He was later than usual today.

Instead of taking a seat, he looked around, peered into the spillover tea room, and beckoned Daisy to the doorway of the other room.

Curious, she met him there. "Good morning, Russ. How are you today?"

"I'm just fine. I know I'm later than usual, but I have a reason for that."

"You do?" Daisy prompted.

He glanced around again and then asked, "Is Iris here?"

"She's in the kitchen baking with Tessa. Would you like me to get her?"

"Oh no. No. That's why I came in later when Iris would be busy. I was hoping to have a word with you."

Now this was an interesting twist. What did he want to have a word about? But she didn't ask. She waited.

Russ was dressed in a plaid shirt with a button-down collar and khaki slacks. He wore sneakers, and Daisy knew he enjoyed a walk every morning after he left the tea garden. His face grew a little redder as she waited to hear his question. He looked uncomfortable and maybe even a bit embarrassed.

"Is something wrong, Russ? Did you buy something you didn't like and you'd like a refund?"

"No, no. Nothing like that. You say Iris is in the kitchen? I don't want her to overhear."

"She won't be able to hear us from there."

"I know this is a little presumptuous of me, but you and your aunt are close."

"If it's a personal question, you should really ask her."

"Yes, well, I know it hasn't been a year since the man Iris was dating was killed."

Now Daisy had no idea where this was going.

"No, it hasn't been."

"That's why I thought I'd talk to you first. I need your opinion. Do you think your aunt would go to a movie with me?"

At Russ's so-serious expression, Daisy almost smiled. But then she knew this was no smiling matter for him or for her aunt. She really didn't know if her aunt was ready to date again.

"To tell you the truth, Russ, I don't know what Aunt Iris would say. But I do know it won't hurt to ask."

Russ didn't look disappointed but rather pleased with that assessment. "You think I should take the risk?"

"I do. What's the worst that could happen?"

He frowned. "She'll say no and I'll have ruined our friendship."

"It doesn't have to be ruined. If she's not ready, just tell her you'll ask again in a few months. That will prepare her and maybe she'll *get* ready."

At that, Russ chuckled. "Aren't you the smart one."

"No, not smart. But I do have a daughter in college and I've gone through several dating scenarios with her."

"And now Jazzi will date soon."

Daisy groaned. "That idea makes me want to lock her in her room or else buy a time machine to go back a few years."

"Tell me you'd give up your life as it is now to return to the past," Russ suggested.

After Daisy considered that idea, she answered, "No, probably not. And I think *you* are the wise one. How about a cinnamon scone and a cup of tea?"

"That should fortify me for a while. I'll think about what you said. When the moment's right, I'll ask Iris."

Soon after Russ had finished his tea and left, business picked up again with springtime tourists. Sightseers from a bus from Westminster, Maryland, spread across the sidewalk out front. They apparently had been dropped off, then had toured the shops. Now they were finishing their visit by gathering at the tea garden. As Daisy served them a Japanese Sencha green tea with a hint of vanilla, one of the women who looked to be near seventy and was wearing a straw hat said, "That is a beautiful teapot."

The blue-patterned teapot was a favorite of many of Daisy's customers. She revealed, "It's Polish pottery—Olympia." She hadn't covered it with a cozy because she knew she'd be pouring most of it.

"My name is Marge," the woman said, holding her hand out to Daisy.

Daisy smiled and shook it. She could tell this was a customer who would like to talk. But that was what the tea garden was all about—chatting, relaxing, and enjoying tea.

Marge said, "I just bought a new teapot. It's one of those glass pots with an infuser. You can see all around it as the tea leaves swish. It came with jasmine-infused tea flowers, but I can use loose leaf tea too," she elaborated. "And I can even put it in the dishwasher, which is a real relief. Many of my pretty pots I can't do that with."

"I know what you mean," Daisy said. "We hand-wash most of our teapots, and many of our cups and saucers too."

"That means you care." Marge's head bobbed as she looked up at Daisy. "If you're that kind to your china, you'll be that attentive to your tea."

"I like to think so," Daisy assured her. "Enjoy your tea and scones."

Marge was happily doing that as Daisy returned to the kitchen.

In the kitchen, Eva was putting porcelain plates into the cupboard. Tessa was busily arranging more pimento sandwiches on a tiered tray, and Cora Sue . . .

Cora Sue was studying her phone. That was unusual. Maybe she'd had an emergency text.

Daisy lifted a teapot from a trivet on the counter and went to Cora Sue. "Is something wrong?"

Cora Sue's face was a little pale. She usually wore a bit of blush along with her lipstick and eye makeup. But right now even the blush didn't make her cheeks look rosy. She touched Daisy's arm. "Can you come into the office with me for a minute?"

Cora Sue was a dedicated worker. She always seemed to be in a good mood, and she enjoyed talking with their clientele. She was full-time at the tea garden and didn't ask for unexpected days off. She also planned her vacations carefully to think about the other servers.

As Daisy followed Cora Sue, she hoped nothing was wrong. Yet that expression on Cora Sue's face told her something was.

Once in her office, Cora Sue handed Daisy her phone. "Look at this. It's Derek Schumacher's blog."

Daisy hesitated to take the phone. "Reading his reviews the other day was enough. I don't know if I want to look any more."

"This isn't a review."

Something in Cora Sue's tone convinced Daisy to take the phone. "What am I looking at?"

"Scan the comments."

Daisy scanned down the comments without reading Derek Schumacher's latest blog. When she reached the tenth one, she gasped. It read:

You've written your last bad review that ruins a business. Write another one, and you're dead.

Daisy was so glad Jonas was coming over tonight. Her argument with Jazzi about Portia still hurt and bothered her. Maybe talking to Jonas about it would help. They'd be able to talk freely tonight. Daisy needed the warmth of his arm around her shoulders, his sensible conversation, his experience as a detective.

When he rang her doorbell and she opened the door to him, she felt as if her heart was twittering a message she'd never heard before. *He is what he seems. He says what he means. You've fallen whether you wanted to or not.*

Trying to hide the feelings that seemed to bubble up when Jonas was around, she said, "It's just us tonight. Jazzi has soccer practice."

She heard a meow from the deacon's bench. "And the cats, of course."

Marjoram stood, stretched, yawned, and then jumped down from the bench. She came over to Jonas as she almost always did. She looked up at him with her cute split-color face—tan on one side and dark brown on the other—meowed again, and sat on his foot.

"I suppose that means something," he said with a smile as he stooped to pick up the cat.

"You understood her very well. Listen, she's purring."

He stroked Marjoram's back until she started to wiggle in his arms. Then he set her down. By that time Pepper had awakened, found her favorite toy—a long catnip-infused fish—and carried it to Jonas. She just sat and looked up at him.

"I'm not sure she wants the same thing," he told Daisy.

"She doesn't. She wants you to throw it so she can chase it."

Laughing, he stooped, picked up the blue fish, and gently tossed it near the sofa. Pepper went scurrying after it with Marjoram right behind her, trying to win the race.

Tonight, Jonas was dressed in a short-sleeve indigo Henley shirt and stone-washed jeans. But after he'd laughed at the feline antics, his face had gone back to serious, lines around his mouth and eyes deep as if he were in thought. She wondered what was on his mind. She knew he'd tell her in his own time. Jonas sometimes had a difficult task expressing his feelings, but when he did, she knew exactly what he felt.

"I made sauerbraten tonight in the slow cooker, and mac and cheese. I hope you like it."

"I like everything you make," he told her. "Is there anything I can do?" He followed her into the kitchen.

That was another thing about Jonas. He helped no matter what the task. She hadn't met many men like that. "The coleslaw is ready. Just pull it out from the fridge. I just have to take the mac and cheese out of the oven."

"Do you want to sit at the island or the table?"

"The island is fine with me."

She and her girls ate there most of the time. They used the table in the dining area when guests were present. Jonas wasn't a guest anymore.

Jonas cut the sauerbraten while Daisy spooned out the mac and cheese. "I made a light dessert, lemon-sponge pudding. So you might want to save a little room."

"Will do. How was your day?"

Daisy had set her phone on the island. Now she picked it up and tapped it open. "Something a little unusual happened."

His brow creased. "Something to do with that food critic?"

"How did you guess?"

"That's mostly what's on your mind these days, except of course, for Jazzi's situation."

Daisy hadn't known Jonas long, but he definitely knew how to read people. "You're right. That's mostly what's on my mind. I'd like your opinion about this." She handed him the phone so he could read the comment.

He scrolled up, then he scrolled down. He stopped on the comment again.

"Do you think that person really means it?" Daisy asked.

Jonas shrugged. "In my experience, comments like that usually come from a relative or a friend of the person who received the bad review. Most of the time, those comments don't amount to anything."

"But what if it does? What if this person means what he says? His user name is 'avidfollower.'"

"I saw that, and yes, he or she could be a crazy stalker."

Daisy never thought about the post being from a woman.

Jonas went on, "My guess is Schumacher probably notified the police and they're looking into it. After all, he is a celebrity of sorts."

"Of sorts," Daisy grumbled.

Jonas patted her hand. "You'll do fine. Your food is good."

"I bet the last tea shop owner thought her food was good too. Don't try to placate me with that everything-will-be-fine platitude, because I'm not buying it." She eyed him because that had just come pouring out. Many times in her life, her intelligence had been underestimated because of her blue eyes and blond hair. So sometimes she was a bit defensive.

Jonas, however, seemed unperturbed. "I really do think everything will be fine in your case. But I do understand how worried you are about it."

Taking a breath, still sensing a serious undercurrent about Jonas tonight, she asked, "Is something causing *you* worry?"

Jonas took a mouthful of sauerbraten and then one of the mac and cheese. "I did learn something today that's worrisome. To me, at least."

She waited, hoping he'd trust her with everything he was thinking and feeling.

Finally, he went on. "One of the detectives I worked with in Philadelphia is taking a job with the Willow Creek Police Department. He's going to be Rappaport's partner."

"Do you know him well?" She couldn't understand why that would be worrisome for Jonas.

"His name is Zeke Willet."

Suddenly, Daisy saw pain in Jonas's eyes. She'd only seen that kind of pain once before when he'd told her what had happened with his partner and lover. She'd been pregnant with his child when she'd been shot and killed. What about Zeke Willet made that pain in Jonas's eyes return?

After a pause, Jonas revealed, "Zeke was friends with Brenda, and he blames me for her death."

Chapter Three

The food critic was coming today. Daisy was beyond nervous as she sliced cucumbers and set them out to drain. She was ticking off the items on the list in her mind of other things she still had to do when Foster came into the kitchen. He was frowning and looked . . . troubled.

There were preparations going on all around Daisy. Her staff was as nervous as she was. Eva was making sure every teapot shone without a water spot, the cups and saucers too. On her left, Tessa was cutting triangles of rye and pumpernickel bread. On her right, Cora Sue drained pimentos, while Aunt Iris and Foster had been taking care of breakfast customers.

"Karina just came in," Foster told Daisy.

This was an all-hands-on-deck day. Aunt Iris would be directing Karina on what she needed to do to ready their reservations-only tea room.

Foster's brown hair fell over his brow when he asked, "Can I talk to you for a minute?"

Not feeling she had any spare minutes, Daisy took a deep breath. After all, she was one of the bosses.

If an employee needed to talk, she had to be there for them.

"Back in five," she told everyone in the kitchen. Then she motioned to Foster to step outside with her. A breath of spring air could calm down her adrenaline . . . maybe.

They were hardly out the door when Foster asked, "Can I leave early today? I'll juggle my schedule with anyone who will cover for me."

"When do you want to leave?"

"I'd like to leave now. But I'll stay until we serve Derek Schumacher."

Daisy looked toward the outside entrance to Tessa's apartment and to the cars parked in the designated area for staff and customers with disabilities. She didn't want to press Foster too hard. She'd rather wait to see if he'd tell her why he needed the day off.

He didn't explain. He just nervously switched from one foot to the other and stared down at the creek at the rear of the property.

"Is there anything I can help with?" Daisy wanted to know.

"No," Foster blurted out. "I just need the time free. That's all."

Daisy could feel the seconds that she needed for prep time ticking away, and it didn't seem Foster wanted to tell her any more than he had. Still she asked, "Foster, are you sure you're okay?"

"I'm fine. I hate to leave you in the lurch, but there's something I really need to take care of."

"All right. If we plan well, we'll be able to serve afternoon tea without you."

After another glance at the cloudless blue sky, at

the budding willows and maples farther down the property, Foster nodded and started back inside.

Daisy thought he'd looked at the world as if he'd never see it in the same way again. Something was going on with him. Maybe his father knew what was wrong. Then again, maybe not. Twenty-year-olds didn't always talk to their parents.

Hoping Foster would eventually tell her why he needed the time off, she followed him inside.

With the arrival of spring, the flow of guests for the afternoon tea service was a parade of mostly pastel dresses and blouses. A few customers even wore fascinators. Tourists had also dressed in jeans.

As Cora Sue checked off the names with reservations, Daisy watched for Derek Schumacher. She had seen his photo on his blog, so she knew what he looked like. She spotted him immediately. After he opened the door and stepped inside, she saw that he was tall and lean and had wavy brown hair that looked professionally styled. His brows were a darker brown that seemed to emphasize his golden-brown eyes. In dark brown slacks with a camel blazer over a cream-colored shirt, he was quite handsome. He sported one of those scruffy beards, the kind that looked like the man hadn't shaved in a few days.

While Derek studied the tea garden with what appeared to be an analytical perusal, Daisy approached him. "Hello, Mr. Schumacher. Welcome to Daisy's Tea Garden. I'm Daisy Swanson. Let me introduce you to my aunt Iris, the co-owner of Daisy's."

Derek Schumacher didn't exactly smile, though he did extend his hand when she did. Then he proclaimed, "Your name, the name of the tea garden, your aunt, and your daughters all have flower names. Very quaint."

From the way he said it, she didn't think it was a compliment. He must have seen her daughters' names on the tea garden's website. There had been a line in the text about her daughters working at the tea garden with her.

After she introduced Schumacher to her aunt, she showed him to his place setting at a table for one.

Seated, he picked up one of her dessert plates decorated with tiny pink roses. Turning it over, he stated, "It's Bavarian. I've seen the pattern before. Quite common."

He still hadn't smiled. Daisy felt like saying, *If you smile, you'll be more handsome.* But the arrogant self-important air surrounding him kept her silent.

From Schumacher's blog, Daisy knew he preferred to have afternoon tea on a day when the tea room took reservations for service. That way he could gauge service style as well as taste food.

After she brought him a pot of Daisy's blend tea and poured it into his cup, the critic took a small camera from his inside pocket. He said, "I'm going to take photos to accompany my blog."

He wasn't asking permission. After he spread his napkin on his lap, he took his camera in hand and took several shots of the group seated in the tea room.

While he snapped photos, she asked, "Would you prefer soup or salad or both?" Usually her customers just received one, but this was Derek Schumacher.

"What's the dressing on the salad?"

Karina answered from the table next to his where she was pouring tea, "It's a sweet and sour bacon dressing."

He focused on Daisy instead of her server. "And what is your soup?"

"It's cheesy cauliflower soup."

"All right. I'll take a small serving of each."

A small course of each would require different plating than her servers had already set out for Derek. Daisy hurried to the kitchen, pulled out a pink Depression ware glass dish for the salad and a bowl for the soup. The pink Depression ware complemented the white plates with pink roses she'd chosen for Derek's service.

Daisy watched as Karina crossed to Schumacher's table with his soup and salad. He looked her over from her pink hair, down her yellow apron, to her neon green clogs.

After Karina hurried back to the kitchen, she told Daisy, "He wants an oolong tea next. He also asked for another glass of water. He drank that first one down pretty quickly."

Daisy wondered what *that* was about. Because the weather had warmed up, she'd turned on the air. It wasn't hot in either of the tea rooms.

Soon Cora Sue was delivering maple and walnut scones to Derek along with a raspberry spread.

Moving to the sales counter in the main tea room that was right outside the yellow tea room's doorway, Daisy unabashedly observed the food critic. He was taking his time eating, not hurrying at all. He seemed to enjoy every bite and every sip. However, he did ask for a third refill of water.

Daisy decided to serve him her fresh fruit plate herself. It held selections of kiwi, pineapple chunks, hulled strawberries, and grapes. She'd included a small silver fork.

When she set it down in front of him, she said, "I hope you're enjoying the food."

He didn't comment on the food, but rather sat back in his chair, stroking his chin. "I'm ready for the next course."

Many women would consider him handsome, but she didn't go for his type. Too polished. His fingernails looked as if he might have had a manicure. His blazer looked expensive. She could tell by the way it fit and the sheen of the material. When he'd walked in, she'd noticed his shoes were a supple leather. And then there was his tie. He was wearing a two-tone brown dotted silk tie and it looked like one from the Armani collection that she'd seen in the window at Men's Trends. The tie bar on it held three nice size . . . diamonds? She really doubted that they were rhinestones.

As Daisy spoke to several customers on the way back to the kitchen, she saw Cora Sue bringing Derek a tiered plate of tea sandwiches. She'd also included a bacon and cheddar puff pastry along with chicken salad sandwiches and the cucumber and pimento pumpernickel triangles. Yes, she'd gone all out today. She hadn't had much choice.

As Derek took in his surroundings, he watched the guests, the servers, and Eva as she cleaned his place after each course. When Karina brought him a tiered plate of assorted sweets including a cream puff, a brownie, Snickerdoodles, and a blueberry tart, he smiled. Daisy wondered if that course was his favorite.

Aunt Iris passed the sales counter where Daisy stood. She leaned close and whispered, "I'm so glad I decided not to serve him. My hands would be shaking. I'd spill something."

"Eva, Cora Sue, and Karina are doing a fine job. With Tessa holding down the fort in the kitchen, we're good. Only the sorbet course to go."

Daisy herself presented Derek a lemon sorbet in a pink parfait glass. She moved away after he said *thank you*, letting him recall how much he'd enjoyed the food and the atmosphere.

Ten minutes later Derek Schumacher approached her at the service desk. "Could I have a dozen of those pimento and cucumber sandwiches? I'll snack on them later. They are different. They'd make a nice hors d'oeuvre. And could you also pack up a half dozen of those Snickerdoodles?"

Daisy had a dilemma. Should she offer him the food for free?

His brown eyes caught hers. "No, I can't accept food for free if that's what you're thinking. Just give me a total." Iris was standing nearby, heard his order, and hurried to the kitchen for the sandwiches and cookies.

As Daisy totaled up his purchase, he said, "I know you're dying to ask when the review will be released. I have a few tea rooms to blog about before yours. As soon as I write it, it will go in my pipeline."

And that was all he said until Iris brought his food from the kitchen and handed it to him. Then he nodded, said *thank you* again, and left.

Daisy gazed at Iris. "I have no idea what he's going to write about in his blog."

That evening Daisy pulled another weed from her back garden. Beside her, Jazzi did the same. It seemed odd that Jonas had never really seen her gardens.

Herbs from last year were sprouting and she'd planted new ones. The oregano and English thyme wintered, but she'd have to replant pineapple sage, lemongrass, chives, marjoram, and basil. She and Jazzi had turned over soil for onions. She would have to wait until May to plant heirloom tomatoes and peppers.

When Daisy heard a car on the gravel at the garage, she knew it was Jonas. They were going to have a late dinner. Jazzi was antsy because she didn't know exactly when Portia would be going away with her husband to tell him that she'd had a baby before she'd met him. A baby she'd put up for adoption. Jazzi seemed to think Portia would call her with details. Daisy wasn't so sure.

Jonas appeared from around the side of the house, and Daisy couldn't help but smile. It was a beautiful spring night, and only a light breeze ruffled her loose blond hair against her cheek. Jonas looked good in jeans and a crew-neck cream-colored shirt.

She told him, "Jazzi and I have been puttering around the garden. I can't wait to have fresh herbs and vegetables again from my own backyard."

After giving Daisy a light kiss, he asked, "Do deer and rabbits bother any of it?"

"The deer mostly munch on the low-hanging tree branches and bushes. And the bunnies? We share our vegetables with everyone."

Jonas laughed, a deep rich sound that had brought a new aspect to her life that she so appreciated.

Jazzi asked Jonas, "Do you want to see where we found Marjoram and Pepper?"

"Of course I do. It's important for me to know the background on my favorite felines."

Daisy heard Jazzi laugh. She also heard her say,

"Mom wants to start up an English garden, but that will take research and ordering plants online. She likes to buy local when she can."

How comfortable Jazzi felt with Jonas. Daisy had the feeling her daughter even trusted him. Maybe that came from Jonas helping her to search for her birth mother. But how would her daughter feel if Daisy and Jonas became more serious? On the other hand, how would Jazzi feel if this new relationship fell apart?

After Jazzi explained how Marjoram and Pepper were only a pound when she and her mom found them, she came over to the patio where Daisy had laid her gardening tools.

Jazzi said, "I'll go in and start the meat for the tacos. You do like tacos, don't you?" she asked Jonas. "Because if you don't, we'll have to order pizza."

"I like tacos just fine."

After Jazzi was inside, Jonas came over to Daisy and held her gently by the shoulders, gazing into her eyes. "Do you think Jazzi went in so we could have time alone?"

Daisy smiled, always tingling with anticipation when Jonas was this close. "It's possible. She's perceptive. She's trying to keep herself busy so she doesn't think about Portia."

"I get that," Jonas said. He brought Daisy a little closer.

Dusk was falling rapidly with only a few solar lights lighting the walkway to the back door.

He murmured to Daisy, "I think we should take advantage of the quiet and the privacy, don't you?"

She hardly had time to nod before he kissed her. This time it was a serious kiss. But as she was melting from the heat of it, the cell phone in her jean's pocket played its tuba sound. "I can let it go to voice mail," she whispered.

"Maybe you'd better see who's calling," he suggested.

Because they were getting too hot and heavy? Or simply because he was considerate that way? She sighed. As a mother, she usually answered calls in case Vi or Jazzi were calling. Now, however, she saw Foster's number on her screen.

She accepted the call. "Hi, Foster. What's up?"

"Mrs. Swanson, I hate to do this to you, but I might be late tomorrow morning. I wanted you to know."

"Can you tell me why?" Daisy asked.

"I just need the time. I'll be back by ten. I promise. I'll make this up to you."

Up until now, Foster had been reliable and hardly taken a day off. "Foster, I'm concerned about you. Are you sure everything's okay?"

His voice sounded a little shaky when he said, "It will be. I'll see you tomorrow. Then I'll make sure I carry double my weight."

"That's not necessary. Just come back safe and settled."

After Foster said good-bye and ended the call, Daisy called Aunt Iris to let her know Foster would be late in the morning. Afterward, Jonas put an arm around Daisy. "What's going on?"

"I don't know and that's the problem. Yesterday, Foster asked me if he could leave early and I let him. But now he said he's going to be late tomorrow. I don't know, Jonas. I hope he's not in trouble of any kind."

Jonas's brow creased as he apparently thought about

her worry. "Foster doesn't seem like the type to get into trouble."

Jonas knew Foster well because Foster had stayed with him for a while when he was deciding if he wanted to rent his own place or stay under the same roof with his family. In the end, he'd decided to stay at home but to start paying his dad for room and board. That way he could save some money but still take on responsibility. Daisy admired him for doing that.

"Why is it so difficult for men to ask for help?" she mused.

"Just men?" Jonas's voice held some humor rather than defensiveness.

"Mostly men. After Ryan was diagnosed, he hated to ask me to do anything for him. And when he had no choice, he deeply regretted asking. When a woman cares about somebody, she wants to do things for the person she cares about." Daisy had to bite her lip because she almost used the word *loved*.

"And my silence sometimes makes you think I don't want to ask for your help," Jonas commented softly.

"Something like that."

"I'll keep that in mind."

She laid her head on his shoulder. "Do you mind when I talk about Ryan?"

She felt him shake his head. "You don't do it very much. No, I don't mind. Seeing inside a marriage is often enlightening."

She wondered *how* it was enlightening. Did it show *her* character? Ryan's? How they'd been committed to each other?

She and Jonas hadn't reached that commitment talk yet, and she didn't know when they would.

* * *

The next morning Jazzi had soccer practice, so Daisy arrived for work early. Iris was already taking cookies out of the oven and Tessa stood at the mixer.

"Those smell delicious," Daisy said, stopping at the kitchen before going to her office.

"Just a shortbread cookie." Iris grinned. "I'm going to sprinkle them with spring colors—pink, blue, green, and yellow."

"That will make them stand out. The customers will like that."

Tessa turned away from the mixer to ask Daisy, "How was your date with Jonas last night?"

Her aunt looked Daisy's way, too, and she felt herself blush. "It wasn't *exactly* a date. He came over and had dinner with me and Jazzi." To change the course of the conversation, she said, "Remember, Foster said he'd be here by ten."

"And you don't know where he is?" Aunt Iris asked, letting Daisy change the subject.

"No idea. He didn't want to say."

"Have you asked Gavin?" Tessa asked.

"I don't want to pry unless I have to. If there's some reason Foster isn't here by ten today, then maybe I will call his dad."

Iris shook her head. "I don't understand young people sometimes. On the other hand, Foster's twenty, old enough to make his own decisions and stand by them."

Just before opening time, Daisy heard a knocking at the front door to the tea garden. Their CLOSED sign was up. Who would be knocking?

"I'll check," she told Tessa and Aunt Iris. "Maybe someone desperately needs a scone," she joked.

However, when she went to the door, peered through the glass, and saw who it was, her smile faded away. It was Detective Rappaport.

She could pretend that she hadn't seen him, but he'd probably glimpsed her or her shadow through the glass. Rappaport was like the proverbial dog with a bone. He didn't give up. That was a good quality for a detective, she supposed, but sometimes it was also a flaw.

She unlocked the door.

Detective Rappaport stepped inside. Morris Rappaport usually looked grumpy, but today his expression was more than serious. His thick, blond-gray hair was ruffled. In his fifties, he had deep lines on his face and grooves around his mouth. He was probably about five-ten, but his expression now made him seem taller and broader.

He asked, "Do you know who killed Derek Schumacher?"

Chapter Four

Daisy and her staff were absolutely shocked at Detective Rappaport's news of Derek Schumacher's death. She hoped he could see that.

"What happened?" she asked.

"That's what I was going to ask you," Rappaport returned.

"Do you think we had anything to do with this?" Cora Sue asked.

He gazed at Daisy's server with a penetrating look. "That's what I'm here to find out. Patrol officers will be here shortly, and we'll question each of you individually."

Daisy raised her chin and stepped forward. "We're running a business here, Detective."

"Oh, I know you are. But it's a business Derek Schumacher had something to say about."

"It's not fair that you make us lose revenue again when this wasn't even the crime scene," her aunt Iris scolded.

To her surprise the detective didn't become irate. Rather he stated, "We can do it one of two ways. I can either take you all down to the station, which will probably take longer, or I can bring my patrol officers in and we'll question you here. An hour tops and you'll be open again, unless I need one of you to answer more questions."

"Do you have your eye on someone?" Daisy asked.

Rappaport was enigmatic about that. "Possibly."

Just then Foster came into the tea garden. Daisy noticed right away that he looked tired and worried. He didn't give her his usual smile and greeting, but rather asked, "Are we having a meeting?"

Before Daisy could answer, Detective Rappaport directed his gaze straight at Foster. "We've had another death in Willow Creek that could be suspicious."

"Somebody we all know?" Foster asked, blinking behind his rimless glasses.

"I don't know how well you knew him. It's Derek Schumacher."

Foster looked shaken by the news. "Where? How? It didn't happen here, did it?"

Aunt Iris put her hand on Foster's shoulder. "No, it didn't. Thank goodness. We're just learning what happened. But the detective isn't giving us too many details. He wants to talk with each of us separately."

"What about serving our customers?" Foster asked indignantly.

"Closing the tea garden for an hour isn't going to bring your business down," Rappaport reminded them. "If one of you is the killer, however, that could possibly do it."

Daisy found if she ignored most of what Rappaport said, she didn't get as angry with him.

Cora Sue turned to Aunt Iris. "Do you want me to stand outside and tell the customers who arrive that we won't be open for about an hour? I'll do it nicely and give them coupons for free tea and a scone."

Iris nodded. "Sounds good. Eva can take over while you're being questioned."

Foster was already taking off his red windbreaker. "Why don't I make us all a cup of chamomile? It should keep us calm." He looked Rappaport straight in the eye. "There's no reason why we can't sip tea while you question us, is there?"

Rappaport studied Foster, from his dark brown hair and glasses to his cleft chin to his white shirt and khaki pants. Maybe he was gauging just how much Foster would defy him. But Daisy knew Foster wasn't usually defiant. This bravado today seemed unusual.

The bell over the door to the tea garden jingled as two patrol officers stormed in. Detective Rappaport gave rapid-fire orders, telling Cora Sue to go with Otis Palmer while Eva and Karina went to another corner of the tea garden with Officer Jim Roland.

Rappaport motioned toward Daisy's office. "Ladies, why don't we go in there? I'll ask the two of you questions. When we're finished, then I'll question Foster."

Foster gave the detective a defiant, dark look.

Rappaport paid no mind and followed Daisy to her office.

The detective started with the obvious questions. He wanted alibis. While Aunt Iris sat in the chair at the front of the desk, Daisy perched on the edge of it.

Rappaport stood in front of them. "All right, Mrs. Swanson, tell me your alibi. I'm hoping it's one I can check out."

Did that mean he really didn't suspect her or Aunt Iris?

"I was at the tea garden late because of the afternoon

tea service with Derek Schumacher and the rest of my guests. After I left, I picked up Jazzi from her soccer game and went home. Jonas Groft was with us last evening for dinner."

"I suppose Jazzi's coach could confirm that you picked up your daughter?"

"She can, and so can Jazzi."

"It's better to have someone impartial confirm the alibi." He directed his focus toward Iris. "How about you? Alibi?"

"I drove home around six. My neighbor was outside and waved when I got home. Then I was alone the rest of the night."

Changing tactics quickly enough to make Daisy's head spin, Rappaport asked, "Do you know where Cora Sue was last evening?"

Daisy shrugged. "My staff doesn't always reveal their lives to me. Why are you asking?"

It was obvious Rappaport was debating with himself over what to tell her.

"Look, Detective, I know you want to keep details of what happened secret. I do understand that. But you also have to give me enough so I can help you if I can."

"All right. But I want you and Iris to keep this to yourselves. If you don't, I'll know where it came from."

"You can trust us," Iris said.

He ran his hand across his forehead. "I have a witness who saw and heard Cora Sue arguing with Schumacher before he came to the tea garden."

Daisy's expression must have revealed her shock.

"You didn't know about that?" he asked.

Daisy shook her head. "Cora Sue didn't mention it. If I had known, I might have questioned her about it."

"That's what I thought. I also want to know about Foster."

Rappaport was reaching, as Jonas would say. And she wouldn't help him reach. From dealing with murder investigations before, Daisy knew the best thing to do was to say as little as possible. "I don't know where Foster was last night. He's my employee. I don't keep tabs on everything about his life."

"He's dating your daughter. I'm sure you know a lot more than you think you do, or that you want to tell me."

Although Rappaport's gaze was steely, Daisy changed the course of the questioning. "Detective, how did Schumacher die?"

The detective eyed her carefully. "That's still to be determined by the coroner and evidence techs."

Rappaport's restrained answer told Daisy more than he thought. His explanation revealed that the manner of death wasn't obvious.

Almost to himself, the detective muttered, "I have to interview Schumacher's colleagues, bosses, and friends. Family too. Believe me, I'm going to be busy for a long while."

He made it sound as if he didn't want to be. Daisy couldn't help but ask, "Detective Rappaport, when you took the job in Willow Creek, did you merely expect to be dealing with jaywalking violations and traffic stops?"

He looked her straight in the eye. "Matter of fact, I did. This job has turned out to be much different than I bargained for. But that could soon be changing too."

"Are you going to leave?" Daisy pressed.

"I always have to remind you that I'm the one asking the questions, don't I?"

"It doesn't hurt to ask," she said with a shrug. "I

know you'll tell me what's going on eventually." She thought she saw the edges of his mouth quirk a bit as if he might be amused by her.

Not to be distracted, the detective said again, "Tell me again about Foster. Where was he yesterday after tea service? Where was he coming from this morning?"

Marshall Thompson, the lawyer she'd consulted during the last murder investigation, had agreed with Jonas about saying as little as possible when questioned. So she stuck to those rules. "I don't know where Foster was."

"Am I supposed to actually believe that?"

"You can believe what you want, Detective. He hasn't been dating my daughter for that long. Their lives are still separate. I don't keep track of him, and I don't think Violet does either. Since she's away at college, he tries to give her her freedom. They're a modern dating couple."

"Maybe. When I talk to him, I'll get it cleared up. For now, try to stay out of this, okay?"

"Detective, you made me close my business and you're interviewing me and my staff. Therefore, I'm in it whether you want me to be in this investigation or not."

"Mrs. Swanson, watch . . . your . . . step." He drew out the sentence so that she'd know he meant it.

Just what questions could she ask and of whom before she fell into trouble with the police?

After the detective and his patrol officers left, Daisy decided she needed to talk with her staff. She wanted to know why the detective was determined to question Cora Sue.

She waved Cora Sue into her office. "Can I talk to you for a few minutes? You're pale."

Cora Sue sank down onto a wooden ladder-back chair.

"I'm getting used to dealing with Detective Rappaport and the rest of the police," Daisy explained. "But I know you aren't. Why was he so interested in your alibi?"

Cora Sue sighed. "I know the owner of a restaurant that Derek Schumacher reviewed last week. She spent the last three years building up her business in Ephrata. She doesn't cook fancy food, but she cooks good food, sort of like Sarah Jane's."

Sarah Jane's was a popular diner in Willow Creek. "So why did Detective Rappaport have a problem with you knowing the owner of the restaurant?"

"On my way to the tea garden for my shift, I stopped for a prescription at the drugstore."

"Presley's Pharmacy?"

"Yes. Derek Schumacher was coming out of the drugstore as I was going in. I was so mad for my friend, afraid he'd hurt her business, so I told him he was unfair to her and he'd better be fair to *you*."

"You didn't threaten him in any way?" Daisy asked.

"No, not in so many words. And if he wasn't going to be fair to you, I don't know what I would have done. Maybe I would have paid his mother a visit. She had sway over him."

"You know his mother?"

"Yes. My aunt and Harriet were neighbors in Harriet's old neighborhood. My aunt and I last visited her at Derek's house just after she came home from rehab for a stroke."

"Derek's mother had a stroke?"

"Yes, about a year ago. She was in rehab for a few months and is doing as well as can be expected. After her stroke, Derek moved her into his house."

"He cared for her?" Daisy asked, surprised.

"Visiting nurses came in to check on her when she first got home. I think Derek's sister-in-law helps out. But Harriet insists she doesn't need help anymore."

Daisy would like to learn more about all that. She wasn't sure why, but after helping the police with two other murder investigations, she knew motives intertwined just like family members and friends. You never knew when you could find a clue that was important.

Clue. Uh-uh. She was not looking for clues, not this time. She remembered the last murder cases she'd been involved in and the consequences of her involvement.

Daisy caught sight of Foster at the sales counter. She wanted to talk to him next.

After Daisy and Cora Sue returned to the main tea room, Daisy captured Foster's eye and nodded to her office. When he gave her a blank look, she said, "Come on. I want to talk to you."

He followed her there, albeit reluctantly. That wasn't like him. Once they were in her office, she closed the door and pointed to the chair in front of her desk. Then she brought around the chair from behind the desk and sat near him.

"How did it go with Detective Rappaport?"

"It went," Foster answered noncommittally.

Daisy pushed on. "I know he wanted to question everyone about their alibis. Is that what he talked to you about?"

"He tried to," Foster mumbled.

"What does *that* mean?" This wasn't usually Foster's attitude. He tried to be helpful and cooperative.

"I didn't tell him where I was."

Sitting back in her chair, she tried to keep the dismay from her voice. "Foster, do you think that's wise?"

"It's none of his business," Foster retorted defensively.

"Foster!" Daisy put her hand on his arm. "What's wrong?"

He wouldn't meet her gaze. "Nothing's wrong. I'm just not ready to talk about where I was . . . with anyone."

"And that includes me?"

"For now, yes, it does," he maintained.

"The detective won't let this go. You know that, don't you?"

Foster gazed down at his shoes. "I suppose."

"There are ways to track people and cars that the police didn't have before. Simply routine traffic cams can snap your license plate number."

"I didn't think of that," Foster murmured. "But he'll be too busy running down other suspects to worry about me."

Daisy knew that was possible. The police would have a good number of suspects where Derek Schumacher was concerned. The problem was—was Foster one of those suspects?

Chapter Five

When Daisy went into the kitchen to check how the preparations for the lunch crowd were going, beef barley soup was simmering. Eva had just taken a tray of maple and walnut scones from the oven. Daisy easily heard Cora Sue telling Tessa, "I don't know what I'm going to do. What if they don't believe me?"

Cora Sue sounded near tears, and Daisy reflexively went in that direction. When she stopped near Cora Sue and put an arm around her server's shoulders, tears did come to Cora Sue's eyes and leaked down her cheek.

"What's going on?" Daisy asked quietly.

While Cora Sue tried to compose herself, Tessa explained, "She's afraid the police won't believe her alibi."

"Actually, I don't have one," Cora Sue said. "That's the problem. I was alone after I went home and the rest of the night. Of all times not to have a significant other."

Daisy could see Cora Sue was trying to smile. She

usually had an encouraging word or joke for anybody. "I don't know if Detective Rappaport will believe a significant other either. Business is slow right now. Why don't we have a cup of tea and we can talk."

Cora Sue glanced around the kitchen. "Are you sure?"

"I wouldn't have suggested it if I wasn't. Come on. I know how talking to the police can freak you out for a while afterward. How about a serving of rum raisin rice pudding along with a cup of Earl Grey?"

"Rum raisin?" Cora Sue asked, interested. "Did you put plenty of rum in it?"

Daisy smiled. "Only extract. But if you pretend it's real rum, it might have the same effect."

This time Cora Sue smiled back. "Sounds good. I'll bring the tea." Ten minutes later, Cora Sue and Daisy sat in the main tea room near the window. They looked out into the street as they sipped their tea.

Cora Sue took a spoonful of rice pudding. "This is really good, Daisy. I don't know how I missed it in the walk-in. Usually I look over everything in the morning. I guess I'm just distracted today."

"Stress can affect your memory, what you see, and what you don't see. I just want you to know that Tessa, Iris, and I have been major suspects with Detective Rappaport, and our situations turned out all right. Yours will be resolved too. Getting angry with someone and telling them off doesn't mean you have it in you to kill them."

Cora Sue's topknot bobbed as she gazed at Daisy and said, "Someone did."

"I know. Tell me more about Derek Schumacher and his mother. Did they have any other relatives?"

"From what I understand, Harriet's husband was an only child. He was his brother Bradley's father but not Derek's."

"So he was Derek's stepfather?"

Turning her blue-flowered teacup around on its saucer, her server responded, "Yes. Derek was the one who convinced his mother to come live with him after her stroke. He put in a chair lift so she could have her own apartment on the second floor. She can do stairs, but he didn't want to worry about her falling."

"So he watched over her?"

"Sort of. As I told you, she went to rehab and then when she came home, a service came in every day. After more occupational therapy and physical therapy, the professionals all decided she could live on her own. But I don't think Derek trusted that. Harriet's a very independent woman, and she doesn't really want anyone taking care of her. This arrangement worked out pretty well. When Derek cooked, he took food up to his mom. Other nights, he brought in takeout . . . or his brother did. From what I understand, Harriet also had containers she could pull from the freezer that Bradley's wife Lauren made. I think Lauren drove Harriet to her doctor's appointments when Derek couldn't. The family seemed to have a system going that was good for everyone."

"I wonder what's happening with Derek's mother now."

"I'm not sure," Cora Sue said.

Daisy took a bite of her rice pudding and then a sip of tea. "Maybe you and I could pay Harriet Schumacher a condolence call. Do you think she'd appreciate that?"

"I imagine she would. I don't think she has many friends."

"Since her stroke?"

"In general. Her husband left her well off. When he was alive, she belonged to the garden club, was on the board of a hospital in Lancaster, and gave cocktail parties to help her husband further his circle of influence. He was a venture capitalist."

"Really? In a town the size of Willow Creek?"

"I think he traveled a lot. I'm not sure how Harriet spent her time alone. She's one of those women who tells you exactly what she thinks."

"I have a mother and aunt who are somewhat like that," Daisy said with a gentle smile.

Cora Sue laughed. "I think your mom and your aunt have more tact than Harriet does. Her bluntness is one of the reasons she doesn't have many friends."

"Yet honesty is the best policy, right?"

"Sometimes I'm not sure about that. Sometimes little white lies go much farther with holding onto a friendship than complete honesty."

That conclusion gave Daisy something to think about.

The following day everything seemed to be going well at the tea garden. The staff seemed calmer, as if they were enjoying whatever they were doing. That was the atmosphere Daisy wanted to promote. If everyone who worked there was calm and peaceful and happy, their customers would feel that too.

At one o'clock, Foster's cell phone dinged. He took it from his pocket and glanced at the screen. Daisy, who was brewing a pot of jasmine tea, looked up. He didn't usually take calls while he was working.

However, he met her gaze and told her, "It's Detective Rappaport. I have to take this."

She nodded. He was right. He did have to take it.

After he ended the call, he said, "He wants me to come down to the police station now. Are you going to be okay for a while? I don't know how long he'll keep me."

"We're fine, Foster. I can always call Karina or Pam to see if they're free. Don't worry about anything here."

"No, just worry about what I'm going to say to him," Foster mumbled. Within minutes he was gone.

Daisy worried about Foster. He was definitely part of the tea garden family now. Besides that, she felt she should watch over him because of Violet.

When Foster returned to the tea garden an hour and a half later, her worry increased. First, she checked the green tea room to make sure customers were taken care of. They were. She nodded to her office and Foster followed her inside.

"How did it go?" she asked.

"It went," he mumbled.

"Foster, what does that mean? I can see you're upset."

Foster paced back and forth. "I can't tell the detective what he wants to know."

"What does he want to know?"

Stopping his travel across the office, Foster admitted, "He says I have to confirm my alibi. He has to be able to verify where I was the evening Derek Schumacher was killed."

"And?" Daisy prompted.

"I can't tell him. Not yet."

"What's so important that you have to keep it to

yourself, that you're putting yourself in danger with the police?"

"I made a promise and I have to keep it." He turned his dark brown gaze to hers, and she could see his eyes were glistening with something she couldn't name. Something was troubling Foster deeply, but he wouldn't reveal what it was.

"You know you can tell me anything . . . anytime. And if not me, you should talk it over with someone, someone you trust."

"I know," he answered, but that was all he said. Daisy could see he wasn't going to say more. There wasn't anything else she could do until he opened up. Except for one thing.

"If the police want to talk to you again—and I'm sure they will to get more information—let me know. I'll call the lawyer that Aunt Iris and I used."

"I can't pay for a lawyer," was the response that flew out of Foster's mouth. That didn't surprise Daisy either.

"Knowing Marshall, he'll give you your first consultation free. There might be a charge if he goes to the police station with you, but I'll take care of it."

When Foster began to protest, she said, "I'm your employer, and if you're in trouble, you're in trouble because you work here. So don't argue with me about this, okay?"

While Foster looked through the glass into the kitchen, they heard the sounds coming from the kitchen and tea room—china clinking, customers chatting, a baking sheet being set into the oven.

When he turned back to Daisy, he seemed determined about something. "All right. If I get called in again, I'll talk to your lawyer. I understand why you think you have to pay, but I'm hoping it won't come to that. Thank you, Mrs. Swanson."

With that, Foster left her office.

She thought they'd gone beyond the formal *Mrs. Swanson*, but maybe, just maybe, she and Foster weren't as friendly as she'd thought they were.

Although Jazzi came in to the tea garden to work after school, Daisy could see that her daughter was distracted, and she knew why. She hadn't heard from Portia lately. Jazzi didn't know if Portia and her husband's trip was still on.

As Jazzi emptied her backpack on Daisy's desk, Daisy brought her a scone and a cup of tea. It was her favorite tea—cocoa Rooibos.

Jazzi looked at the snack and asked, "Don't you want me to work?"

"We had two busloads of tourists this afternoon, and they all filed out about a half-hour ago. Do you have much schoolwork tonight?"

"I do, but I can still work if you want me to."

"Why don't you eat your snack and then decide."

"Are you being nice to me because I haven't heard from Portia?" Jazzi's expression said she wanted the truth.

"I'm being nice to you because I'm your mom and I'm concerned about you."

"You don't have to be. I sent a text to Portia at lunchtime, but she didn't answer me. I don't know what to think."

"I know you don't. And I know you believe that I don't want her to get in touch with you. But I do. I don't want you in this limbo. But this isn't a situation you can force."

"I thought about just turning up on her doorstep."

It took all of Daisy's self-control to keep quiet.

Jazzi went on, "But I know that could push everything the wrong way instead of the right way. But I hate waiting."

"I know. I'm not fond of it either."

Jazzi pointed her chin toward the Plexiglas in the hallway. "I think somebody wants to talk to you."

Daisy turned in her chair and saw Jonas. She couldn't help but break into a smile.

"Go on, Mom. I know you want to. And I'm fine. I'll eat, then think about cleaning tables or doing homework. I lead such a glamorous life."

There was sarcasm in her daughter's voice, but humor too.

As Daisy stood, she squeezed Jazzi's arm. "You're a good kid, do you know that?"

"Yep, I do."

On that positive note, Daisy left Jazzi to her snack and went to meet Jonas. At first his smile said he was glad to see her, but then his expression turned serious.

"This isn't simply a social call, is it?" she asked.

He frowned. "You're learning to read me too well."

"Do you want to go out back and talk? We'll have privacy there."

He motioned toward the kitchen's back door. "Sure. Lead the way."

They stepped outside, then kept walking across the paved area to the grass. The sun was warm on Daisy's head. She loved spring. She really did. The season was all about new beginnings, and she was hoping there would be good ones.

They walked for a while in silence, heading toward the creek. The sound of the water gurgling over rocks was calming. Neither of them spoke until Jonas said, "I have investigation news for you."

"Good news or bad news?"

"It was bad news for Schumacher. You need to keep this information under your hat . . . or under your apron."

Daisy chuckled. "So you got it from Detective Rappaport?"

"I did. No matter what you think of him, he *is* a good investigator."

"Except when he's investigating the wrong suspects. He has Cora Sue and Foster in his crosshairs."

"He'll investigate everyone the same way, finding out exactly what he wants. Rappaport is one of those detectives who doesn't just go on gut instinct. His motto is—follow the evidence."

"In some ways, that's good, and in others, I'm not so sure. What has he discovered so far?"

"He didn't tell me anything about suspects. I wouldn't expect him to, especially when he can't seem to single one out. But he did find out that Derek Schumacher had a low blood pressure problem."

"Low blood pressure," Daisy murmured. "I don't know exactly what you would do for that."

"Apparently there's not much that can be done. He was under a doctor's care. Eating more salt can help, but that has to be under the direction of a physician. He also needed to drink lots of non-alcoholic beverages."

"That day he ate here, he was drinking glasses of water and cups of tea."

"That makes sense if he cared about his health. The

third thing the doctor advised him was never to rise to his feet too fast. He could be dizzy."

"I didn't see any signs of that. Low blood pressure won't kill you, will it?"

"No, it won't," Jonas replied. "But arrhythmias or seizures *can* kill a person."

"Low blood pressure can cause seizures?"

Jonas shook his head. "No. That's why this has been categorized as a suspicious death. Rappaport told me he's called in favors to have the forensics expedited."

"Do you think that will happen?"

"I believe Rappaport will stay on their backs until it does."

"So they don't have any idea what killed him?"

"Not until they analyze stomach contents, blood work, and tox screens. But all that takes time, even when the process is expedited."

"So what you're telling me is that this murder isn't going to be solved any time soon."

"That depends. Rappaport could get a break in the case some other way. A slip of the tongue . . . an unexpected clue."

Jonas gave Daisy a sideways glance. "Do you intend to get involved?"

She knew Jonas wanted honesty, and that's what she gave him. "I'm not sure yet. It depends if Cora Sue or Foster become Detective Rappaport's main suspects. Either way, something *is* going on with Foster. I don't think he had anything to do with Derek Schumacher's death, but he's troubled about something. I told him if the police call him again, he needs to take Marshall with him."

"Good advice."

Daisy took a deep breath, drawing in the scents of

leaves budding, damp earth renewing, grass growing. "I should take a walk out here every day at lunchtime just to renew my energy."

"That sounds like a good idea." Jonas's deep voice was a bit husky when he added, "What else renews you?"

"Spending time with you," she said a little shyly.

Jonas took her hand and kissed the top of it. Then he swung their hands between them. "Maybe we should take walks together and get doubly renewed."

As Daisy laughed, Jonas turned to face her . . . and then bent his head to kiss her.

Jonas stayed for a blueberry tart and a cup of peppermint bark tea. Then a busload of tourists arrived, and Jonas waved to Daisy as he headed for the door. Foster left an hour early to attend an evening class. After consulting with Iris, Daisy told Cora Sue and Tessa that they could leave too. Inventory had already been taken for the next day. The prep was done for salad dressings. Mini cheesecakes were in the walk-in. Vegetables had been scraped and diced for tomorrow's soup.

Daisy was cleaning the last of the tables in the spill-over tea room and Iris was pushing the broom, when there was a knock at the front door. Once before, someone had asked to be let in after hours. That had become a life-and-death situation.

Daisy hurried to the main tea room and saw Iris going to the door. "Are you sure you want to open it?" Daisy asked.

"It's your dad, Daisy. Of course, I want to open it."

A minute later her dad walked in, saying hello to both of them.

"Dad, what are you doing here?"

His blue eyes glistened with amusement. "Is that any way to greet your father after I've been gone?"

Daisy smiled. Maybe she did have PTSD after being involved in a few murder investigations. Post-traumatic stress can certainly result when a person goes through something dreadful and terrifying. She wrapped her arms around her dad and gave him a huge hug. He hugged her back, the bill of his baseball cap hitting her cheek.

"Sorry about that," he said, and pushed the bill of his cap up.

Her dad was a flannel shirt kind of guy. Now that the weather had turned warmer, he usually wore snap-button plaid shirts and a flannel jacket.

"How was your fishing trip?" Iris asked.

"It was good," he said. "I relaxed but mostly thought about a lot of things."

"I'm surprised Mom didn't call me to tell me you were back."

"That's because she doesn't know it yet," her father stated with resolve.

Iris took a step back and gave him a piercing look. "Tell us what's going on, Sean Gallagher. This isn't like you at all. Rose is upset enough without you coming here first."

"Upset?" her dad asked.

Daisy sighed and decided to spill the truth. "Mom came in here scolding Aunt Iris because she told you that you should go on this trip. Mom couldn't understand why you'd leave her alone this time of year, busy as it is."

"She had plenty of help," her father grumbled. "I made sure of that."

"But none of that help is *you*," Daisy said softly.

Her dad pulled out a chair and removed his ball cap and set it on the table. "I know you're closing, but I really could use a cup of tea."

"I didn't turn off the hot water keeper yet," Iris said. "Do you have a preference?"

"How about that pear spice concoction?"

"Coming right up," Iris said. "And if you don't want me in on this conversation, I can make myself scarce."

"Maybe I just need a little advice . . . about Rose. Who better to get that from than her sister and her daughter?"

"We'll listen, Dad, but I don't know how much advice we can give you." Daisy knew relationships had to work themselves out. Advice from others often put a wrench into what might happen naturally.

Daisy was worried because whatever her father was contemplating sounded serious. Once more she wondered if he had a health issue he hadn't told her mother about. Maybe there was a financial problem with the nursery? She could ask the questions, but she wanted to give her dad the chance to explain the situation himself.

Iris soon returned with three cups of tea and blueberry muffins with a lemon curd spread.

"Just what I needed," her dad said. "I'm tired of trail mix and peanut butter and jelly sandwiches."

"You didn't cook on this fishing trip?" Iris asked.

"If cook means making coffee over a campfire, yes, I did that. I didn't catch any fish, so I roasted hot dogs. But not much else. I wasn't there to eat but rather to think."

"And just what were you thinking about?" Daisy

prompted, believing her dad was stalling because this might be a difficult discussion.

"I was thinking about my end years and your mother's end years."

She suddenly felt panicked. "End years? What are you talking about, Dad?"

He reached across the table and patted Daisy's hand. "I don't want to alarm you, and I don't want to alarm your mother, but we aren't getting any younger. At your age, you still have dreams and hopes and places you might want to travel to."

"Are you saying you can't have those anymore? You're not even sixty yet!" Daisy pointed out.

Her dad looked at Iris and then back at Daisy. "Think about what that means. If your mother and I are lucky, we'll have maybe fifteen, maybe twenty years together yet. And I have to figure out the best way to spend them."

Daisy was incredibly shaken. She never thought of her parents as old. Maybe she still thought of them as she had when she was a little girl. She wanted to deny, deny, deny that someday her parents would be gone. Suddenly, the reality of what her father was saying struck home.

It seemed that her aunt Iris had made the decision to keep quiet at this juncture. She didn't want to overstep her bounds or make her sister more cross with her than she already was.

Daisy took a deep breath, then asked, "So what are you thinking about, Dad? Do you have health issues that I don't know about . . . that Mom doesn't know about?"

"No, I don't," he said. "Arthritis here and there but that can be expected. However, any day something could crop up. Your mother and I have a retirement account that doesn't have nearly enough in it. I consulted with an elder lawyer to consider the things I should be doing at my age."

"You consulted an elder lawyer without Rose?" Iris asked.

"I can't discuss anything like this with Rose without her getting all upset. I thought it was better if I did research and then summed it up for her. That's why I needed the trip to think about all of it."

"And what did the elder lawyer suggest?" Daisy asked, curious.

"She suggested long-term care insurance. We're at the age now when it's good to consider it. It's expensive, but with the price of nursing homes and home health care these days, it could be essential to have. I won't go into the ins and outs of it now. I have all of that summed up so I can go over it with your mother. I don't think she'll fight me on that if I can just get the discussion going."

"What do you think she'll fight you on?" was Iris's next logical question.

"I had an offer to sell the nursery."

Daisy and her aunt exchanged a look. It had been so much a part of her parents' lives. What would they do without it?

"It was a good offer," he added. "If we put that money into a retirement account and don't draw from it right away, we could have a no-frills decent income for the long term."

Daisy knew how she worried about finances as she studied the income the tea garden brought in week by week. She had sleepless nights when the sum was lower than she expected, but she rejoiced when it was higher.

Sean pointed at Aunt Iris. "In a few years you're going to have to think about this too."

"Ah, yes," her aunt said. "But then I can come to you for advice."

Sean's lips twitched up. "I can give you good advice now. Make a will. And not only make a will. You need to have a medical power of attorney and a durable power of attorney. I'm sure Marshall would do that for you and be reasonable about it."

"Do you have all that?" Daisy asked.

"Your mother and I do, but we need to update everything. We also have to make living wills."

"This is an awfully big discussion you want to have with Rose," Aunt Iris commented. "Maybe you should think about dividing it up. Talk about what you think is most important first, then slowly step into the other matters."

"Aunt Iris is right, Dad. This is an awful lot to throw at Mom."

"I suppose it is. I've been gathering information for a few months. I can't expect her to absorb it in one night. I just wish—"

"Wish what?" Daisy asked.

"I just wish your mother would be more practical about it. She thinks I'm a worrywart, but I want to be prepared."

Daisy was shaking her head. "I don't believe she thinks you're a worrywart. I think she's afraid to lose you, and that's why she doesn't want to talk about it. Talking about it makes it a possibility, and she doesn't want to consider it. She loves you, Dad, and she'll do anything to keep from thinking about the time when you won't be at her side . . . or she won't be at yours. Maybe you can compartmentalize much easier than she can."

"Maybe so," her father agreed. "Do either of you have any suggestions on how I should broach this?"

"I suggest you make a special time to talk to her about it," Daisy suggested.

"A special time. Do you mean a date?"

Daisy smiled. "Exactly. Don't tell me you're too old to have a date."

"I'm leaving now," Aunt Iris said with a laugh.

"We won't go there," her father agreed with a chuckle. "Maybe you're right. And I can make your mother feel special after being gone like I've been. Maybe we'll set up a series of dates, and we can talk about something different at each one."

"That sounds like a plan," Daisy said.

"And I won't tell her I stopped to have a blueberry muffin and tea with the two of you." Her father winked as if complete honesty wasn't always the best policy. Daisy would have to consider again whether or not that was true.

Chapter Six

Daisy stood beside her friend Rachel, adding tea cozies to a shelf for display. She'd known Rachel since she'd been a child. The Esh family, who were New Order Amish, had let Daisy's parents start bushes and shrubs on their property for the nursery. Daisy had wandered the fields on that farm as freely as Rachel. Their differing lifestyles hadn't mattered. Rachel wore the traditional cape dress and black apron with a kapp over her hair. Her family traveled in a horse and buggy. However, Daisy had never felt different from Rachel in any way that mattered. They were friends then, and still were.

"These quilted cozies are so cute," Daisy said to Rachel, although she knew her friend, like most Amish, was uncomfortable with praise. "I especially like the one that slips on from the bottom and then ties around the spout and the handle of the teapot."

She adjusted the cozies among the teapots that she had for sale.

Rachel lifted her head and sniffed the sudden waft

of baked goods that made its way into the spillover tea room. "Tessa must be baking chocolate scones. They smell wonderful *gut.*"

"Do you have time to try one with a cup of tea?"

"Another time, ya?" Rachel asked. "Hannah went to visit a sick friend with soup and biscuits. I told Sarah I wouldn't be gone long."

Two of Rachel's daughters, Hannah who was twenty and Sarah who was sixteen, assisted her at Quilts and Notions.

Suddenly, there was a woman standing in the doorway to the yellow tea room. She asked, "Daisy Swanson?"

Daisy turned toward the strawberry-blond, tall woman with high cheekbones and a long, thin face. She was wearing jeans and a cowl-neck short-sleeve coral-colored sweater.

Daisy answered her, "I'm Daisy Swanson. How can I help you?"

Rachel patted Daisy's arm. "I will come in soon for a cup of tea and a scone, I promise. But now I have to scoot."

Daisy gave her friend a hug and watched her walk away, as her long skirt brushed the heels of her sneakers.

The tall woman approached Daisy now. "Your assistant said I'd find you in here."

Daisy waited.

The woman shifted her purse from her left hand to her right and held out her hand for Daisy to shake. "I'm Clementine Hankey from Atlanta."

"Are you interested in tea rooms?" Daisy couldn't figure out why she was here.

"You could say that, but what I'm really interested in is information about Derek Schumacher."

Daisy wasn't sure she wanted to talk to this Clementine. "Are you a reporter?"

"I am. But I don't want an exclusive story from you or anything like that."

"What do you want?" Daisy asked bluntly.

"Can we sit for a few minutes?" Clementine asked her.

Daisy checked the main tea room and it seemed to be running smoothly. She motioned Clementine to a table. Just because she was suspicious about the woman didn't mean she should be rude. "Would you like a cup of tea while we talk?"

"I'd appreciate that," Clementine said, looking around as if for the first time.

Five minutes later Daisy returned with two cups of Earl Grey tea on a tray with sugar, as well as honey, and a dish with two chocolate scones. She placed the tray on the table and then sat across from Clementine. "You do know Derek Schumacher is dead."

"Yes, I do. I'm not usually an investigative reporter, but this is a little different."

"In what way? Do you intend to find out who murdered him?"

"If I can. I knew something was going to blow up, though I really didn't expect it to end in his death."

"Why don't you start at the beginning?" Daisy advised her.

Clementine took one of the chocolate scones. After breaking off a piece, popping it into her mouth, and chewing, she took a sip of tea. "I followed Derek's cable show when he was a famous chef, and I've been following his blog as long as he's been writing it."

"You report on food?" Daisy asked, curious.

"I'm a freelancer. I report on anything that I think will end up with a good story. I like working on five things at once, so Derek's story was always in the back of my mind."

"What story?"

"I became personally interested in him when he switched partners on his TV show. He and his co-host had been doing very well, but suddenly he switched from one female host to another."

"And no one knew why?"

"That in itself is curious because news always gets out. But everyone was hush-hush about this. One day Miranda Senft was in, and the next day she'd been replaced by Birgit Oppenheimer, a blonde with much less talent."

Daisy thought about her partnership with her aunt. "Is it possible that Derek Schumacher made a stronger connection with this Birgit?"

"Anything is possible, and TV is as cutthroat as anything else."

"Did you ever meet Derek?" Daisy was beginning to feel that she knew him, so it was easy to use his first name.

"I didn't actually meet him, but I was in the same proximity a few times."

Daisy hoped she wasn't talking to Derek Schumacher's stalker.

Clementine was shaking her head. "I know what you're thinking. No, I didn't have a crush on him or anything like that. I never went to his personal residence. I was interested in his professional career because something just wasn't right."

"What gave you that idea?"

"Ever since his show was canceled and he became a

food blogger, a mean streak emerged. And it seemed to get even worse after his mother had a stroke."

"You know about that?"

"Chefs and everyone in the cooking industry gossip. News makes its rounds as if it were a small town like Willow Creek. But stories also became distorted, so I decided to write a piece on Derek and get to the bottom of what was happening with him."

"You couldn't just set up an interview and ask him?"

Clementine took another sip of tea. "It's never that simple. Believe me. With the reasons for the changes on his show so hush-hush, as well as why the show was canceled, I knew he wouldn't tell me outright. I decided first to see if his reviews had merit. I ate at some of the same restaurants he ate at. But the last place I actually saw him was a coastal town in Maine when he was reviewing seafood restaurants. The reviews on one restaurant by other critics were stellar. Derek gave it a terrible review. So I drove to Maine, ate at the restaurant, and found the food delicious. I began to wonder if Derek was just burdened with too much responsibility. I heard his mother had moved in with him, but I'd also learned she was doing well. Still, when he traveled, he had to make sure she was taken care of. He had a home health aide, but his mother threw her out, so on his last few travels, his sister-in-law had stayed with his mother. It's quite possible his mental state had something to do with the tough reviews, but I wanted to know."

Clementine's story pushed Daisy to wonder what review Derek had given the tea garden.

As if Clementine read her mind, she asked, "Do you know what review Daisy's Tea Garden received?"

On Derek's website, he listed upcoming reviews and

posted expected dates when his opinion of the eatery would go live.

"I hadn't received his review yet," Daisy said. "Maybe the police know what it is, but I probably never will."

"My guess is that they've confiscated Derek's computer," Clementine said, and Daisy knew she was right.

"So why are you pursuing this story now that Derek is dead?"

"None of the rumors I've followed about the show being canceled, about why he changed co-hosts, have panned out. I thought that was a bit suspicious. If there was a scandal, that type of thing always resurfaces . . . or something else happens. I'd like to be the first reporter to break the story. Since Derek was from Willow Creek, since his chef show began in Lancaster, since he died here, I think it's a good place to start."

Daisy summed it up. "So what you're saying is that Derek's bad professional history led to his murder."

"I believe it's an exceptional possibility." Clementine ate the remainder of her scone. Wiping crumbs from her mouth, she declared, "This is delicious. If Derek didn't give you a good review, then either something had spoiled his palate . . . or his peace of mind."

Daisy knew either of those reasons could lead to murder.

The following evening at Daisy's direction, Jazzi cut butter into the flour mixture in the bowl in their kitchen. "Why can't I just use the mixer for this?" Jazzi asked.

"You probably could," Daisy answered. "But the dough would be a different consistency after it bakes. I know baking is supposed to be all about science, but

I just know what works when I want something to come out a certain way."

"The chili smells good. Did you make it spicy?"

Daisy returned the glass lid to her slow cooker after stirring the chili con carne. "If you mean did I put three tablespoons of chili powder in there, yes, I did."

Jazzi gave her mom a smile, then went back to cutting the butter with the pastry cutter.

All of a sudden Jazzi's phone played a Gwen Stefani song that Daisy recognized. Jazzi changed her ring tone every week or so.

"Is it okay if I get it?" Jazzi asked Daisy.

Daisy had made a rule that none of them would take phone calls or texts while they were sitting down at dinner. But since they were still in the food preparation stage . . .

"See who it is," Daisy said.

Jazzi wiped her hands on a paper towel, tossed it into the waste can under the sink, and then checked her phone. "It's Portia," she said, a bit breathless.

"Go ahead and take it. I'll spoon the biscuit dough onto the cookie sheet."

As Daisy did just that, she could hear the slow rumble of Jazzi's voice in the living room. She couldn't make out the words, and that was just as well. Jazzi needed her privacy as much as Daisy sometimes needed hers. This relationship between Portia, Jazzi, and herself was complicated at best, headed for disaster at worst. Had Portia spoken to her husband about her youth and how she had given Jazzi up for adoption? If so, it was a momentous moment in all of their lives.

Daisy slipped the cookie sheet into the oven and set the timer for fifteen minutes. Then to distract herself from Jazzi's voice that had risen a little, she opened the refrigerator and picked up the bowl of coleslaw that she'd made earlier. They could eat as soon as the biscuits were a golden brown.

Thinking about dessert, Daisy pulled two whoopee pies from the refrigerator. These were chocolate with peanut butter filling, Jazzi's favorite. Maybe she'd put on the teakettle so they could have tea with their dessert. Suddenly, dessert seemed very important after Jazzi's phone call, or maybe it was the conversation that having tea together usually produced that was important. Sometimes after a phone call with Portia, Jazzi clammed up. Sometimes she told Daisy about it in detail. The more detail, the more serious the conversation.

As soon as Jazzi entered the kitchen, Daisy could feel her daughter's sadness. When she looked at Jazzi's expression, Daisy just wanted to hold her in her arms. But she needed some signal from Jazzi on what she should do next.

"What happened?" Daisy asked.

Jazzi found her way to a stool at the kitchen island, sank down to it, and turned to face her mother. She shook her head. "Portia's husband didn't take the news well. He's staying at a motel for a few nights while he thinks about everything. Portia was crying almost the whole time we talked. I feel so bad. I feel responsible."

Crossing to the stool beside Jazzi, Daisy pulled it out and sat. Facing her daughter, she took Jazzi's two hands in hers. "Portia's marital difficulties aren't your fault."

"Yes, they are. Maybe I pushed too hard for her to tell him. Maybe she should have waited."

"And maybe she should have told him before they were married," Daisy decided firmly.

"Mom, that's *so* judgmental."

Yes, it was, Daisy conceded to herself. However, it was also what she believed would be the right thing to do. You couldn't keep secrets from a marriage partner and have a good marriage.

"A marriage is based on trust, Jazzi. If one person lies or omits something important before taking vows, it always comes back to haunt them."

"She thinks she would have lost him if she'd told him when they were dating."

Oh, so they'd talked about that. "And what did *you* say?"

"I told her I didn't know. I don't know anything." Tears began cascading down Jazzi's cheeks and Daisy took her into her arms. She didn't say anything more. What could she say? That everything would be fine? She didn't know if it would be, and she wasn't going to give her daughter false hope.

After a while Jazzi pulled away. "I still think this is my fault, and I should do something. Maybe I should talk to her husband."

"No, you shouldn't," Daisy insisted. "This is between the two of them. *They* have to solve it. You can't do that for them. What did Portia say about contacting you again?"

"She said we should give it time. Now she doesn't want to call me on the sly. She wants Colton to know about it when she does. But if he's in a hotel and she's at home, he wouldn't know anyway."

"Remember what I said about secrets. She probably feels she'd be lying if she did that. The only thing you can do for the moment is to give Portia and her family space as well as time. I know that's going to be difficult, but you can't push or it will only make things worse."

Daisy took Jazzi's hand again. "Do you understand? It's sort of like when Aunt Iris and your grandmother have a fight or an argument. Camellia and I or even Dad can't step in and fix it. They have to do it on their own."

"Do you believe love conquers all?" Jazzi asked with hope in her voice.

"I believe sometimes it can." Yet Daisy thought to herself that most of the time, it couldn't conquer what couldn't be changed.

On Sunday after working at the tea garden with Daisy, Jazzi decided to go out to dinner with Iris. That gave Daisy the opportunity to go with Cora Sue to pay a condolence call to Harriet Schumacher.

Cora Sue drove. After chatting about tea services that afternoon, Cora Sue pointed out, "This is Derek's neighborhood. Nice, isn't it?"

From what Daisy could see in the dusk, the neighborhood was more than nice. But that didn't surprise her. Schumacher had been a star at one time. If he'd saved his money and invested it wisely, he could have still afforded living here. The neighborhood was one of those on the outskirts of Willow Creek, much farther out than Daisy's barn home. The area would have been rural if not for the development. It seemed like a small community with a convenience store, a gas station, and a pizza and sub shop. Daisy was glad Cora Sue had driven since she knew all about the area and exactly where she was going. Schumacher's house was located at the end of a cul-de-sac.

As Cora Sue pulled into the driveway, she said, "I understand that Derek bought three lots—the one in the middle of the cul-de-sac, and one on either side so that he'd have privacy."

Daisy whistled. "That must have cost a bundle."

The house was a Colonial-style, a square with an emphasis on the entry door in the middle of the front of the house. There were paired chimneys, and the windows were framed by shutters, black against the white siding.

"The second floor has four bedrooms," Cora Sue explained. "But Derek had the floor renovated for his mother. There's a small kitchen and a full bath up there. He knocked out a wall to make a more open sitting area. The great room in the back of the house on the first floor became his master suite."

"Is there a reason he didn't give his mother the first floor if she has problems with steps?"

"That's why he put in the chair lift. Since she likes quiet, he thought she'd have more privacy upstairs. I understand he sometimes had other chefs in and out, cooking up a storm. He also had friends who liked late nights. I think he felt more free being on the first floor himself with a large kitchen with the island to cook at. After all, the kitchen used to be the center of his life."

Used to be. Again Daisy wondered what had happened that Derek's show was canceled. Just low ratings? Or something else. Maybe something more sinister?

Cora Sue and Daisy exited the car and walked to the front door. There Daisy noted the video camera doorbell. It was probably part of a security system.

Cora Sue pointed to it and rang the doorbell. "When I press the doorbell, Harriet receives an alert on her phone. The app shows her who's at the door."

A voice came through the small intercom. "Cora

Sue? I see you. Who's with you?" Harriet Schumacher's voice was clipped and terse.

"It's Daisy Swanson from Daisy's Tea Garden. She wanted to come along to pay her condolences too."

Daisy thought she heard a harrumph, then there was a loud click at the doorknob. Harriet's voice came over the intercom again. "Come on up. I just opened the door for you."

"I'm surprised she's using high-tech security," Daisy noted.

"Just because Harriet is in her sixties doesn't mean she's not up on the latest trends. I think she's the one who found the system she wanted Derek to put in."

Daisy could understand why Detective Rappaport was looking at Cora Sue closely as a suspect. She had ties to the family. Did many people? Maybe Daisy would soon find out.

After Daisy and Cora Sue entered the house, they closed the door behind them and heard it click. The stairway was directly in front of them and cut the second floor in half. As Daisy peered up the stairs, she spotted the chair lift at the top. She also saw a woman standing there with a four-pronged cane.

"Come on up," Harriet said. "I have enough sweets that could kill a person with diabetes. Fortunately, I don't have it. You can eat some of them so I don't have to throw them out."

Cora Sue leaned close to Daisy. "Harriet can be crotchety, but I like her. You never have to guess what she's thinking."

After Cora Sue and Daisy climbed the stairs, Cora Sue introduced Daisy to Harriet. Daisy took Harriet's hand and said sincerely, "I'm so sorry for your loss. I got to know Derek just a little when he came into the tea garden."

"Did he give you a bad review?" Harriet asked brusquely.

"I don't know," Daisy responded honestly. "He hadn't put it on his blog yet."

"That blog," Harriet grumbled. "It's probably what got him killed." The older woman motioned to the living room. "I need to sit. My legs still get shaky now and then."

The living room was decorated in shades of claret and pale pink, from the sofa and faux-suede recliner to the flowered valances. Even the marble-topped tables had a bit of pink in them.

Harriet sat in the recliner, put her cane along the chair, and then pressed a button so that the footrest came up. Daisy recognized the type of chair. It was one of those recliners that raised its seat so standing up was easier.

Cora Sue commented, "I thought your family would be here with you."

Harriet took the chair's control in hand and adjusted her sitting position. "I sent them all home. They were more of a bother than a help. The police have still been in and out, asking all types of questions. I wish they'd all just leave me alone."

Daisy and Cora Sue exchanged a look. If Harriet could be blunt, then Daisy could be too. "They're trying to figure out who killed your son."

"Maybe so. But some of the questions they ask have nothing to do with me, and I didn't know the answers. Derek had a life before I had my stroke, and I didn't know much about it. Even after I moved in with him, we kept our lives separate. That's just the way we lived.

When I tell the detective that, he looks at me as if I'm crazy."

"Detective Rappaport might just be trying to get a rise out of you," Daisy pointed out. "He feels he can elicit information that way."

"Do you know the detective well?" Harriet asked, narrowing her eyes.

"More than I'd like," Daisy said wryly. "My aunt and I were involved in a murder at the tea garden, and since then Detective Rappaport and I have crossed swords at times."

Harriet gave Daisy a more penetrating look. "So you're not just a pretty face with long blond hair and blue eyes."

Daisy almost laughed out loud. "No, ma'am, I'm not."

Harriet pointed a finger at her. "I suspect everyone, especially men, underestimate you."

"That's true," Daisy agreed.

"Do you know what that detective asked me?" Harriet asked huffily.

"What?" Daisy countered, wondering if she'd be shocked.

"He had the nerve to ask me if I could do the stairs if I wanted to. Can you imagine?"

Was it possible that Detective Rappaport suspected Harriet of murdering her son? What could ever give him that idea?

"Do you have children?" Harriet asked Daisy.

"I do. I have two daughters. One's in college and one is still in high school."

Harriet shook her head. "I imagine daughters are twice the trouble as sons—makeup, hair, highlights, and clothes. What those young women wear now is disgraceful."

It was obvious that Harriet had strong opinions about everything.

Derek's mother said to Cora Sue, "Why don't you go into my kitchen and grab one of those cakes. There are three of them there."

"Do you like tea?" Daisy asked. "I can make us all a cup."

"That would be lovely. My daughter-in-law doesn't care much for tea, so she doesn't think to make it for me. And of course, my sons never think of tea." She said in a lower voice, "At least, Derek never did."

Daisy remembered how Derek had drunk lots of tea. Did he just not care that his mother might like it? Had he been oblivious to her needs? Is that why Detective Rappaport thought Harriet might have something to do with the murder?

Chapter Seven

As soon as Foster's brother Ben pushed open the door to the tea garden on Monday morning and stepped inside, Daisy predicted trouble was brewing. Ben could see his brother at home, so why come to the tea garden? One reason—privacy so other family members couldn't overhear.

Ben was about twelve and his eyes were usually sparkling and animated, his walk full of energy. However, today he looked around for Foster, spotted him in the spillover tea room, and crossed to him faster than Daisy could blink. She knew Foster would be upset that Ben was interrupting him while he was working. Foster had a sense of responsibility two miles wide that spilled over into work and his relationships with his family. Daisy didn't want to interfere. But as she stood at the sales counter, she could hear their raised voices. She knew Foster's voice, and Ben's younger voice was distinguishable.

She peeked around the corner into the room and saw Ben and Foster were in the corner by the bay window. There was only one table filled with four customers, but it was obvious that those customers were listening because they kept looking toward the two young men. Daisy truly didn't want to intervene, but she couldn't let the Cranshaws' personal situation affect the guests who came to the tea garden for calm and quiet. Arguments just weren't good for business.

She bit her lower lip, debating whether to act or not. Aunt Iris, Cora Sue, and Karina were easily handling the main tea room. If anything, Daisy should help Tessa in the kitchen with baking and prep.

She heard Ben say very loudly, "No."

As Foster shushed his brother, she decided to break up their conversation.

However, she'd only taken one step forward when Ben, looking miserable, brushed past her and headed for the door. He was gone before she could say his name. At the same time, her four guests in the spill-over room rose from their table to leave. On their way out, they told Daisy how much they'd enjoyed their tea service. She was glad they were satisfied, but her mind was on Foster.

She smiled and said everything she should to them including, "Feel free to stop in anytime." She handed them each a coupon for a free scone. She kept the coupons in her apron pocket just in case she needed one. After they'd left, she caught sight of Foster who was now staring out the bay window. She doubted he was seeing anything.

Instead of going to Foster, she caught sight of Ben lingering on the sidewalk to the left of the tea garden. Foster hadn't been telling her anything about his moods, and Ben just might.

She signaled to her aunt Iris who was at the kitchen

doorway that she was going outside for a few minutes. Iris nodded and gave her a thumbs-up.

Daisy quickly looked left as the tea garden door closed behind her. Ben was still there, staring at something in his hand.

She hurried past the colorful potted planters filled with pansies that decorated the porch, ran down the steps, and swerved to her left. When Ben saw her, he looked as if he was going to walk away.

She called to him. "Ben! Ben Cranshaw. Can I talk to you for a minute?"

She and the twelve-year-old had had a few conversations. She didn't know him well, but she did know that he looked up to Foster. If he was arguing with his older brother, then something was wrong. He looked unhappy as he shifted his billed cap on his head and stared down at his sneakers.

Daisy motioned around to the garden side of the Victorian where no one was sitting. It was still a little chilly for outdoor service, though some residents of Willow Creek requested it. Ben looked like he didn't care where they sat.

He took the white wrought iron chair at a small table and still didn't look up at her.

"Ben, I'm worried about your brother."

Ben's eyes snapped up to hers. "Why?"

"Because he seems different the past week. He appears to be distracted, and he won't tell me what's distracting him. He won't even tell Detective Rappaport where he was at a certain time. That could get him into real trouble."

She thought she had to be honest with Ben to coax out any information he might have. Her next step, if she couldn't get anything out of Ben or Foster, was to go to their dad.

At first Gavin hadn't wanted Foster to work at Daisy's Tea Garden. He thought it was beneath his son and that he should be concentrating on his studies. But Foster wanted to earn money to become more independent. He believed he was too old for all the rules his father demanded. So they'd come to an agreement. Foster paid room and board but could come and go as he wished. Daisy thought the arrangement had been working out. Now she wasn't so sure.

"What did you have in your hand when you were standing on the sidewalk? I saw you had it when you were talking to Foster too."

Ben pulled a crumpled cocktail napkin from his jacket pocket and laid it in front of Daisy on the table.

Curious, she slowly opened it. It had come from Bases, Willow Creek's sports bar, which was a singles' hangout, especially at Happy Hour.

"Foster dropped that in the kitchen when he came in last night. He came in late, but he wouldn't say where he'd been. That's not like him."

Both she and Ben knew that Foster wasn't twenty-one yet, the legal drinking age in Pennsylvania.

"Do you think Foster has a fake ID?"

Ben shook his head. "When he was getting a shower this morning, I went through his wallet."

"Ben, you should have just asked him."

"The way he's been acting, I knew he wouldn't tell me the truth. When I asked him about it in there just now, he said of course he doesn't have a fake ID. There's no *of course* about it. I know kids my age who have fake IDs. So if he had one, he'd want that for drinking liquor, right?"

Daisy suspected Ben's conclusion was probably true. "Did you see him when he got home last night?"

"I did. I talked to him. I made up the excuse that I wanted to borrow one of his binders for a school project."

"*Had* Foster been drinking?"

"I don't think so. After Mom died, Dad did drink, even in front of us. And we saw the symptoms of that—slurred speech, sweating, the smell of alcohol. If he'd been to Bases, he always smelled like smoke when he came home because he'd been in one of their private rooms playing poker."

"He told you this?"

"After he got back on his feet, after he realized he needed us as much as we needed him, he told us he'd just go in there and drink and play poker until he couldn't think about Mom. I get it. Foster got it. But Foster just won't get real with me now. I don't want to have to snoop. I want him to just tell me what's going on. I don't want to worry he's drinking and driving."

"Maybe Foster has a romantic dilemma and thinks you wouldn't understand."

"You mean like breaking up with Vi? He'd better not do that."

Daisy smiled. "See what I mean? I think we'd better let Foster figure out on his own whatever's troubling him. The best thing for you to do is just be available to listen. Try to be helpful to him, not critical. Sometimes when someone annoys us, we tend to criticize everything they do. That's not the way to get them to open up."

"So I should just listen," Ben acknowledged.

"Yes, just listen if the two of you talk. If you just

listen, something might spill out. Don't jump on it, but just let Foster explain slowly. Think you can do that?"

"I guess I can." But Ben didn't sound as if it would do any good.

"Okay, Ben, I'll tell you what. You do that, and I'll approach Foster and see if I can get anything else out of him."

"Will you let me know if you do?"

Being truthful, Daisy said, "That depends on what's troubling him. But if I can, I'll tell you."

"I don't have a cell phone," Ben admitted. "So you won't be able to call me."

She could see how much that bothered him. She patted his arm. "That's okay, Ben. Call me at the tea garden, and I promise I'll tell you if I've learned anything."

Ben stood. "Thanks, Mrs. Swanson. I didn't know what I was going to do. I didn't want to go to Dad."

"You still might have to. *I* might have to."

Ben nodded. "Dad will be upset if we go to him."

Daisy knew Foster would be beyond upset too.

It was late in the day when the busloads of tourists stopped arriving. Daisy saw Foster busing tables in the yellow spillover room. The customers had emptied out except for two tables in the main tea room. Now was as good a time as any to talk with him.

As Daisy approached him, Foster frowned. She must have had an I'm-going-to-have-a-word-with-you look on her face, and he could read her quite well. He kept silent as he loaded a teacup and saucer onto a tray.

She walked up to the table and asked, "Can I talk to you, Foster?"

He set down the tray as if he knew he couldn't evade her. "You saw my brother here this morning. I'm sorry we argued in the tea garden. That won't happen again."

"Siblings argue. I'm not concerned about that, Foster. But I am concerned about what Ben told me."

"What exactly did he say?"

Daisy added dishes with crumbs on them to Foster's tray.

"He told me you came in really late last night and you dropped a cocktail napkin from Bases."

"He tried to blackmail me this morning. If I didn't tell him why I went to Bases, he'd go to Dad."

"He still might. He's worried. He said you didn't answer your cell phone last night, and if you're going to be out late you tell everyone that. Why was last night so different?" Her motherly instincts were kicking in, and she was going to eventually get to the bottom of what was bothering Foster.

"I just had some things to think about," he explained.

"And you had to stay out late to do that? When Ben found the cocktail napkin, I think he was worried that you'd been drinking and driving."

Foster stopped loading the tray and turned to face Daisy. "At home, it's hard to think with Dad, my brother, and my sister. I needed quiet."

"And the bar was quieter?" Usually a TV was blasting, and chatter could be loud among the customers.

"I guess I mean I needed time to myself. There was a replay of a game on the TV. I had soda water with lemon. I just needed time alone." His words were almost pleading.

"Is this about work? Are you considering taking another job?"

"Absolutely not. I like what I do here."

He seemed sincere about that, and suddenly Daisy wondered if he *was* thinking of breaking up with Vi. Trouble in Paradise could cause this kind of angst. Should she ask if this was about Vi? Should she try to dip her finger in the pool of teenage romance? She knew how heartbreaking it could be. She knew how every missed call and offhand remark could be misconstrued. A breakup at this stage of their relationship wouldn't be uncommon. They were separated by distance, though Vi *would* be coming home for the summer.

However, maybe Vi had a job she wanted to take elsewhere and Foster didn't want her to. Daisy didn't want her to, either, if that was the problem, but she wouldn't stop her. She couldn't stop her if she wanted Vi to fly with her own wings. That also meant she couldn't interfere in her daughter's relationship with Foster. She absolutely had to stay out of it. She hadn't talked to Vi for a week. She usually let Vi call her. But Vi hadn't called. This time maybe Daisy would have to create the opportunity to speak to her daughter.

In the meantime, she told Foster, "If you ever need to talk . . . about anything, you can come to me. You know that, don't you?"

Foster nodded. "You've been good to me, Mrs. Swanson, and treated me with respect. I don't want anything to change that."

Daisy wondered why Foster had reverted to the Mrs. Swanson title again, but she wouldn't point it out now. She simply said, "Nothing could change that, Foster."

But as she left Foster busing the table, she considered what could possibly change the way she thought of Foster. The only thing she could think of was him being involved in a murder!

* * *

The volunteer fire company in Willow Creek had long ago built a community social hall that was attached to the engine house. The social hall was used for everything imaginable, from Spring Fling dances to wedding receptions to private parties and other social events by businesses in the community. Today the hall was being used for a chamber of commerce breakfast.

Daisy stood in the short line at the buffet table with her aunt Iris. The meeting always started early in the morning, around seven o'clock, so business owners could get back to their work environments. This occasion was nothing fancy, but the chamber of commerce president Bridie Stoltzfus had asked Daisy to provide scones, muffins, and her brown sugar biscuits.

Daisy knew that Bridie didn't want anything too refined. Still she'd used a white tablecloth over a long table, put a bouquet of flowers in one of her tall teapots in the center of the table, and down the center she placed a quilted runner Rachel had sewn. Daisy displayed the scones, muffins, and biscuits on tiered dishes. The hot water urn would serve anyone who wanted tea. She had provided a wooden box of selected quality tea bags. There was, of course, a coffee urn for the coffee drinkers. Instead of the teacups Daisy would have preferred, insulated cups bought at the local discount store served the day.

Aunt Iris chose a biscuit, put it on her paper plate, then slathered it with the raspberry jam that they used at the tea garden. "I wonder if Bridie ever thought about having a meeting in the evening instead of the early morning. We might get a whole different bunch of store owners and business operators, don't you think?"

"You can make the suggestion," Daisy assured her aunt.

"Bridie won't listen. She always thinks she knows what's best."

Daisy tried to hide a smile. Bridie, white haired, petite, with huge blue glasses and running suits in a variety of colors, ran the chamber of commerce like a ring master. She did rarely accept suggestions, but she was a good organizer. When something needed to be done, she was sure to see it through. But Bridie and Daisy's aunt had clashed on more than one occasion because they both belonged to the same social women's group at the local church. There Bridie didn't run the show but had a hard time letting go of being boss.

"When's Bridie's term up?" Daisy asked, though she knew very well when it was.

"In August," her aunt answered airily.

"You could run for chamber of commerce president."

"You can't be serious." Her aunt looked astonished that Daisy would even think of such a thing.

"You organize very well. How difficult would it be to run a meeting once a month?"

"It's not just meetings once a month," her aunt protested. "There are the weekends we have special events to coax more tourists to drive through Willow Creek. Then there are the Christmas decorations around town, whether or not a stoplight needs to be retimed, and just the general business of keeping records."

"The mayor makes decisions on some of that."

"That's true, but Bridie is good at what she does."

Daisy smiled at her aunt's concession. Though she might cross swords with Bridie at times, Aunt Iris respected the woman.

Suddenly, Daisy felt a hand on her shoulder. The gentle firm grip was one she had come to know. It was Jonas.

Turning toward him, she smiled. His thick black hair looked like it might still be damp from his shower. This morning he wore a steel gray pullover with black jeans and black shoe boots. She wanted to give him a hug, maybe even a kiss, but they were in a public place. She spotted Elijah behind Jonas. As well as selling his furniture through Jonas's shop, Elijah Beiler also oversaw the shop from time to time when Jonas's manager couldn't be there.

"Good morning, Jonas. Hi there, Elijah. I suppose this meeting is to get us ready for Tourist Appreciation this weekend."

"Ready is a relative term," Jonas commented. He leaned close to Iris. "Your sweets this morning look good. Better yet, I know they'll taste delicious."

Iris's eyes were twinkling as she said to Jonas, "My blueberry scones are the best. If you want more than one, you'd better grab them while you're up here because there won't be any if you come back."

Jonas laughed. "I'll keep that in mind."

As soon as he had put two scones on his paper plate, his gaze wandered to the back entrance of the social hall. He leaned over Daisy's shoulder and asked her, "Since when does Detective Rappaport come to chamber of commerce breakfasts?"

"I don't know." Daisy realized worry tinged her voice. "Do you think it has something to do with the murder?"

"We'll soon find out."

It didn't take long until everyone who was at the breakfast was seated. They all had stores or work of some kind to get back to. Daisy, Jonas, Iris, and Elijah had ended up seated next to Arden Botterill.

The first thing Daisy asked Arden was, "How are sales at Vinegar and Spice?"

Arden had opened the shop in the beginning of winter, not the best time for an opening. The boutique was an amazing shop, and Daisy stopped in often. Arden sold flavored vinegars. Daisy liked the peach vinegar the best, and she often used it on her own salads. She also made dressings with it for the tea garden. Other flavored vinegars were strawberry and cranberry walnut balsamic. Along with the vinegars she sold flavored olive oils such as blood orange and basil lemongrass. Combinations of spices also drew cooks to Arden's shop. The orange pepper was Daisy's favorite, although there were many more.

"Sales have picked up in the past week," Arden said. She had a piquant face and short red hair. She looked to Daisy like a pixie. But she was in her forties and business-savvy despite the inopportune opening of her shop.

"The tour buses have done a great deal for business," she said. "Apparently, the tourists have experienced stores similar to mine in other towns. Hanover has two—one in their Amish market and one downtown."

"Why do you think interest in this has picked up, not only among chefs, but among ordinary people?" Aunt Iris asked.

Arden's answer was quick in coming. "It's the cooking shows. My goodness, I don't think I could even count them all now. There's the Food Network, of course, but then there are cooking shows from home chefs to master chefs on other TV networks too. Women especially see how they can enhance their family's dinners, so they use something different. I'm grateful for that. I believe business will only pick up."

Jonas interjected, "I hope that's true. When one business succeeds, it helps others succeed."

Although Jonas had experienced deep heartache and seen absolutely vile things as a detective, he was one of the most positive people Daisy knew. And his positivity was another attribute that drew her toward him. Jonas Groft was so much more than a handsome man who could be a *GQ* model or a macho hunk on the front of a mercenary magazine.

Now what had made her think of that? His background and the fact that he'd carried a gun?

Bridie took her position at the podium with the microphone after almost everyone attending had finished eating and they'd gone back to the serving table for their second cup of tea or coffee. Iris had been right. There weren't any more blueberry scones, just a few biscuits.

Bridie tapped the mic to test it as she usually did. Then she bent down. "Hello, everyone. Thank you for coming today. I hope you've enjoyed a little camaraderie in preparation for the meeting. We really do want all great minds to think alike."

Everyone chuckled. Bridie didn't like dissention or confrontation, and they all knew it.

"Before we start with our business about Tourist Appreciation Weekend that's coming up faster than we probably want it to, Detective Rappaport has asked me if he could speak a few words. Since the chief of police called me ahead of time and told me this was going to happen, I said of course he could. How could I ever turn down Eli Schultz?"

Again, a chuckle went through the room. Chief of Police Schultz was always gruff and unsmiling. Though he used to be mostly a paper-pusher, that had certainly changed over the past year with the murders that had landed on his desk.

"Detective Rappaport, it's your turn," Bridie said, "but do please keep in mind that these folks have to get back to work."

"And so do I, Miss Stoltzfus. So do I."

Bridie reddened a bit at that but stepped aside so he could stand at the podium.

He took a minute for silence to settle in—an unsettling silence. Then he said, "Most of you know me or know of me." His glance fell on Daisy's table and a few others. "Knowing that you are all store owners, I consider you as responsible adults in this town."

Daisy leaned close to Jonas. "What's he talking about?"

Jonas shook his head. "I don't know, but I'm sure we'll find out."

"I have a murder to solve, and I'd like to solve it quickly. Tourist Appreciation Weekend could slow me down just because of having more people in Willow Creek. But also because of emergencies and situations that might call me away from my desk because of it. So I'm going to ask all of you to keep your calm hats on this weekend. Try not to let fights break out, screaming matches start, or anything that would require you to call the police. If someone needs help and you can help them, please do that. I guess what I'm saying is, try to take some of the burden off the police. You know we patrol more and contract additional security officers for these weekends. I would consider it a big help in going forward if stores could install security cameras. They would be a huge aid if a crime occurs."

A man in the back shouted, "Big Brother is watching."

Rappaport scowled. "Maybe so. But just remember, you are your brother's keeper, and your brother could save your life."

He looked over at the business owner again and added, "Also with more people milling about, you're bound to overhear conversations. Keep an ear out. I'm sure Daisy's Tea Garden will have curious tourists who'll want to see the last place Derek Schumacher ate food. Whether they come into the tea garden or stop at other stores, take note of their conversations. I'm going to set up a tip line. I will give all of you the number. If you hear anything that might have something to do with the murder, call that line. I have cards here with the number printed on it, so I'll put them on the table at the entrance. As you leave, pick one up. Then you'll have the number with you. Are there any questions?"

No one raised a hand. Rappaport gave them all a level look. "Remember to pick up your cards on the way out."

Arden, who was sitting next to Daisy, said, "I know the Schumacher family. My grandparents were friends with Harriet's parents. Her parents were bakers, and they took goods to be sold to the farmers market. My grandparents who sold produce had a stand next to theirs."

"Do you know much about the present-day Schumacher family?"

"I know that Harriet has a hard shell."

"Hard as in . . ." Daisy prompted.

"Would you believe Harriet has a sister, June, that she hasn't spoken to in about thirty-five years?"

Daisy couldn't imagine it. She and her sister Camellia didn't always get along, but they never would think about going without talking for a year or longer.

"Do you know the basis of the split or anything about June?"

Arden shook her head. "No, I don't. Truthfully, I don't think anybody does. Harriet can be very closed-mouthed. I do know Bradley, Derek's brother. He's a bit rigid but a good guy. His wife is decent too. She's been kind to Harriet since her stroke."

"How about Derek? Did you know him?"

"Not well. He was hardly in Willow Creek, cooking at this restaurant or that, then with his cable show."

Daisy watched Bridie as she took her place at the podium, intending to make her next announcement.

Jonas asked Arden, "Is an inheritance from Derek in the offing?"

Arden glanced at Jonas and must have realized that he wasn't asking out of mere speculation. "You were a detective, weren't you?"

"Once," he said, leaving it at that.

"I don't know the exact contents of Derek's will, but I did hear he's definitely leaving his house to his mother to sell or keep as she wishes."

Bridie was at the microphone and tapped it several times. Without preamble she began, "You know I don't like discord. I hear there's a squabble over whether there should be a DJ at the social for Tourist Appreciation Weekend. If we can't come to a consensus, we will have a vote and that will settle it."

Jonas's shoulder leaned into Daisy's. "Maybe someone didn't want Harriet to have Derek's house."

"Maybe the murder had nothing to do with an inheritance."

She exchanged a look with Jonas that said only time would tell. Then they turned toward Bridie who intended to maintain order no matter what.

Chapter Eight

From a vantage point across the street, Daisy cast her glance toward the tea garden. Sometimes it was so hard to believe that she and her aunt owned it and were making a success of it. On Saturday of this Tourist Appreciation Weekend, she realized how the Victorian stood out set among the other businesses. The pale green exterior with its white and yellow trim looked fresh, as fresh as spring. She'd filled huge ceramic pots with herbs and flowers, especially lavender and rosemary. It was early yet for the herbs to reach their full stature, but they still looked beautiful surrounded by purple and pink pansies and daffodils. By summer's end, the lemongrass would grow as high as the top of the bay window.

She felt a hand on her arm and turned to see her friend Rachel.

The strings on Rachel's white kapp floated a bit in the spring breeze as she said enthusiastically, "Doesn't the town look wonderful *gut*?"

With her family and close friends, Rachel often lapsed into Pennsylvania Dutch dialect. Daisy understood it because of the time in her childhood spent with Rachel's family. She remembered wishing she and Rachel could go to school together. But the Amish school was separate from the public school. Still, during planting season, Daisy and her dad had made weekly trips to the Esh farm to pick up plants they'd grown there for sale in their nursery.

Glancing down the street again at the bright-colored canopies lining the main road on both sides, Daisy felt the excitement of a weekend for crafters and store-keepers that was going well. The weather couldn't be any more perfect. This was the second day of their event, and although everyone was harried and busy, they wore smiles on their faces that told Daisy many customers were buying.

"I only have a few minutes' break," Daisy said, "or I'd come in and look around at the quilts I saw Levi bringing in yesterday."

"Table runners too," Rachel said with a nod. "I thought of you when I saw them."

"Uh-oh. Now I'm hooked. Still, I promised Jazzi I'd bring her a funnel cake from the Kings' stand. As if we don't have enough baked goods in the tea garden. But Jazzi insists scones and muffins are not funnel cakes."

Rachel laughed. "And you feel obligated to bring one back because she's working for you today."

"She is. I'm trying to keep her busy so she doesn't think too much about Portia and what's going to happen next."

As if Daisy had summoned Jazzi, her daughter came running over from the tea garden. "Mom, we need you. We don't have an empty chair."

Daisy patted Rachel's arm and said, "See you later."

Daisy handed Jazzi the plate with the funnel cake

dusted with powdered sugar. As she and her daughter waited to cross the street, she spotted Harriet Schumacher headed toward her in a wheelchair. Her son Bradley was pushing her, and a woman walked beside him.

Harriet called, "Mrs. Swanson."

Daisy crossed to where Bradley had stopped the wheelchair. She was surprised she'd never made the Schumacher name connection before. Since Jazzi and Violet had attended the high school, she'd just considered *Schumacher*, the principal's name, a common name in this area.

Immediately Harriet said, "This is my son Bradley who you might know if your girls are at the high school. And this is my daughter-in-law Lauren."

As soon as Jazzi saw her high school principal, she blushed. She was obviously embarrassed at seeing her principal in an out-of-school setting. She quickly said, "Remember, Mom, we need you," and rushed down the street away from the group.

Daisy stared after her daughter. "I'm sorry if she seemed abrupt. Apparently, the tea garden had a surge of customers, and she called me in off of a break."

Bradley said, "My students like to forget I'm their principal."

Lauren laughed. "Authority figures and teenagers don't go together very well. I'm glad we're not at that stage yet."

"They have a daughter," Harriet interjected. "She's three."

"That's a wonderful age," Daisy said. "You ought to frame lots of photos so you can remember as many days as you can."

Lauren nodded. "Exactly."

"Where is she now?" Daisy asked.

"She's with a sitter," Lauren responded. "This was a bit too much for her. Fortunately, a responsible teen lives next door to us, and she can babysit when we need her."

"I know it's a little early after Derek's death for me to be out and about," Harriet said. "But I can mourn Derek and still live my life."

Lauren and Bradley exchanged a look.

Daisy knew what Harriet said was indeed true, and yet . . . After Ryan had died, she'd found it hard to get on with life. Part of her had been missing. It was as if she still had one hand but not the other. The only thing that had kept her moving forward had been her girls. She couldn't even imagine losing a child, not even a grown one. Maybe Harriet was pushing grief away with bravado. But it would catch up with her.

"You have to do what you feel is right," she said tactfully. "You also have to take care of yourself. If coming out, interacting with people, stopping at craft stands, can ease your sorrow, then that's what you need to do, no matter what anyone says."

Harriet nodded. "I like that philosophy."

Harriet studied the people strolling up and down the street, stopping to buy potholders, a flower arrangement, or a wood carving. "Derek would have loved this," she mused.

"Derek did like to be in the center of the action," Bradley agreed.

Daisy could tell from the expression on Harriet's face that she was reminiscing. "He was so upset when his show was canceled," Harriet said.

Although Daisy remembered the tea garden needed her, she couldn't help asking a question to learn more about Derek. "Why didn't he try to propose another show if he had a good following?" Daisy asked. "His blog alone gets a million views."

Bradley shook his head. "That just wasn't possible. Burned bridges and all that."

Harriet gave him a sharp glance as if she were puzzled by what he'd said. "You and your brother were just very different."

Lauren added, "Although Bradley's around eight hundred students most of the time, he's more of an at-home, quiet person and doesn't seek the spotlight."

Studying Derek Schumacher's family, Daisy wondered exactly what Bradley knew about Derek's burned bridges. She also suspected that seeking the spotlight could have been one of the things that had gotten Derek killed.

As Daisy glanced across the street, she spotted Jazzi again, waving at her from the doorway. With an apologetic smile, she said to the group, "I really do have to get back to the tea garden. Why don't you come with me? Tea and a free scone for each of you, your choice."

Bradley leaned down to Harriet. "Mother?"

"Can you accommodate a wheelchair?" Harriet asked Daisy.

"Yes, we can. We have a handicapped entrance at the back. You can come right through the hallway and into the tea room. No muss, no fuss. I promise."

Harriet nodded. "A cup of Earl Grey and a scone would hit the spot. But there are a few craft stands I'd like to visit first."

"The invitation is open-ended. Come in anytime."

She hoped that they would. She also hoped that

maybe she'd learn more about Derek Schumacher from this trio who each had very different personalities.

After a round of good-byes, Daisy crossed the street, took one glance at the gingerbread trim on the tea garden's porch and second floor, then quickly ran up the few steps to the covered porch of the Victorian. Once inside she easily realized why Jazzi had beckoned to her more than once. Both tea rooms were crowded, and there was a line at the counter that her aunt and Karina were attempting to manage. Daisy had called in extra help to bus tables with Jazzi, but everyone was scurrying, pouring, serving, or taking orders.

Had she expected today to be such a success? She wasn't sure. She'd been on a committee in the winter to promote Quilt Lovers Weekend, and the promotion had increased their winter traffic significantly that weekend. But not like this.

She went to the kitchen first because if the tea garden didn't have enough baked goods, salads, and soups to sell, they might as well close.

Tessa looked up from the carrot salad with grapes and pecans that she was stirring in a huge stainless bowl.

"How are we doing?" Daisy asked.

"Another batch of Snickerdoodles will come out of the oven in about three minutes. I have more scone batter ready to go. Eva said she'd roll and cut it for me. We're almost out of beef barley soup, but I think we still have enough vegetable to get us through 'til the end of the day."

"Where do you need me most?" Daisy asked.

"Can you mix up a batch, maybe a double batch, of apple cinnamon bread? We can sell that in slices. We have more chocolate chip cookies in the freezer. You might want to put those out to thaw."

As her kitchen manager, Tessa did a wonderful job. And Daisy let her. This was the type of business where everyone did their part and chipped in when they needed to help someone else with theirs.

Daisy asked Eva, "Are you keeping up with washing the teapots?"

"It's a good thing we bought extras for the summer," Eva said. "I'm good for now. Jazzi was helping me, but she disappeared a few minutes ago."

Disappeared. Just what did that mean?

After Daisy did everything Tessa had requested, she checked both tea rooms and the counter line. Everything seemed to be under control, but Jazzi wasn't in sight. She also popped into her office, but it was empty. She didn't think Jazzi would go far without telling her. Maybe she'd needed a bit of privacy.

Returning to the kitchen she told Tessa, "I'm going to check out back for Jazzi."

Tessa gave her a quick nod and a smile, then a thumbs-up sign. Daisy knew what that meant. They wouldn't have to worry about profits this week, or maybe even this month.

Unless . . .

Unless Derek Schumacher had written a bad review for the tea garden and it was somehow published. She knew blogs could be timed to post. Maybe he'd set hers up and the word would go out whether the tea garden was a place to visit or not.

Daisy stepped outside into the sunshine and heard birdsong along with the chatter of conversation around the corner at the outside garden. She checked around there first. They weren't serving outside today.

They knew that would require even more help. However, the customers who bought baked goods at the counter and tea could bring their selections outside and sit at the tables.

Russ Windom was seated at one of the tables closest to her. She asked him, "How are you enjoying the weekend?"

"I'm enjoying it a lot. I've even caught up with some of my former students. They themselves have children now. It makes one feel old."

"Think of it as feeling productive, not old. I'm sure you touched their lives in a positive way. That's what matters. When they raise their kids, they might pass on something they learned from you."

"A very good point," Russ remarked with a smile.

"Have you seen Jazzi?"

"Why, yes. She exited the side entrance a little while ago and went around back."

Daisy waved at what he was having. "Enjoy your chocolate chip cookies and tea."

His smile said he would.

Moments later, she found Jazzi at the door that was the entrance to Tessa's apartment. Steps led up to the second floor where her friend lived. Tessa used the third floor as her artist's studio.

But Jazzi wasn't trying to enter Tessa's apartment. Rather she had her phone out and looked upset. Daisy didn't hesitate to go to her.

"Is something wrong?" she asked her.

Without any hesitation at all, as if she just needed to blurt it out, Jazzi answered, "I've been trying to call Portia, but she isn't answering."

Daisy saw the tears in Jazzi's eyes, and her heart hurt for her daughter.

"Portia probably won't answer until she's ready to answer . . . ready with some kind of decision," Daisy told her daughter again. "You can't push this."

Jazzi took one more glance at her phone and pocketed it. "You know the social tonight?" Her voice was husky, and Daisy knew that Jazzi still might be fighting back tears. "I don't want to go. I just don't feel like it, Mom."

Daisy had a date with Jonas for the social. This was always the single mom's dilemma. Should she go? Or should she offer to stay at home with Jazzi? However, she thought about the whole situation.

"I'll cancel with Jonas if you want me to stay home with you."

"Don't do that, Mom. We have a security system, and I have Pepper and Marjoram for company."

"Can I take you to your grandparents?"

"I'll see them tomorrow for dinner."

"Can I help you look at this relationship with Portia another way?" Daisy asked.

"What way?" Jazzi asked petulantly.

"If you stay home tonight, what will you do? Try to constantly call Portia? Think about calling Portia? Be upset about Portia not calling you? Isn't that going to be underlying everything you try to do?"

"Probably." Jazzi pushed her straight black hair over her shoulder. "But what's the alternative?"

"Come along with Jonas and me to the social. I know you don't want to be stuck with us, and I don't expect you to be. Make arrangements with friends. Decide you're going to have a good time. Forget for a little while about Portia and what's happening or not happening."

"I don't mean to be snotty," Jazzi said, "but you just

want to go with Jonas and you don't want to feel guilty if I stay home."

Jazzi's feelings had been so much on the surface lately that Daisy didn't come down on her this time for the snottiness. "Jazzi, look me in the eyes."

"Mom . . ." She drawled out the word.

"I'm serious. Look into my eyes." She pointed two fingers at Jazzi's eyes and then the two of hers.

Finally, Jazzi's gaze was direct. "I told you, if you want to stay home, I will stay home. You and Vi come first in my life. Your needs come first. I just have to know what they are. I think it would be good for both of us tonight to socialize with friends."

Maybe Jazzi could see Daisy's sincerity, and maybe she knew from experience that Daisy did what was best for her and Vi.

"Let me see who's going tonight," Jazzi murmured. "Stacy texted me a list." She checked her text and then she looked up at her mom. "Okay. It's a good crowd. I should be able to find somebody to hang out with."

"And you'll try to have a good time."

"I will. I don't have to tell *you* to try and have a good time with Jonas." Her daughter's smile was a little sly.

"Break over," Daisy said. "Back to serving tea."

Jazzi laughed, a genuine laugh. "You don't want to talk about Jonas, but sometime we're going to have to do that too."

"Sometime," Daisy promised, then headed for the door to the kitchen.

When Jonas rang her doorbell that evening, Daisy let him in and smiled. He was wearing a suit tonight and a tie too. His green eyes twinkled, and he looked relaxed.

He checked out her outfit, a mint green two-piece linen suit. She'd wound her hair on top of her head in a messy topknot. Her jade earrings trimmed in gold dangled low while her gold bracelet watch determined that this was a special occasion.

A little crease lined Jonas's brow when he caught a glimpse of Jazzi descending the stairs, Pepper on one side of her and Marjoram on the other. Daisy knew what his perplexed look was about. Jazzi hadn't dressed up, at least not in her Sunday best. She'd worn a new pair of torn jeans, a royal blue T-shirt, and a tan boyfriend sweater on top. Only, of course, she didn't have a boyfriend. Her sneakers were her favorite ones with rainbow laces, but those laces were barely tied. That was because she knew Daisy didn't approve of them hanging loose.

Jonas leaned close to Daisy's ear. "You look very pretty tonight. I'm not exactly sure what to say to Jazzi."

"Neither am I," Daisy said with a chuckle.

As Jazzi crossed the room to them, the two felines split off and headed toward the kitchen and their kibble bowls. "I hope they're not lonely while we're gone," Jazzi said as if she was still thinking about staying home.

"They'll probably nap all evening," Daisy assured her.

"Yeah, then they'll be up half the night," Jazzi complained.

"You can always close your door," Daisy reminded her daughter.

"No way. I'm not shutting them out. Is it okay if I leave a light on for them?"

"That's fine," Daisy agreed indulgently. "It would probably be best if you left the upstairs hall light on.

That way it will glow into your room as well as down the stairs. I'll leave the light on over the sink as I usually do."

Jonas said to Jazzi, "I'm glad you're going along. Have you picked out which board game you're going to play yet?"

Jazzi scoffed. "It's not that I don't like board games, but it's a party."

"Are you taking Catopoly along?" Daisy suggested.

With a sigh, Jazzi said, "I'll get it. At least that one I enjoy. I enjoy it more when the cats can play with the dice."

As Daisy tried to hide a smile, she shook her head. "I'm not sure how the board games are going to go over with English teenagers."

"The Amish teens will enjoy them as well as the smaller kids. No, it's not dancing to a DJ, but there could be communication around those tables . . . and fun. It was a good suggestion that Rachel's husband Levi gave and a partial compromise."

"I suppose. Amish and English have been living together in Willow Creek for the past two centuries. The times are changing so fast that sometimes I don't know if we have anything in common anymore. If we want them to be part of our world, and we want to be part of their world, then we have to make concessions."

Jonas nodded. "Most of those concessions are good ones because we go back in time a little. The English kids will get enough of DJs and dancing, playlists and parties in the years to come."

"And the Amish?" Daisy asked.

"Except for their Rumspringa, they'll still be establishing their social bonds the way they always have—more quietly, around the table, with family, working together and playing together."

Jazzi returned from the kitchen with what almost looked like a purple tote bag, its handle thrown over her shoulder. Although Daisy's purse carried her phone, keys, lipstick, and not much else, Jazzi's tote should have enough supplies for a weekly camping trip.

Once they arrived at the community room at the firehall, Jazzi asked if she could go meet her friends. Daisy gave her the okay.

Jazzi was off, waved to the group she was meeting, and smiled. Daisy was happy to see that smile.

"I'm glad she came tonight," Daisy told Jonas.

He directed her toward a table where they could sit and talk for a while before they decided if they wanted to participate in any of the games.

"She looked happy enough to see her friends," Jonas pointed out.

"I don't know if she's faking it or not."

"Would she do that?"

"Maybe. So I won't worry."

Jonas dropped his arm around her shoulders and passed his hand up and down her arm. She liked the feel of him close like this. She liked the bonds that seemed to be growing between them. But here wasn't the place to submit to her attraction to him.

She cleared her throat. "I'm going to take Jazzi to get her learner's permit. She's been studying the questions. Maybe that will distract her from what's happening with Portia. The problem is when I talk to her about restrictions that accompany a learner's permit, she becomes annoyed with me."

"I could casually do that some evening that I come over."

"She might listen to you."

"Male authority figure and all that?" he asked with a smile.

"I think the two of you have a bond because you found her birth mother."

Jonas turned his chair to face Daisy more directly. "Do you resent the fact that I did that?"

"Of course not," Daisy was quick to assure him. "I'm the one who came to you, remember?"

"Oh, I remember. But that doesn't mean you didn't want it to happen. That doesn't mean you don't see me as putting a wedge between you and Jazzi."

"Portia isn't going to be a wedge unless I make her one," Daisy insisted, thinking about what Jonas had just said.

"Sometimes you can't control what you feel." His eyes were a darker green, maybe telling her things he couldn't say in words, at least not yet.

"I know," she whispered softly, and she knew he caught her meaning. No, she didn't resent him for finding Portia. He'd made the situation easier.

He leaned close and kissed her temple.

A short time later, they stood in line at the buffet table and picked up snacks and drinks. By then more people had arrived. They chose a table, sitting with Amelia Wiseman and her husband. The couple managed and operated the Covered Bridge Inn. Daisy had worked on a committee with Amelia and enjoyed her company. Arden Botterill was there too. Soon Rachel and Levi joined them along with Elijah and his wife Darla. Eventually they chose a table where the people were playing word games. Jazzi on the other hand was playing Catopoly with her friends.

Around ten, Daisy said to Jonas, "I don't think I can keep my eyes open much longer."

"We can go if you'd like. Tonight has been enjoyable. Maybe there should be a games night here every Saturday, or at least once a month."

"I'll tell Jazzi we're leaving." Daisy went to Jazzi's table and put her hand on her daughter's shoulder. "Are you ready to go, honey?"

Jazzi looked around the table at her friends. One of them nodded to her. Daisy saw it but didn't know what it meant.

Jazzi asked, "Can I stay another hour, please? Sherry's older sister Olivia is here, too, and I can catch a ride home with them."

"How old is Olivia?" Daisy asked.

"She's twenty. She goes to Millersville too. Maybe Foster knows her. Anyway, please, Mom? I don't get a chance to do this often."

Daisy suspected Jazzi meant she didn't get the chance to stay out later. Sure, she had sleepovers with friends, and they often went to the movies. But this was a little different.

"All right. I won't set the alarm, so you can get in easily. Do you have your key?"

Jazzi patted her tote bag that was sitting beside her chair. "Sure do. Don't wait up for me, Mom. I'll let you know when I'm back."

Daisy had to accept the fact that Jazzi was growing up. She didn't like it. She didn't like it at all.

Jonas drove Daisy home, both of them enjoying the quiet in the car and each other's company. There, he walked inside with her and gave her a long good night kiss.

After he left, she brewed herself a cup of tea. Jazzi had said she'd be home in an hour. By the time Daisy had tea, watched the news, and dressed for bed, her daughter would be coming in the door.

However, eleven came and went and Jazzi wasn't home. Eleven thirty came and went. At midnight Daisy was still sitting on the sofa waiting, ready to call the parents of Jazzi's friends.

Then she heard a car. She made herself stay seated. She didn't go to the window and look out. She trusted her daughter.

Except Jazzi was an hour late. Daisy would hear her story before she made any assumptions.

Daisy heard the key in the lock. She saw the door open. Before Jazzi spotted her, *she* saw Jazzi and she didn't like what she saw. Jazzi was clutching her tote bag and seemed to have trouble closing the door. When she turned around to head to the kitchen, she didn't even glance through the living room. Her gait seemed unsteady, and she didn't walk in a straight line.

Daisy stood and called to her. "Jazzi?"

Startled, Jazzi dropped the tote bag and turned to face her mother.

"Have you been drinking . . . or worse?" Daisy wanted to know.

Jazzi just stood there and stared at her mom, her mouth opening and closing as if she had no idea where to start her explanation.

Chapter Nine

Before Jazzi could answer Daisy, her face practically turned green. She left her tote bag where she had dropped it and made a beeline up the stairs. Daisy could hear her in the bathroom getting sick. As far as Daisy knew, Jazzi didn't drink. She didn't even know if her daughter had ever had a beer. Maybe that was naïve, but, on the other hand, she hoped Jazzi had never felt the need to drink before.

Why now? Peer group pressure? Or was it a lot more than that?

Marjoram and Pepper, who had been sitting on the sofa with Daisy, roused from their nap and trotted up the stairs. Daisy picked up Jazzi's tote bag and followed.

A half hour later, after holding Jazzi's hair away from her face, after pressing a cool washcloth to her daughter's brow, Daisy helped her wash up, then guided her to her room. Jazzi crumpled onto the bed like a wet sheet of paper. Daisy hadn't scolded her at this point, just ministered to her. In her mind, she was running over all the things she should say . . . and do.

Pepper had perched on Jazzi's dresser to watch whatever came next while Marjoram stretched along the side of Jazzi's bed, waiting for her to lie down.

Daisy went to Jazzi's dresser and lifted out a pajama set of a tank and boxer shorts.

"Do you need help getting undressed?"

Jazzi glanced up at her mom and then down at her hands. She took the tank and shorts from Daisy. "You don't have to stay. I can get ready for bed."

Daisy took hold of the bedroom chair and pulled it over beside her daughter's bed. "It's not going to be that easy. You're not going to bed as if nothing happened."

"Mom . . ." Jazzi drew out the word as if her mother should know what that meant.

"I'm going downstairs and make us both a cup of tea. You get changed. Then we'll talk."

"I have a headache."

"No kidding! Believe me, it will be worse in the morning if you had as much to drink as I think you did." Daisy couldn't keep the bit of anger from her tone, and Jazzi heard it. She looked away as Daisy went downstairs.

Daisy knew how Jazzi liked her tea, mild with a spoonful of sugar. So she brewed a light green tea and carried the tray with the mugs upstairs. Jazzi was sitting in bed propped up against her headboard. Her eyes were closed.

"What did you have to drink?" Daisy asked.

Jazzi wrapped her hands around the mug as if the warmth of the tea could give her comfort. "I had beer."

"How many? I saw a can in your tote."

"Three or four."

Daisy gave her a penetrating look.

"And two shots of something else. I don't know what it was. Sherry had these little bottles of something. I've seen them in motel room snack bars."

"And *where* did you drink? Certainly not in the community room."

After Jazzi took a sip of tea, she took another. "We went behind the building where the fire engines turn around. A couple of us slipped out. Nobody noticed. The beer was waiting back there for us. When Natalie and I went back in, two more of the kids slipped out."

There was another fact Daisy needed. "Was this planned? When you joined Jonas and me, was it your intent to get drunk tonight?"

"No! Not at all. Sherry planned it. Honest, Mom, I didn't know about it before I went. Somebody asked if we wanted to go out for some fresh air, and I thought maybe a couple of the girls were going to smoke."

Daisy rubbed her hand across her forehead. She was getting a headache now too. Her temples throbbed.

She slid to the edge of her chair and took Jazzi's free hand in hers. "All right, so I know what you drank and where you drank. Now tell me *why* you drank."

Jazzi set the mug on the nightstand and blinked fast. Daisy could see the tears welling up in her daughter's eyes. She squeezed Jazzi's hand again. "Come on, honey, talk to me."

After she ducked her head, she murmured, "I just felt so bad, Mom. I wanted to disappear. I feel like I caused the trouble in Portia's marriage. Now I don't know if I'll ever see her again. Everything is such a mess. I should have let well enough alone and forgotten about searching for birth parents. Maybe this is my punishment for hurting you."

Uh-oh. Where did Jazzi pick up that heavy guilt?

Daisy moved onto the bed beside Jazzi and wrapped her arm around her. "Let's start with the last thing first. You didn't hurt me, Jazzi. I always knew the day might come when you wanted answers. Sure, I worried about it. I didn't want to lose the closeness we have. But you didn't hurt me. Searching after your own happiness can never hurt me."

Jazzi was openly crying now.

Daisy plucked a tissue from a white wicker holder on the nightstand and handed it to Jazzi. "I've also told you before that you did *not* ruin Portia's marriage. If anything, her secret did. And if it's a good marriage, it won't be ruined. It might be damaged, but she and her husband can mend the rift if they both want to."

When Jazzi just shook her head, Daisy knew her words weren't going to fix this.

"And as far as never seeing Portia again—I really can't imagine that. I can't imagine that she wouldn't want to stay in your life. You're a beautiful, smart, kind young woman. If she doesn't want you in her life, she's really missing out."

"Oh, Mom." Jazzi laid her head against Daisy's shoulder and held on to her like she once had when she was a child.

After hugging each other for a good while, Daisy asked, "What would you think about seeing a counselor?"

Jazzi tilted up her head. "You mean a shrink?"

"No, not necessarily a psychiatrist. I can talk to your guidance counselor at school. Mrs. Cotton probably has a list of therapists she recommends. It might do you good to talk to someone about this who isn't involved. You don't believe what I tell you because you know I have a stake in it. What affects you affects me.

A counselor can look at the situation objectively and help you deal with it."

Jazzi thought about it. "Would it be like on TV, lying on a couch?"

Daisy chuckled. "I don't think so. In fact, there are art therapists and play therapists and just plain talk therapists. You express your feelings as if you're talking to a friend or writing in a journal or drawing for your own benefit."

"Would you go with me?"

"If the counselor would recommend that, I would."

After another pause, Jazzi asked, "Can I skip church tomorrow and dinner at Gram's? I really don't feel good, and I don't want Gram looking at me like she does and asking all kinds of questions."

Daisy wouldn't mind avoiding those questions herself. "I'll tell you what. I think it's important that you get up, shower, dress, and eat something in the morning. We'll go to church. I'm sure your grandparents will be there, and you can tell them yourself you're not feeling well. We'll both stay home tomorrow night."

Jazzi shot a quick glance to her mom. "Am I grounded?"

In the upcoming weeks Daisy knew Jazzi had practices for the talent show. That show would be good for her, and Daisy didn't want to prevent her daughter from experiencing it. On the other hand . . . "Let's just say your activities are going to be curtailed. I'll approve of them or cut them out one by one for at least the next two weeks. How does that sound?"

Jazzi didn't answer but hugged Daisy tighter. It was the only answer that Daisy needed.

* * *

On Sunday morning, Daisy took Jazzi to church. Jazzi had looked so pale when she'd come down the stairs that Daisy had thought about letting her stay home. However, a night like last night had consequences. After coaxing her daughter to eat a piece of toast and drink a full glass of water—she knew Jazzi needed to hydrate—she seemed to have a little more color. Daisy had wanted to talk to the moms of the other girls who had been drinking last night. These girls weren't Jazzi's close friends, and Daisy suspected that's why what had happened happened.

Before the service, Daisy spotted Sherry and Olivia who had driven the girls home last night. When she started toward Olivia, Jazzi grabbed her arm. "Mom, you aren't going to make a scene, are you?"

"No, I'm not. Trust me, Jazzi."

Jazzi didn't have much choice but to tag along. When Daisy stopped by Olivia's side, the twenty-year-old turned a little red. "Hi, Olivia," Daisy began.

"Mrs. Swanson! How are you?"

"I'm just fine. Jazzi was feeling a little peaked this morning though."

Jazzi gave her a death stare.

"But I want to thank you for bringing her home safely last night. I just wanted to ask you a question. Did you have anything to drink?"

Olivia lowered her voice and leaned close to Daisy. "I did not. I give you my word. I didn't know what they were going to do. When I went looking for them to bring them home, there were the empty beer cans and they were tipsy."

"Were any of the other mothers up when you dropped off their daughters?"

"Not that I know of. The houses were dark except

for yours, and I didn't get any texts or calls that parents were mad or anything. Mrs. Swanson, if something like that happens again, I'll call you. I promise. Last night I wasn't sure what to do."

"Thank you for that, Olivia. Calling parents would be the responsible thing to do. But I do appreciate the care you took bringing Jazzi home."

Olivia nodded, Daisy smiled, and Jazzi followed her into the church.

Jazzi elbowed her. "She's never going to talk to me again. Neither is Sherry."

"Olivia seems sensible. Are you telling me she's not?"

"Olivia *wasn't* drinking. Her boyfriend was there, and they were making out somewhere."

Daisy rolled her eyes. Of course.

"I'm surprised your usual friends, Stacy and Susan, weren't there last night."

"I told them I wasn't going. I didn't think I was. And you know what, Mom? They would have walked away from that beer."

"So you might have walked away from it too," Daisy pointed out.

"Yeah, I guess, even if I was feeling bad. I suppose the friends I hang with are important."

"Yes, they are."

"That's why you and Tessa still hang together, right? Because you trust each other?"

"We do. We have a long history." She and Tessa had attended high school together and had stayed friends even through long distances.

As Jazzi and Daisy sat in a pew, Jazzi leaned her shoulder against Daisy's. "Gram and Gramps are over there . . . on the right."

"We'll talk to them after the service. Are you still sure you don't want to go to dinner tonight?"

"I'm sure. My stomach's going to be queasy for a while. I don't want to have to turn down her food and explain why."

After the service, Daisy's mom and dad found them in the back of the church. Rose took one look at Jazzi and said, "My goodness, honey, you look pale. Are you feeling all right?"

Sean put his hand on Jazzi's shoulder as if that would help her feel better. Rose couldn't have provided a more appropriate opening. Jazzi kept her eyes a bit downcast but told her grandmother, "I'm not feeling so great. After we go home, I'm probably going to rest for the day."

Daisy told her mom, "I think we're going to stay home tonight. I don't want to leave Jazzi alone. You, Dad, and Aunt Iris can have a quiet dinner together."

Daisy's mom wrinkled her nose and patted the curls at the back of her head. "I suppose so. It will be quiet as long as Iris keeps her opinions to herself."

It would be downright silent if they both did that, Daisy thought.

Daisy wanted to talk to her dad and ask if he'd spoken to her mom about everything he was mulling over. But this wasn't the place or time to do it.

After walking to the open church door, Daisy, her mom, and her dad shook hands with the minister, told him what a great sermon he'd delivered, and then went out to the parking lot. There Jazzi and Daisy walked her mom and dad to their car.

After hugs all around, her mother said to Jazzi, "Feel better, honey," then climbed into the car.

Her father put down his window and reminded them, "We love you."

As Daisy and Jazzi walked to Daisy's PT Cruiser, Jazzi asked, "Gram and Gramps are happy, aren't they?"

"Yes, they are. When you think about it, they're together almost twenty-four hours a day. And they seem to enjoy it."

"Do you think that's good for a marriage?" Jazzi asked. "Working together and living together?"

Daisy responded, "I guess that depends on the couple."

"Would you have been able to work with Dad?"

When Jazzi said the word "dad," pictures of Ryan floated in front of Daisy's eyes. "I don't know if we could have or not. We gave a workshop together once. He spoke about organic products multiplying on grocery shelves, and I talked about healthy diets. But after Vi was born and we adopted you, I stayed home to take care of you. When you went to school and I went back to work, your dad's work path and mine never crossed again."

"Do you think Dad would have ever moved back here?"

"I don't know, honey. I just don't know. Your dad didn't like to take risks. Coming back here and starting anew would have been hard for him."

Ryan had been an only child, and both of his parents were deceased. If Daisy wanted family support, moving back to Willow Creek had been her best choice. Now that her parents were getting older, it made even more sense.

She had no regrets about making Willow Creek her home once more. She did regret that she and Ryan hadn't had more years together.

* * *

Daisy and her aunt Iris had barely opened the tea garden on Monday when someone came in who Daisy didn't want to see—Detective Rappaport. He never looked jolly, but this morning he looked downright serious.

Daisy circled their cash counter and met him. "What can I do for you, Detective? A cup of tea and a scone?"

"You know I'm a java man. Nothing for me now. Can I see you in your office?"

Daisy glanced at her aunt Iris, and her aunt gave a nod. Eva and Tessa were in the kitchen, and Cora Sue was setting up the spillover tea room for afternoon tea. Her aunt could take care of the counter.

Once in the office, the detective didn't waste any time with niceties. He closed the door and faced Daisy. "We have a cause of death."

"And?" she asked.

"You know those cucumber sandwiches you served with the pimento filling?"

She had a sinking feeling in her stomach. "Yes."

His gaze was piercing as he announced, "They had more in them than cucumbers and filling."

"I don't understand. I made them here myself."

"Listen to me before you jump to conclusions," Detective Rappaport advised her. "I don't conclude anything until I have all the facts. You should be the same way."

She kept quiet.

"Two drugs were found in Derek Schumacher's stomach contents as well as in the filling of the sandwiches that we confiscated from the Schumacher house."

Daisy sucked in a breath, not expecting any of this. "He purchased sandwiches to take along."

"I know. You and your aunt Iris told me that."

After Daisy thought about the detective's news, she repeated, "You said there were drugs. Not poison?"

"No poison. Both drugs are heart medications. Because Derek Schumacher had low blood pressure—we surmised that from his medical records—the drugs dangerously lowered his blood pressure until his heart rate became erratic and he had a seizure. The question now is—who put the pills in the filling?"

Daisy felt her face go pale. "You don't think I did it?"

Detective Rappaport didn't directly answer her question. "It either had to be somebody here at the tea garden or someone who had access to Schumacher's refrigerator. In both cases, a limited number of people had access. I need to speak with each of your employees again and warn them not to leave town."

"Detective Rappaport, none of my employees had a reason to kill Derek Schumacher."

The detective's face was grave. "I don't know that for certain. I haven't checked through their backgrounds to see if they crossed his. And I'm sure somebody's did."

Daisy thought about Cora Sue.

Apparently, the detective did too. "Cora Sue Bauer is the first one I want to talk to again. I'll do it one by one in your office. That shouldn't disrupt your business. Are all of your employees here?"

"Foster has classes this morning and won't be in until this afternoon."

"I'll catch him another time, possibly later today. I'd like you to keep what I told you under your hat, so to speak. I understand Jonas heard a little bit about this from somebody down at the station, but not the final results. If you want to tell him, that's fine."

"What about my aunt?"

Detective Rappaport looked toward the ceiling as if he expected help from heaven. "I knew if I told you anything, this would happen."

Daisy wasn't going to back down this time. "We run the business together, Detective. She'll know something's wrong. My aunt Iris knows me very well."

"Do you think she can keep a lid on what I told you?"

"Of course, she can. After all, we've both been involved in investigations before."

His sigh could have been heard through the closed office door. "You certainly have, and I don't want you involved in that way ever again. No civilians should have their life put in danger because of a murder investigation. So, no matter how much you want the tea garden cleared of any suspicion, don't go asking questions."

Daisy couldn't make that promise, and he seemed to see that. "I mean it, Mrs. Swanson. If you interfere, I might have to bring charges against you."

"You wouldn't."

"Don't try me." He went to the office door. "I will have to tell the press a few details. The public will know your food was the cause of death."

"If you let that information go public, it will affect our business."

"I'm sorry about that, but I'm hoping letting that much info out will shake things up and the right suspect will surface." He opened the door. "Send Cora Sue in first."

Daisy felt something like panic as she started to leave the office.

The detective stopped her with his next words. "By the way, Schumacher's review of the tea garden sucked . . . except for the cucumber sandwiches."

When Daisy studied the detective's face, she noted that his brows were arched. He'd be putting all of them under his magnifying glass.

Chapter Ten

Even after all these years, the high school halls still smelled like wax if not chalk. As Daisy realized everything was about interactive boards now, she heard the clank of one locker and then another on Monday afternoon.

The high school guidance counselor's office was open. Daisy checked her watch—right on time. She stepped inside. She had to keep her mind on Jazzi now, not on what Detective Rappaport had told her.

Stella Cotton smiled at her and gestured to the vinyl chair in front of her desk. When Daisy sank down onto it, she felt as if she were back in high school again. Stella was probably as old as Daisy's aunt Iris, in her late fifties. But there, any resemblance ended.

Stella's hair was coal black, straight, and angled from the back of her nape to her chin. Her eyeliner and mascara were heavy, and her red beads and bangle bracelets were bold. The two-piece suit she was wearing was yellow with red geometrical shapes dancing across it. As Daisy had walked in, she'd noticed the guidance counselor's red platform sandals. She was a short woman, about five-foot-two, and the chunky heels on the shoes added a few inches to her height.

Daisy in her mauve short-sleeve sweater and slacks felt bland compared to Stella. The guidance counselor had helped Vi make a good college choice in Lehigh University. More than once, Violet had mentioned how Mrs. Cotton was good with the kids and spoke their language.

After Daisy was seated, she dropped her purse to the floor. "Thank you for fitting me into your schedule. I know you're busy with graduation functions."

"I am," Stella admitted. "But this sounded urgent. The welfare of each of our students is our main priority at Willow Creek High. Now tell me what's happening with Jazzi. You mentioned significant changes in her life, and that you feel she needs outside help handling them."

Tension crawled up Daisy's spine as she wondered how much to say. "I don't want to overload you with information."

"I made time for you. Go ahead and overload. You're not the type of woman who talks just for the sake of talking. Believe me, I have a lot of parents who do."

Mrs. Cotton's half smile relaxed Daisy a bit.

She didn't know why she was nervous. Whatever happened here . . . or didn't . . . should help Jazzi find her way. She started with, "As you know Vi went to college this year."

"I hear she's doing well," Mrs. Cotton said.

Daisy nodded. "She is—four-point-oh her first semester, and I think she's enjoying it too."

At the guidance counselor's nod, Daisy went on.

"But Jazzi misses her. They've been together since we adopted Jazzi."

"Yes, I remember that Jazzi is adopted. That's in her records, and I went over those before you came in. Jazzi is a good student, though according to her teachers, she has seemed moody at times this year."

"And that's the essence of why I'm here," Daisy explained. "In the fall, Jazzi decided to search for her biological parents."

"Ah," Mrs. Cotton breathed, as if that said it all.

"With help from a friend, we found her mother," Daisy went on. "She lives in Allentown. She and Jazzi have had phone conversations, and Portia has visited us twice."

"How is Jazzi feeling about her?"

"She likes Portia. But I think she feels guilty she's hurting me by being friendly with Portia. Of course, I'm worried about their relationship and worried that Jazzi will get hurt."

"Why are you worried if this Portia is accepting Jazzi as her daughter?"

"That's the problem. She hasn't accepted Jazzi completely. Her husband and children don't know about Jazzi. At least they didn't until a short time ago when Portia went away with her husband on a business trip and she told him. It didn't go well. He moved out. Now Jazzi feels responsible for splitting up their marriage."

Mrs. Cotton looked aghast. "Jazzi is an intelligent, caring young woman with a sense of responsibility. I can see that from the service projects she takes on and the clubs she's joined, not to mention the fact that she works for you now and then at the tea garden. Correct?"

"Yes, she does. And on top of all the rest, I don't think we spoke of my husband's death enough. Violet was vocal in her grief. Jazzi wasn't. When we moved back to Willow Creek, I was involved in opening the business. I feel Jazzi stuffed it all inside because she didn't want to bother me with it."

"Or she didn't want to go through the pain of the grief," Mrs. Cotton commented.

Daisy had considered that. "Yes, that too. On top of everything else, I'm dating someone. He's the one who helped me find Jazzi's biological mother. Jazzi says she doesn't mind. She likes Jonas and she trusts him. But I think it's just one more thing for her to deal with."

Both women were silent for a few seconds. Then Mrs. Cotton asked, "And how would you like me to help with all of this? Do you want me to talk to Jazzi?"

"You have so many students to think about, and I believe Jazzi needs more than a session here and there. I was wondering if you could suggest a good therapist."

"Art therapist, play therapist, talk therapist?" Mrs. Cotton asked.

"I'm not sure about that. I know it can take time to get in to see somebody. I was hoping with your recommendation, Jazzi could start sooner rather than later."

Mrs. Cotton's Rolodex sat on her desk. She pulled it over in front of her and fingered through it. "I have several suggestions, but . . . if I remember correctly, Violet and Jazzi have two cats, don't they?"

Daisy had no idea where this was going. "Yes, we do. They're part of our family."

"I know a therapist who's very good with teenagers. She has a cat who sits in on most sessions. She finds that Lancelot relaxes her clients. He's very loving, and in that intuitive way cats have, he knows whether to come closer or stay away."

"It sounds like he might be an icebreaker," Daisy remarked.

"Exactly. Let me give you Tara Morelli's number. Call her and tell her I recommended that you contact her. If that isn't enough to get you an appointment soon, I'll call her myself. Just let me know."

Mrs. Cotton wrote the name and number on a sheet of paper from a notepad and handed it to Daisy. "Do Violet and Jazzi talk on the phone or do they text mostly?"

"Mostly text."

The counselor shook her head. "That's the problem these days . . . too much impersonal finger use and not enough actual face-to-face communication. If you talk to Violet about this, you might want to emphasize that actually having a conversation with Jazzi would be more beneficial to her than texting."

"I'll do that. I'm hoping Vi will get home for the talent show, but that depends on her end-of-the-year workload." Daisy picked up her purse and stood. "Thank you."

"Don't thank me yet," Mrs. Cotton admonished, standing also. "Jazzi might have to go through rough sessions and come out feeling better on the other side. Just keep that in mind while she's going through therapy."

"I will," Daisy assured the guidance counselor. "Thank you again," Daisy said as she went to the door.

"You can just leave the door open," Mrs. Cotton advised her. "I have an open-door policy."

Mrs. Cotton's words warmed Daisy. She was a kind woman doing a difficult job. But her years of experience showed she knew how to handle most situations.

Daisy was hurrying down the hall when she spotted Bradley Schumacher walking toward her, looking preoccupied. As she approached him, she said, "Good afternoon, Mr. Schumacher."

He stopped and blinked as if he had come back from very far away.

"My mind isn't as alert as it should be," he said with a grimace. "I just received a call. Derek's body has been released and the funeral is in two days."

"I know I've said this before, but I'm sorry for your loss. It must be hard to lose a brother. I can't even imagine." She thought again about Camellia and the love they shared, even though they fought now and then.

But there was an expression on Bradley Schumacher's face that made Daisy wonder just how close he and Derek had been. "Will two days be enough time for you to notify everyone?"

"There aren't that many people to notify," Bradley insisted.

"Derek wasn't romantically involved with anyone?"

After a beat, he shook his head. "My brother wasn't involved with anyone seriously at the present time."

Daisy suspected that could mean that Derek might hop from one woman to another, and not really get involved with anyone. She had to wonder if Detective Rappaport would be pursuing that angle.

"Take care of yourself, Mr. Schumacher. Grief is much more difficult to handle than the worst flu."

"You sound like my wife," he said with an almost-smile. "Thank you for your concern. Eventually it will be all right, especially after the police capture whoever hurt Derek."

Hurt was a funny word to use with regard to murder, but she supposed Bradley didn't believe that anyone could hate his brother enough to kill him.

That evening Daisy was thinking about her conversation with Tessa before she'd left the tea garden.

"Is something going on with Foster that I should know about?" Tessa had asked.

"He won't say, but I'm sure something is. I just hope it has nothing to do with Derek Schumacher."

"Why do you think it would?"

"Foster has computer skills. My guess is he knows how to hack into networks and e-mails. I'm just wondering if he could have hacked into Derek's blog and seen the bad review."

"What bad review?"

"When Detective Rappaport was in, he told me that the review Derek gave us sucked."

"But he didn't say how bad it was?"

"No. Actually, he did say Derek liked our cucumber sandwiches."

"There you go, something positive to think about."

Now Daisy didn't know whether to laugh or cry because those were the same sandwiches that had killed him.

A white crossover van came up the lane. That was

Jazzi, home from debate practice. When Jazzi came in the door, Daisy went to the living room to greet her. After she hugged her, she said, "I invited Tessa to supper. She likes my sausage and potato casserole. I thought we'd have a girls' night and watch a movie."

Jazzi wrinkled her nose. "I have homework, Mom."

"Do you think you could get it done while Tessa and I clean up after supper?"

Jazzi gave Daisy a thoughtful look. "Maybe. I do have a study hall tomorrow morning."

Usually, Daisy didn't suggest putting off homework until the morning or before class. But this was a little different. She sat down on the sofa and petted Marjoram who was sitting bread-loaf-style on one of the cushions. The tortie stretched out and rolled over.

Daisy fluffed her tummy hair. "I saw Mrs. Cotton today."

"What did she say?" Jazzi removed her backpack, setting it by the staircase.

When Daisy hesitated, Jazzi pushed. "Be honest with me, Mom."

"Have you heard from Portia?"

"No, I haven't. Nothing. Not a text, not a call, not an emoticon."

Daisy knew her daughter lived on emoticons . . . with her friends anyway.

"First of all, Mrs. Cotton said you're a good student, and that you're responsible and caring."

"How does she know?" Jazzi brushed her hair back over her shoulder. "She's not around me that much."

"She knows from comments teachers make on permanent records, from clubs and activities you participate in. Willow Creek is a small town and gossip travels. The school is an even smaller community. Good and bad things spin around."

"I know that. What else did she say?"

Sometimes Jazzi was too perceptive. "She said some of your teachers have remarked that you've been moody since fall. I explained about Portia."

Jazzi sank down on the sofa and lifted Marjoram onto her lap. The feline stayed there as if she sensed Jazzi needed comfort. "Does Mrs. Cotton want me to go in and talk to her? I just can't see it. We have nothing in common."

Daisy thought of Stella's dyed black hair, her intense makeup, her bold outfits. "You don't have to have anything in common with someone for them to be a good listener."

She could see Jazzi was still doubtful. "But really, that's not what she suggested. I think you need more than a drop-in session."

"Mom—"

"I mean it, Jazzi. You need to get your feelings out. If you can't do it with me, you have to do it with someone."

"*Not* Mrs. Cotton."

"No, I didn't think you'd want to do that. As I said, the whole community is a small one. So I asked her for the name of a good therapist."

Jazzi sighed. "And what did she come up with?"

"It's interesting, really. She asked if I thought you'd be interested in play therapy or art therapy or just talk therapy. I told her I wasn't sure. So she suggested a therapist, Tara Morelli, who brings a cat to her sessions. Apparently, Lancelot is a yellow tabby and a sensitive feline. He can tell when her clients need comforting or want to be left alone."

Daisy saw Jazzi's dark brown eyes sparkle a bit. "Really?"

"That's what she told me. I have Mrs. Morelli's number. Do you want me to set up a session? Mrs. Cotton said if I tell Mrs. Morelli that she recommended her, she'll get you in sooner rather than later."

Jazzi studied Marjoram for a moment. The tortie gave a soft meow. At the sound, Pepper came running in and wound around Jazzi's ankles.

"Do you really think this is best?" Jazzi asked.

"I do. And if Portia gets in touch with you again, this therapist can probably give you strategies to handle that too. I'm warning you, though. She's not going to have answers."

"Then what's the point of going?" Jazzi whined.

"The point of going is for her to lead you to find your own answers."

Jazzi scooped up Marjoram and set her on the sofa beside her. Pepper jumped up on the couch too.

Finally, Jazzi said, "Okay. Call and make the appointment. I want to stop feeling so sad every day, and I want to stop being mad at Portia for not letting me know what's going on."

"That will be a good place to start."

When Jazzi stood, Daisy went to her and gave her a long, tight hug. "I'm proud of you. For the most part, you've handled all of this really well."

"But not by drinking."

"No, not by drinking. Trying to escape never solves a problem. Why don't you try to get some of that homework done? I'll call you when dinner's ready."

Jazzi nodded and headed toward the staircase, both cats jumping off the sofa to follow her.

As Daisy crossed to the kitchen, she hoped she was doing the right thing for Jazzi. If Portia cut Jazzi out of her life altogether, Jazzi was going to need more help than Daisy could give her.

When Daisy and Tessa entered the funeral home Wednesday morning, they saw right away that it was packed. *Were all these people Derek's friends?* Daisy wondered. Or were they simply nosy onlookers who wanted details about the murder or about the case?

Daisy spotted Detective Rappaport and knew it wasn't unusual for him to attend the viewing and/or funeral of a murder victim. He arched his eyebrows when he spotted her as if to ask—a nosy onlooker?

No, she wasn't. She had a reputation to uphold and a business to protect.

Noticing Harriet sitting in her wheelchair along the velvet rope next to the closed casket, Daisy said to Tessa, "I'm going to give her my condolences." Aunt Iris hadn't come along, because funerals brought back too many memories. Memories returned for Daisy too.

"I'll come with you," Tessa said. "Do you know who the woman is standing beside Harriet?"

The woman standing beside Harriet's wheelchair was dressed in a black suit and sturdy black shoes. She looked older than Harriet. Her hair was laced with as much white as gray. Her face, lined with wrinkles, told Daisy she was probably in her late fifties or sixties.

As Daisy and Tessa waited in the receiving line, they could hear bits and pieces of conversations.

"Derek could be quite snippy. Did you follow his blog?" one woman asked another.

"Yes, I did. Do you think that person who made the death threat is the one who killed him?"

Daisy had forgotten all about that death threat. She wondered if it had been brought to Detective Rappaport's attention. Maybe his tech support people were tracing it back to whoever had posted that day.

"Derek was a wonderful chef," a man sitting on an aisle seat commented. "A couple of years ago, he invited me over. He made shrimp scampi to die for."

Bad use of the phrase, Daisy thought. As the line inched closer to the front, she saw the woman in front of her cup her hand around her mouth and say to the woman directly in front of Daisy, "That's her sister. She hadn't seen her in thirty-five years!"

That was news. Daisy elbowed Tessa. "Do you believe they really weren't in contact for thirty-five years? That must have been some rift."

"Anything's possible," Tessa replied with a shrug.

Soon Daisy and Tessa were standing in front of Harriet's wheelchair. Daisy took Derek's mother's hand in hers. "I'm so sorry."

Harriet took a deep breath. "This is harder than I thought it would be."

Had Harriet thought she could sail through the viewing and the funeral without feeling anything? Why would she want to?

Harriet squeezed Daisy's hand. "I appreciate your coming. Let me introduce you to my sister, June."

After Daisy and Tessa were introduced, the woman in the black suit stretched her hand out to Daisy. "It's good to meet you. It's good to know Harriet has people who care about her."

Harriet's son and daughter-in-law were standing next to June. Harriet's daughter-in-law frowned.

Daisy didn't know what to ask without being nosy, but June herself started the conversation. "I haven't been back in Willow Creek for thirty-five years."

Daisy wanted to ask why, but of course she couldn't, at least not here. "Do you feel it's changed much?" Daisy asked.

"That's the thing about towns like Willow Creek," June said, "they don't change much in even *fifty* years. Oh, there might be a new restaurant or a motel, one of those discount stores, and maybe even an extra streetlight, but for the most part they stay the same."

"Do you feel that's a good thing?" Daisy asked.

"The thing is, Daisy, the town doesn't change, and neither do the people."

"I'm not sure about that," Daisy disagreed. "The younger generation brings new ideas."

"Possibly. But I'm not sure they're better ideas. I like the fact that there are still horses and buggies on the streets of Willow Creek. The farmers market has stayed viable. Many of the families I knew when I lived here still own farms that their families lived on for a century or more. Somehow they've kept them up and running."

"Not an easy task," Daisy agreed.

"Especially when you're older, it's hard to keep your own place. That's why I moved into one of those retirement communities. Harriet should do the same."

Harriet's gaze met Daisy's. "She's my older sister, can't you tell? Always has an idea or a suggestion for what I should do."

June gave Harriet an indulgent smile. "For now, I'm going to stay with Harriet so I'm sure she has everything she needs. Then she can decide if she wants to sell the place or not."

That brought up a lot of questions. Who did Derek leave his estate to? Maybe no one knew yet.

The line behind them had grown longer again. Daisy gave her condolences to Bradley and his wife Lauren, and then she and Tessa went to find a seat. As they did, she noticed a woman come in who didn't speak to any of the family members. She looked to be in her thirties, well dressed in a yellow linen dress with a jacket and spiked heels. She took a place in line and waited until it was her turn to gaze down at the picture on top of the casket. Suddenly, she frowned and turned away. Without giving condolences to the family, she left the funeral home.

"I'll be back in a minute," Daisy said to Tessa. After she rose to her feet, she went to the vestibule. No one was at the guest book, so she took a look but didn't see a woman's signature in the last four entries. Interesting. The stranger hadn't signed the guest book either.

On her way back to her seat with Tessa, Daisy spotted Clementine who was sitting at the end of the side aisle. She was tapping something into her phone. Since the seat beside her was vacant, Daisy slipped into it.

Clementine turned to her and smiled. "Hi. I thought I might see you here."

"Since Derek recently visited the tea garden, it seemed the proper thing to do."

Clementine grimaced. "So you're one of those."

"Pardon me?"

"One of those women who do the proper thing. I never could do that."

"Sometimes I wish I didn't have to, or I wish I could rebel against propriety. The way I was raised has stuck."

Clementine vehemently shook her head. "Nonsense. I was raised to be the proper Southern girl, and look what happened to me. I turned into a journalist digging up secrets."

Daisy kept her voice low. "Have you discovered any secrets?"

Clementine shook her head again. "I'm reaching all dead ends. How about you?"

"I learned Harriet has a sister."

"Yeah, I wonder what the story is behind that."

"We might never know. Do you know who the woman was who walked away from the casket without greeting the family?"

"Oh, yes, I know who that was. That was Miranda Senft. Didn't you ever watch Derek's cooking show?"

"I was in Florida then, working, raising the girls after Ryan died. I didn't have time for cooking and cable shows. Was Miranda part of that?"

"Miranda had been Derek's co-host on his cable show. She traveled with him everywhere."

"Why didn't she offer sympathy to his family? They must have been close."

"I don't know. Miranda won't talk to me. I tried after she left the show. She wouldn't talk to me then, and she won't talk to me now. She either hangs up or shuts the door in my face."

"Shuts the door? Where does she live?"

"Near Lancaster. When she and Derek were an item, that was convenient for them."

Daisy wondered if Miranda Senft would shut the door on her.

Chapter Eleven

Daisy and Tessa didn't attend the graveside service. Tessa went back to the tea garden while Daisy stopped in at Woods. For some reason, she just needed to see Jonas. She told Tessa she wouldn't be long, and she wouldn't be. But in some ways, Jonas had become her touchstone, her balance, a perspective when hers was skewed. Right now, she felt it was skewed.

Jonas's store had a unique flair that she usually appreciated. Huge cubicle shelves lined one side of the store. In each of those cubicles stood a ladder-back chair, each in a different color or finish—lemon, robin's egg blue, distressed green. The wood furniture in the rest of the store—cherry, dark walnut, and pine—always shone with a glossy finish. Not only had their crafting been done carefully, but they were kept polished. She passed pedestal tables, library tables, occasional tables, which stood along the other side of the room. Armoires, chests, and highboys were the most beautiful Daisy had ever seen. All of the furniture was handcrafted by local craftsmen including Jonas.

Elijah, who sometimes clerked at the shop, was one of the major contributors. Daisy could see that Jonas wasn't at the counter at the rear of the store, but rather his store manager, Tony Fitch, was. Tony was in his thirties. He was a bachelor and lived in an apartment in a row house back on Hickory Street. He had blond, almost white hair and a smile that could help sell furniture to someone who might not need it.

He greeted Daisy. "Hi, Mrs. Swanson. Are you looking for Jonas?"

"I am. Is he here?"

"In the back. He was sanding a set of bookshelves."

"Thanks," Daisy said as she opened the back door that led into the workshop.

Jonas was crouched down, sanding the inside of the lowest shelf. He was wearing goggles and a tool belt, and she had to smile. Whether he was dressed as a woodworker or a detective, he made her heart do a flip.

He must have heard her footsteps because he pushed the goggles to the top of his head and stood. "This is a surprise." He checked his watch. "Is the funeral over already?"

"Tessa and I didn't go to the graveside service."

"Any particular reason?" Jonas asked with a cock of his head.

"I was . . . I was . . ." Her voice trailed off.

Setting the sander on top of the bookshelves, he came closer to her. "You what?"

She shook her head. "I don't know. I guess I should have just gone back to the tea garden."

His expression was kind when he pressed, "You came here for a reason. What was it?"

"I don't like funeral homes," she blurted out.

Still studying her carefully, he said, "Most people don't."

She fluttered her hand as if it could catch her thoughts and make sense of them. "Something just got to me today. Maybe it was the flowers. There was an arrangement there with lilies that was so much like the one Ryan's colleagues had sent. It just threw me back."

"Not just the bouquet, I imagine, but the scent too."

She nodded. "I really can't stand the smell of lilies anymore. There were several bouquets with them."

"At Ryan's funeral or at Derek's?"

"At Ryan's," she said softly.

Jonas lifted his goggles to the top of his head and came even closer, close enough that she could see the dusting of sanded wood on his forearm. "And you came here because . . ."

Taking a deep breath, she admitted, "Because I needed you to bring me back to the present. I don't want to be stuck in the past."

Jonas put his arms around her and hugged her. That was exactly what she needed. They stood there for a while just holding each other.

When she leaned away, he asked, "Did you learn anything while you were there?"

Daisy summed up new facts. She told Jonas about Harriet's sister June, about what Clementine had said, about the woman, Miranda, who hadn't stayed.

"Do you think she came out of curiosity?"

"I don't know. Her face was . . . hard. I'd like to talk to her."

"Think about it. I'd be glad to go with you if you'd like."

"Do you want to get involved?"

"Rappaport uses me as a confidant sometimes, so I'm aware of what's happening, whether I want to be or not. But if you decide you're searching for clues, I'll help you."

She smiled up at him and felt the connection she'd felt from the first time she'd talked with him.

"I'm glad you stopped in. There's something I wanted to ask you."

"What?"

"I'm driving to Philadelphia over the weekend, and I'd like you to come with me and meet my friends. They're having a barbecue."

"I'd love to come," she said immediately, knowing it was true.

"Will it be a problem with Jazzi grounded?"

"No. She can stay with Aunt Iris or my parents."

"Great. I'll reserve two rooms at a B and B I like."

Two rooms. Although that's what he said, she wondered if he might have a romantic time in mind. Was she ready for that? She wasn't sure, but she *did* know she wanted to spend more time with Jonas Groft. And if romance wove a spell around her while they were in Philadelphia, she just might give in to it.

When the morning rush slowed the following day, Daisy mixed up a second pan of rum raisin rice pudding and slid it into the oven. She always had to be careful that the water didn't splash up into the pudding. It was more like custard really. She used Carolina rice, golden raisins, eggs, sugar, and milk. The important fact about it was knowing when to take it out of the oven. She, Tessa, and her aunt knew exactly what consistency it was supposed to be.

Daisy signaled to Tessa. "I set the timer for the rice pudding. I'm going to see if Iris needs help at the counter."

With Tessa's nod, Daisy exited the kitchen and crossed into the green tea room. She was taken aback with what she saw there. Detective Rappaport was sitting at a table near the window where he could see outside as well as inside. His mouth was full of a chocolate whoopee pie, and a glass of iced tea sat beside his dish. Daisy had seen Iris come into the kitchen for the tea but hadn't thought much of it.

Iris met Daisy in the middle of the room. "He said he came to talk to you. I told him you were busy. When he said he'd wait, I offered him a whoopee pie. He agreed to iced herbal peach tea. Seems he's on the road to enjoying tea."

Daisy almost smiled. But then the thought struck her that Detective Rappaport had not come to the tea garden for a whoopee pie. She would bet money on it.

There were only a few customers at tables. She told her aunt, "If you can handle the counter, I'll go talk to him."

"Better you than me," Iris said. Her aunt Iris had had run-ins with Rappaport, too, and she didn't particularly want to spend time with him.

Going to the detective's table, Daisy pulled out the chair around the corner from his and sat.

He was licking the creamy filling from his fingers after eating the last of his whoopee pie.

"That was great," he pronounced as if he hadn't expected it to be.

That surprised her. But Morris Rappaport didn't

seem like a man who enjoyed adventure . . . or even new foods. "You never had one before?"

"Nope. Never felt the urge to try one. But I've got to admit, I'm thinking about taking a few of them along."

"You'll have to come in on a morning when we have the chocolate ones filled with a peanut butter cream instead of vanilla cream."

He pointed his fingers at her. "You do know the way to a man's heart."

"No," Daisy said, "just his stomach."

The detective actually smiled.

"Did you come today to keep your eye on us, or ask us more questions?"

He shook his head. "Sometimes I just like to observe human behavior."

"Which humans?"

He shook his finger at her. "You're way too smart, and that's one reason why I don't really have my eye on you and your aunt. I've dealt with the two of you before, and my gut tells me you wouldn't do something so stupid as to kill Derek Schumacher."

"I caught a glimpse of you at the funeral. Did you find anything out while you watched the grieving family?"

Rappaport stayed silent.

"Are you seriously considering anybody on my staff as a suspect who killed Derek?"

"Truth be told, I'm not finished looking into backgrounds yet. I'm curious about Cora Sue and her connection to Schumacher."

Daisy knew for the most part she should keep her

mouth shut, but maybe if Rappaport understood the connection, he'd see Cora Sue differently.

"Cora Sue knows Harriet Schumacher through her aunt. Her aunt lived close to Harriet in her old neighborhood. My guess is that Cora Sue ran into Derek over the years too."

The detective gave her a penetrating look. "You're not usually so forthcoming. Why now?"

"Because I thought if you knew Cora Sue's history with the Schumachers, you'd understand it wasn't unusual for her to stop Derek and scold him."

"Even if he's a celebrity?"

"I don't think that meant much to Cora Sue. Besides the fact that he hasn't been a celebrity for a while."

"He still got paid for appearances, big money too. Even as a food critic he acted as a chef at pop-up restaurants and made the owners big money. So his celebrity really isn't in question."

"What is?" Daisy asked.

"Everybody's motives for wanting him dead. You wouldn't believe how many people there are who had a grudge against him. And, no, I'm not going to tell you who they are. Let's just say, I need help with this investigation and I'm going to get it."

She easily remembered what Jonas had told her. "Is Zeke Willet going to partner with you?"

"So Jonas told you."

"He told me that he and Zeke used to be friends."

"And?" Rappaport prompted.

This was when she kept her mouth shut. "No, Detective, I'm not telling you anything else. If you want to know you'll have to ask Mr. Willet or Jonas. But while we're on the subject of suspects, what about Foster?"

Rappaport took a few gulps of his iced tea and then set down the glass. "Not bad," he said. "I added sugar."

"It's better for you without the sugar. What about Foster?"

Rappaport sighed and sat back in his chair. "I don't know. That kid is hiding something, but he won't spill it. I'm keeping my eye on him. I know his schedule. I know when he's here if I want to talk to him."

"How do you know his schedule?"

"Because of my great investigative skills," Rappaport said. Then he did smile. "Mrs. Swanson, you're too naïve. I just asked him."

Was she naïve? She didn't think so. Maybe her fault was that she did like to trust the people she cared about. She'd always thought she could trust Foster, but now she wasn't so sure.

Fifteen minutes later, Detective Rappaport left after buying six whoopee pies. Daisy was ringing up a customer when her phone played its tuba sound, and she slipped it from her pocket to check the screen. Violet was calling. She could just let it go to voice mail, but she hated to do that when one of her kids needed to talk to her.

Her aunt Iris was at a nearby table, and she caught her eye. When Iris came over, Daisy said, "Mr. Clemson would like two dozen Snickerdoodles. Do you think you could box them for him? Vi's calling and I think I'd better take it."

Iris nodded and Daisy accepted the call. It was unusual for Vi to call her at this time of day. She usually called in the evening when they were both free. Maybe it had something to do with Jazzi. Maybe Jazzi was confiding in her sister when she wasn't confiding in Daisy.

"What's up, honey?" Daisy asked. "I thought you had class all morning on Thursday."

Silence met that statement, but then Vi said, "I'm coming home this weekend because I need to talk to you."

Daisy's heart lurched. So she was honest with her daughter. "I'm supposed to go to Philadelphia with Jonas. Can it wait until next weekend?"

"It really can't, Mom. I need to talk to you this weekend." Her daughter's voice broke.

"What's wrong, Vi?"

"I really don't want to talk about anything now, okay? I'll be home tomorrow. I'll text you when I'm almost home."

Daisy wanted to say, *No texting while you're driving*. But Vi knew that. Instead, Daisy asked, "Are you driving home yourself . . . no carpooling?"

"No carpooling this weekend."

Daisy wondered if there was a message in that. Was her daughter breaking up with Foster? Is that what this was about? But as she did most of the time, she knew she had to wait to see what Violet wanted to talk about. What was so important that she had to do it *this* weekend?

As Daisy walked toward Woods when she took a short break that afternoon, she felt Jonas would understand about this weekend. She'd been looking forward to it, and she'd have to make that clear. Spring was in the air, and that made the task of telling him she couldn't go even more difficult. Everything was budding, maybe even beginning to bloom. Just like their romance. And now . . .

It was just one weekend. They could go another time.

Elijah greeted Daisy when she walked into Woods. She could see he was noting measurements on a legal pad. In deference to spring, he'd switched from his black hat to a straw one. However, he still wore his long-sleeve blue shirt with black suspenders and pants. Jonas was on the phone at the sales counter in the rear of the store.

"How are you, Elijah?" Daisy asked.

"I'm *gut*," he answered with a smile. "The *kinner* are liking this warmer weather. They can be outdoors more and not just for chores."

Daisy nodded. "I know what you mean. I've decided no matter how busy we are, I need to step outside at least three times a day and just breathe."

"That is a *gut* idea, certain sure." Elijah motioned to Jonas. "He's talking to a man about reclaimed wood. We have more orders than we can finish for tables and islands."

"That's because you and Jonas do such a marvelous job."

Elijah blushed a little. Some Amish thought it was prideful to accept compliments, and Elijah was one of them. But she knew it didn't hurt to say what was the truth.

"You'll need a waiting list," she teased.

"That we will, and maybe we need to hire another woodworker here on site to help Jonas."

Jonas ended his call and crossed the showroom to Daisy. "This is a surprise."

Although she was glad to see him, she didn't want

him to think this was a social visit. "I have something to talk to you about."

He looked puzzled. "Would you like to go into the workshop?"

"That would be good."

Once in the workshop, Jonas motioned Daisy to his office. It was just a cubicle in the corner of the room, walled off with a door with plate glass. He left the door open now as they went inside. There was hardly room for the two of them because his desk took up space, but they managed. She stood by the computer station and he stood by the printer.

"Is this about the investigation?" he asked.

"No. Jonas, Vi called me. She told me she's coming home this weekend because she needs to talk to me. I asked her if it could wait until next weekend, but she says it can't. From the way Foster's been acting, I'm concerned it's about them breaking up."

"Are you telling me you can't go with me to Philadelphia?" His question didn't have much intonation, and his expression was stoic.

"I just can't go *this* weekend, Jonas. Is it possible to postpone?"

"No, it's not. Peg and Vince have already asked a group of friends. It's too late to cancel the barbecue."

"But *you* can go," Daisy said.

"Yes, I can, and I will. But that wasn't the point."

She took a step closer to him. "I know that. But Vi wouldn't ask me to cancel without a good reason."

"You don't even know what that reason is."

"No, I don't, but I trust her and her judgment. If she says she needs me, then she does."

His reply was quick and terse. "Do you always drop everything for your children?"

There was an edge in his voice and, truth be told, Daisy took the question as an insult. "If you had children, Jonas, you'd understand. My children will always come first, especially now that I'm the only parent they have."

Jonas didn't look sorry for what he'd asked, and Daisy didn't feel sorry for how she'd responded. The look he was giving her now was cool or maybe it was merely disappointed. She backed away from him because she was so tempted to throw her arms around him to keep him close. She felt him emotionally pulling away. Yet, she didn't quite feel that freedom, and especially not with what they'd just said to each other.

"I'd better go," she murmured.

He merely stuck his hands into the back pockets of his jeans and nodded.

She felt terrible as she left his office and then the workshop and then the store. He didn't call to her . . . or follow her. But she'd meant what she'd said. Her children did have to come first.

Sighing, she realized too late that a comment about him not having children probably hurt. The way he and his partner had lost their baby was tragic. Brenda had been shot in the line of duty and killed. She'd been pregnant when it happened. Jonas had told Daisy about it, but she wasn't sure he'd healed from it, not emotionally anyway. She'd thought they could work on that together. But if he didn't understand the responsibilities of being a mom and a single parent, she wasn't sure their romance would ever take off.

As she hurried up the street past Vinegar and Spice and waved to Arden inside, she liked the feeling of community this town gave her. Not all of the shop owners were friends, that was true, but they had something in common that united them and helped the businesses in Willow Creek thrive.

She stopped for a moment at the candle shop's window. All of Betty Furhman's candles were made by hand with beautiful natural scents. She'd have to stop in soon. Her aunt had a birthday coming up . . . maybe she'd just like something to put in the house that smelled good. She'd hoped her dad would call and tell her how his conversation with her mother had gone, but he hadn't.

She didn't know if that meant it went smoothly or if there were problems. She'd most likely see them this weekend. When Vi came home, they all had dinner with her parents on Sunday evening.

She hurried her pace back to the tea garden, but when she stepped inside, she knew immediately something was wrong. Foster's voice was raised.

Mr. Johnson was a regular customer; he had bristly gray hair that stood straight up and a belligerent look on his face. "It's smaller than Daisy's scones usually are. I should get *two* of them."

Foster gestured to the sign behind the cash counter. "That's not what the sign says. A scone costs the same no matter how big it is."

"You'll lose customers that way."

"Most of our customers understand that Daisy packs goodness into each scone she makes."

Uh-oh. This wasn't like Foster at all. He was a PR expert, a social media guy. He could tell her what she should tactfully say on her website and how she should comment when customers weren't flattering. *This* Foster she almost didn't know.

Did he miss Vi so much that it was affecting his schoolwork, his life, and his work here? Or did he know trouble was coming when Vi came home, and he couldn't stay focused on what he was doing?

Walking up to the two men, she put her hand on Foster's shoulder. Aunt Iris was watching from the counter, shock written on her face, so much apparent shock that she hadn't intervened.

"Foster, you know that when I'm making scones sometimes I get distracted. If there's a discrepancy, I'll be glad to give Mr. Johnson another scone."

After an angry moment, Foster bit out, "Fine. I'll get one."

But Daisy stopped him. "Why don't you take a walk outside for a few minutes? I'll get Mr. Johnson a scone and another type of tea if he'd like it."

Mr. Johnson sat back down on his chair. "Maybe I made something out of nothing," he apologized as Foster turned and headed toward the kitchen and the back door.

"I apologize for Foster's behavior."

"He's usually such a polite young man. But just look at that scone. Isn't it smaller than they usually are?"

Daisy had to admit it was a bit smaller but not enough that all her customers would notice. She knew Mr. Johnson was on a tight income and he didn't spend his money foolishly. "There *is* a discrepancy," she assured him. "Now what kind would you like? A cinnamon scone or a chocolate scone?"

"A chocolate scone and some of that orange spice tea."

"Coming right up."

As Daisy passed Cora Sue, she gave her the order for the tea, then she went to the scone case herself and chose an especially large chocolate scone. She set it on a flowered plate and took it to her customer's table.

"You enjoy this, Mr. Johnson. Cora Sue will bring out your tea in a few minutes. Don't hesitate to ask if you'd like a refill."

After he thanked Daisy again, she headed for the kitchen and the back door. When she went outside, she spotted Foster almost the whole way down the yard at the creek. She'd intended to try to talk to him, but he was moving at a fast pace, as if he was trying to walk off something. She just hoped after Vi came home this weekend, he'd return to being the young man she'd originally hired.

Chapter Twelve

On Friday morning, Russ Windom entered the tea garden. Daisy noticed him immediately because business was slow today. An article had appeared in the *Willow Creek Messenger* about the murder. It had mentioned the sandwiches as the cause of death and the fact they came from the tea garden. Daisy glanced into the kitchen where Iris was helping Tessa. She motioned to Cora Sue that she'd take Russ's order.

When she crossed to his table, he smiled sheepishly. "Hi, Daisy."

"Did you ask Iris out yet?"

"Not yet," he said with a shake of his head.

"Are you still afraid she'll say no?"

"Maybe, but when I come in like this, we can have a little quiet conversation if she's free."

"Do you want me to get her?"

"No, I want it to be natural . . . that she just stops to talk to me because she wants to."

Daisy shook her head and scowled at him. "Is that how you asked girls out when you were in high school?"

"When I was in high school, I had more confidence and a lot more hair," he answered grudgingly.

Daisy laughed. "Sorry," she apologized, "but you still have a lot of hair."

"Not on top."

She bit back another smile. "If you don't want me to get Iris, what can I bring you today?"

"How about lemongrass green tea and a bowl of your beef barley soup?"

"Early supper?"

"Yep. I don't feel much like cooking tonight. A couple times a week I stop by Sarah Jane's and order takeout. Usually, one of her meals lasts two nights, but the refrigerator's pretty bare. I have to go grocery shopping tomorrow. I might take along a few of your blueberry muffins too."

"Three?" she asked.

"No, make it a half dozen."

After Daisy brought Russ his order, she asked him, "Do you want company? Business has been ridiculously slow today."

"Yes. Join me. I hate eating alone."

Daisy wondered if her aunt Iris felt the same way. If Russ didn't soon make a move, she might have to play matchmaker.

"Any word on the murder investigation?" he asked her.

"The detective asked me to keep the specifics of Derek's death to myself."

Russ dipped his spoon into the beef barley soup and swished it around. "No problem. I understand confidentiality. As a teacher I had to deal with it a lot. Times have sure changed since I began teaching."

"Were you a teacher under Bradley Schumacher?"

"I was."

"How was he as a principal? Vi never said much about him, and Jazzi doesn't now."

"He was firm but fair. He has great organizational skills. Being a high school principal is a lot of paper pushing. The assistant principal usually takes care of the discipline if the teacher can't handle it himself or herself."

Daisy nodded. "Does Bradley get along with all of the teachers?"

Pulling his teacup in front of him, Russ added a teaspoon full of sugar and a bit of cream. "He made it a point of his to get around to all the teachers every day and talk to them about something. He didn't play favorites."

As soon as Russ said that, she frowned. "Was it a problem, not playing favorites?"

"No, not at all. It's just that . . . Bradley didn't hesitate to sit down at the lunch table in the lounge with other teachers and chat. The impression I got when he told childhood stories was that he was the favorite brother. In fact, I don't believe Harriet gave Derek as much attention. Bradley didn't say that, but it was what his stories revealed. It's very odd since Derek was the firstborn."

That was odd and yet . . . "Did Derek get along with his stepfather?"

"From what I understand, the stepfather tried to take Derek under his wing, but Derek was a hard kid to get to know. In high school his grades were all over the place. He was cited for truancy, but he was popular with the girls. Maybe it was that bad boy persona he wanted to project."

"It sounds as if he might have been the opposite from Bradley."

"As a father and a teacher, I know each child has his or her own personality. It could be as simple as that."

"Do you know anything about Harriet's sister June?"

"Not much. I do know they hadn't spoken since before Derek was born."

Daisy decided that tidbit was worth saving.

The bell over the door jingled and four women stepped inside. As they took a table near Russ's, Daisy pushed back her chair. "I'd better help serve. Everyone in the kitchen is prepping for tomorrow."

"It's always good to talk to you, Daisy."

"It's good to talk to you too. Now remember what I said, make your move."

Russ's face turned a little ruddy. "I'll keep your advice in mind."

Daisy suspected Russ might need a few cups of black tea with lots of caffeine to make his move.

Foster arrived early for his shift. Because Vi was coming home tonight, Daisy thought he'd be more cheerful than he had been recently. But he seemed as edgy as ever. Yesterday, he'd told her he was going to update their social media site and answer any questions customers might have. Right now, as he stared at Daisy's computer, he looked downright sober.

"What's the matter?" Daisy asked.

"Business has dropped off today for a very good reason. Have you checked your comments on the tea garden website lately?"

"No, I haven't. Why?"

"Come look," he said as if she might not believe what was there if he simply told her.

A chill ran up Daisy's spine because she had an inkling of what this might be about.

"The newspaper article?" she asked Foster before looking at the screen. "I suspected it would cause a few rumors."

Daisy sat at her desk and began scrolling down through the comments. That chill up her spine transformed into a slow panic. "The public thinks we poisoned Derek Schumacher."

"They've been reading between the lines of that article. Of course, they think it was poisoning of some type."

"What are we going to do?" Daisy asked rhetorically, but Foster took her literally.

"There's not much we can do until this case is solved. We could put coupons in the paper. We can give out coupons to the people who do come in so that they come back. It might even be necessary to do that in the York paper and even Harrisburg, because you know the rumors are going to circulate farther than we expect them to."

"You're giving me a dimmer outlook than I want to see," she scolded.

He looked as if he was about to say something but then changed his mind. "I'm only telling you what I think about it. You should check with your aunt Iris and Tessa and see what they think."

"Do you want me to deny all these rumors?"

"I think the comments need to be addressed. Can you somehow keep the responses positive? Something like—*We hope Derek Schumacher's murder is resolved by the police quickly?*

Daisy nodded. "We might have to repeat the comment several times. I'll respond to these comments now. We'll have to check tomorrow to see if the tide has turned, but I doubt my responses are going to do it. Only solving the case will do it. I might have to take a more active role."

Sighing, Daisy rolled her chair away from the computer and changed their topic of conversation. "Did Vi tell you what time she'll be home tonight?"

Foster answered, "She had loose ends to tie up. She probably won't get here until after eight."

Daisy thought about that and the comments on the tea garden's website and where she could discover more clues. "Cora Sue mentioned visiting Harriet Schumacher this evening. Maybe I'll tag along."

"Is Jonas helping figure out who murdered Derek?"

"Not right now. He's away this weekend." Her heart felt heavy when she thought about their argument.

She spoke in spite of the tightening of her throat. "I'll ask Tessa to close up for the day. She knows to put the cash from the register in the safe. I'll take it to the bank when I come in tomorrow morning." She stood and untied her apron. "And I'll see you later or tomorrow." Daisy smiled at Foster with a wink.

But he didn't smile or wink back.

Daisy told Cora Sue that she'd drive to Derek's house. Cora Sue's husband had brought her to work this morning, so Daisy could just drop her off after their visit and then head home. On the way to Harriet's, they talked about the comments on the website.

They had almost arrived at Derek's house when Cora Sue said, "We could take down our website for a while, and comments wouldn't be spread as fast as they're spreading now."

"I thought about that," Daisy agreed. "But Foster doesn't think that would help. He said people who know each other are still going to gossip, and there are other blogs about tea rooms where the rumors can spread just as fast. I'm still thinking about it though. Your inclination was my first inclination, but it isn't just Facebook anymore or my website. There's Twitter too."

"You sound discouraged," Cora Sue said.

"I don't want to be. Every time we get pushed down, we seem to pop back up. But watching the sales numbers this week is challenging."

"We can hope another big story takes the place of the murder."

"Yes, or I can make better strides solving this case."

"I don't feel I can help because of Detective Rappaport. I feel he has his eye on me. He comes into the tea garden about once a day now."

"You're helping me tonight."

"This kind of help I can give. Even Detective Rappaport couldn't find anything wrong with wanting to visit Harriet so she isn't so lonely."

A few minutes later, they stood at the door of Derek's house. June let them inside.

Daisy explained, "We thought Harriet could use a little company and maybe soup." Daisy held up the bag.

"That's kind of you. We were just having a cup of tea and talking about old times."

"Your childhood?" Cora Sue asked.

"Yes, and our teenage years. How does time pass so fast?"

"My dad insists time goes faster the older you get," Daisy said.

"Your father's a wise man. I agree with that. Monday turns into the following Sunday, and I don't know where the week went. Staying here with Harriet is giving me balance again, and something to do each day."

Using her walker, Harriet came down the hall to meet them at the top of the stairway. Daisy, Cora Sue, and June climbed the stairs. "Cora Sue. Daisy. What a nice surprise."

Harriet looked genuinely pleased to see them. Because being with her sister after all these years might be a little too much company?

"Come into the living room," she invited. "June, can you put the kettle on?"

"I certainly can. I don't know if our tea will be as good as what they sell at the tea room. I bought all kinds of teabags. I'll bring in the box so you can choose."

Harriet seemed to be in a contemplative mood when she said, "Derek didn't like all the flowers in here . . . or the pink backgrounds. He would have put geometric stripes on the wall if I'd let him."

"That could be the difference between a man's and a woman's décor," Daisy said.

"I suppose. But he said something that always made me wonder."

"What was that?" Cora Sue asked.

"He said I was too hard for flowers."

That statement just hung in the air, causing tension in the room and awkwardness that wasn't there before.

Daisy felt as if she had to step in. "It's possible he meant that you were strong, not hard."

Harriet shrugged. "Maybe."

They talked about the antique marble-top tables until June returned with a teapot and two mugs on a tray. Under her arm, she'd wedged a box. She set the mugs on the table beside Cora Sue and Daisy and then poured the hot water into them. When she held out the box with teabags, Daisy chose a country peach.

She didn't know what had happened between the two sisters, but they actually seemed close now, as if thirty-five years apart hadn't happened. Daisy suddenly wondered if Derek could have been June's child and she gave him to Harriet to raise, promising no contact. But why? What could that possibly have to do with Derek's murder?

Daisy knew she wasn't going to collect much information if she tried to coax particularly personal information from the sisters.

June fixed Harriet another cup of tea. As she handed the cup and saucer to her sister, she said, "For some reason, tea brings comfort. I suppose that's why you and your aunt opened the tea garden."

"Yes, it was. And we need that comfort now. All kinds of gossip about what killed Derek is circulating around town. It's affected our business."

"I imagine," Harriet said. "That's not fair."

"Fair or not, that's what's happening," Cora Sue agreed. "So we want to try to figure out who might have hurt Derek. If the case is resolved, there shouldn't be any more gossip."

"How are you going to figure it out?" June wanted to know.

"I guess we'll start where we have the most information. There's a reporter from Atlanta, Clementine Hankey, who was doing a story on Derek. She asked me questions, which also gave me information. Can you tell me anything about Derek's show and his co-host?"

"Sure, I can," Harriet said. "His show started right here in Lancaster. Derek and a friend from culinary school, Miranda Senft, started out with a home base. Sometimes they would invite cooks from other states to come here and cook with them. Then the audience would vote on whose dish was best. After that first year, Miranda and Derek traveled to other states and cooked with home cooks from those areas. It made for lots of laughter, good times, and audience appreciation."

Daisy nodded. "I can see that it would. That sounds like a fun show."

"The ratings were terrific," Harriet added. "Derek was making money hand over fist. He even had a line of cookware on a home shopping channel. That's when he bought this big house."

"What happened next?" Cora Sue asked.

"Yes, what happened next?" June asked too. Apparently, she and Harriet hadn't caught up to this level yet.

Harriet took a few sips of tea. "I'm not sure how to put this because I don't know exactly what happened. As I said, Derek was making money, not just from the show and his product line but from appearances too. Then suddenly, I watched the show one week and Miranda was gone. Somebody named Birgit took her place. The truth is—Miranda was a class act. She was a serious cook and could be funny at times. She and

Derek played off of each other well. Birgit was a tall blonde. Derek's ratings started tanking, and then the network wouldn't renew his contract."

"Is that when he began his blog and became a food critic?" Daisy asked.

"That's exactly when. He didn't even take much time to think about it. I guess anybody can build a blog. As a celebrity chef, he already had lots of followers. He started visiting restaurants, tasting other chefs' food, then he would comment on it. I have to admit, his attitude about food seemed to change."

"What do you mean?" Daisy prompted.

"Once upon a time, and you could see it on his show, he enjoyed every bite of dinner, no matter if he cooked it or another chef cooked it. The experience of eating was just as important as the food. Suddenly, as a food critic, that was no longer true. He ate critically, as if he was tearing apart every recipe in his mind. If it didn't meet his standards, then he gave it a harsh review."

"Whatever happened to Birgit?" Daisy imagined Birgit could be one of the keys to this puzzle.

"I really don't know," Harriet concluded. She exchanged a look with her sister. "Derek and I weren't close. You might as well know that. I thought as an adult he'd found his place and maybe we would become closer. But his success drove him, and the more successful he became, the more he became distant. He had lots of friends. I wasn't necessary." Harriet shook her head.

June patted her hand. "But Derek took you in after your stroke. He made a place for you, and he looked after you."

"*Looked after* is the way I'd put it," Harriet agreed with sadness in her eyes and her voice. "He was doing his duty. Lauren was the one I'd call if I needed groceries or a driver for a doctor's appointment . . . or just some company. Lauren and Bradley's little girl is a joy. I liked having Chrissy around. After my rehab experience, Lauren would bring her over and the two of us would play with blocks. That would help my hand-and-eye coordination. Three-year-olds are just the cutest." Harriet seemed to be looking back and remembering her sons at that age.

June said softly, "Children give us hope that a new generation will treat the world more kindly than we did."

Daisy supposed that was true. Vi and Jazzi had given her hope after Ryan died. Ryan had often said, "No matter what happens, keep on truckin'." That's what they'd all done . . . one day at a time.

When Daisy's front door opened, she was in the kitchen with Jazzi. It was almost nine o'clock. Vi had told her not to wait supper, so she hadn't. But she had brought home a selection of baked goods, as well as two quarts of potato and leek soup. Vi often said she wasn't hungry when she got home, but then she would rummage in the refrigerator for something to eat.

Daisy gave Jazzi a thumbs-up sign as she went to the living room to greet her daughter. However, she stopped mid-stride when she realized Vi wasn't alone. Foster was with her. How were they going to have a conversation about whatever Vi wanted to talk about with Foster here? Maybe he just came to say hello and was going to leave again.

Foster said formally, "Hello, Mrs. Swanson," and set Vi's duffel at the base of the stairs.

They were back to *Mrs. Swanson* again. That gave her an uh-oh feeling.

Daisy stepped forward to hug Vi, and Vi hugged her back tightly with a low mumbled, "Hi, Mom."

Daisy stepped back when Jazzi came into the room to hug her sister. Vi hugged Jazzi, but it was a shorter hug. Then she stepped away from Jazzi and closer to Foster.

Violet had highlighted her medium brown hair with lighter streaks. She was wearing a maroon lipstick and her cheeks were rosy. In spite of her T-shirt and jeans, she looked beautiful.

Yet her expression warned Daisy that she wouldn't like the news that was coming. She was dropping classes? Maybe she'd flunked a class. Some subjects like physics she simply didn't like. All of it rolled through Daisy's mind so fast she hardly caught what Violet was saying.

"Mom, can we sit down? I really want to talk to you about something."

Daisy's gaze flickered to Foster. "With Foster here?"

"Yes, with Foster here." Vi held on to his hand as if it were a lifeline.

Vi and Foster went to the love seat while Daisy and Jazzi sat on the sofa. Jazzi wasn't saying a word, just watching the couple. Daisy focused on them too . . . especially their sober expressions.

Foster patted Vi's hand, and Vi took a big bolstering breath. "Mom, I'm pregnant, and Foster and I are going to get married as soon as possible."

Chapter Thirteen

Daisy was absolutely speechless. From the expression on Jazzi's face, Daisy could tell *she* was shocked too.

Pregnant. Violet was pregnant.

She wanted to get married.

Daisy felt as if she'd had a fall and all the breath had been knocked out of her. Was this the absolute last thing a mother wanted for her child?

No, no, no. No one had died. Some of her breath came back.

Recovering first, Jazzi blurted out, "You can't get married, because you're both in school!"

Even in her shocked state, Daisy could see Violet squeeze Foster's hand even tighter.

Daisy realized why when Violet insisted, "I'm going to quit school. If I get a job, then Foster and I can find a place to live."

Her daughter looked happy and hopeful, and Daisy didn't believe either emotion would last.

Quickly Foster claimed, "I'll take on more and more computer work as well as working at Daisy's. If I can't earn enough that way while going to college, then I'll quit school for the time being and return later."

It was a toss-up whether Daisy wanted to cry or yell. Yet from experience she knew neither would do any good. She needed facts.

Finding her words again and trying to keep her voice calm, she asked Vi, "How far along are you, honey?"

"Six weeks. I told Foster two weeks ago when I asked him to come to Lehigh midweek."

Again, Foster took the next part of the explanation. "That was the week of the murder. Now I can give Detective Rappaport an alibi."

Daisy wasn't sure what to address or how to do it without alienating this young couple. She might even need outside advice. "You've both known about this for a little while. I need time to absorb everything you've told me. Then I want to talk about it. Can you both come to dinner on Sunday?"

After the couple exchanged another look, Vi answered, "We can come. I came home this weekend to talk about our plans with Foster and with you."

Jazzi shook her head. "I can't believe you did this. How could you be so stupid . . . so careless?"

Daisy had had the "talk" with both of the girls. At about eight, they'd talked about where babies came from. At twelve, they'd discussed birth control. She had gotten them books for their age levels to read about the subject. Her daughters hadn't been hesitant to ask her questions. She thought they were good.

But Violet's answer told her why they weren't.

"You don't understand, Jazzi. Wait until you fall in love with someone you can't see all the time. Every minute is precious. Only once. We only forgot once."

"Well, I'm going to wait until I'm married," Jazzi almost shouted back. "That's what you're *supposed* to do."

In a perfect world, Daisy thought.

Vi shot back, "Grow up, Jazzi. When you start dating, you'll understand."

Daisy knew she had to be the tempering force no matter what her own feelings were on the subject, no matter her own past history. She held up her hand and waved it. "This is why I want to wait until Sunday to discuss everything. I want you two to think about what you're going to do, what you want to do, what's most practical to do. Jazzi, I want you to try and understand the way Violet's feeling right now."

Jazzi crossed her arms over her chest. "I'm going up to my room. Seeing Violet's point of view isn't going to do either of us any good." She crossed the living room and ran up the stairs.

Foster looked up at Daisy. "Mrs. Swanson—"

"It's Daisy," she said softly.

"I didn't think I should call you that since I caused this."

Violet took his arm. "You did *not*. We were both there."

Again, Daisy stopped the flow of the argument with her hand. "Foster, you're still my employee, and you're a young man who I like very much. I understand you want to do the honorable thing. That's one of the reasons I like you. But you need to think about it."

"We've thought about it for over two weeks, Mom."

"Two weeks is a blip in your lifetime."

Foster turned to Violet and gently touched her cheek. "I'd better go. I'll see you tomorrow at the tea garden, right? And we'll go out to dinner tomorrow night and talk."

At Vi's nod, Daisy became hopeful. Maybe she could talk some sense into Vi after Foster left.

Violet walked Foster to the door and gave him a long kiss.

Daisy wasn't a voyeur, at least not yet. She went to the kitchen to make tea. Chamomile. It was probably the only thing that would calm her down right now. She'd also warm up the soup. Maybe Vi would open up more over a light meal. This was her older daughter, the daughter she'd always been able to talk sense to. Violet had only ever cared about her studies and going to college. More than once, when a new boy had asked her out, she'd said she wasn't going to get serious because she had a future to think about.

A future that might now include Foster and a baby. A baby. Daisy had to smile at the thought. She'd be a grandmother. Alarm set in. Or maybe more than a grandmother.

Daisy heard the front door close and the beep when Violet set the alarm. Then she heard Violet's footsteps as she wandered into the kitchen. She had that just-kissed look and was smiling. Young love. Daisy hated to put a damper on it, but reality was reality.

She motioned to the island where she'd set the scones and two bowls for the warming soup. "I have the pot on for tea. I thought you might want a snack."

"I'm not really hungry, Mom, but tea sounds good."

"Nausea?" Daisy asked.

Vi looked surprised that Daisy had caught on so quickly. "It comes and goes all day. I thought a woman was only supposed to be sick in the morning."

"Each woman is different. Sit down and we can talk."

But Vi was already shaking her head. "Oh no. You're not going to try to brainwash me while Foster's not here."

"I would *never* try to brainwash you. Why do you think I would do that now?"

"Because you think you know what's best. Foster and I have to make our own decisions. I won't talk to you about my pregnancy without Foster being here."

That was a shutdown on conversation if Daisy had ever heard one. But she had to acquiesce. This wasn't the time to push Violet away.

"Fine," Daisy said. "We won't talk about the pregnancy. Can we talk about your finals and classes and when you'll be coming home?"

To Daisy's relief, Vi took a seat at the island. "Sure. We can talk about that."

Daisy was certain that Violet and even Foster didn't understand the import of what they wanted to do. All of their lives were going to be changed forever.

Daisy pulled a scone pan from the oven at the tea garden on Saturday and burned herself as she set it on the counter. The problem was—she was totally rattled. Going to the pantry, she reached for the bottle of aloe vera gel. At the sink, she dripped it over the side of her hand.

Tessa came to take a peek. "It doesn't look too bad. Do you need a bandage?"

"No. It's simply one of those slashes we all get."

More than anything, Daisy wanted to talk to her aunt Iris or to Tessa about Vi's pregnancy. She couldn't do it here because Foster, Vi, and Jazzi were all working.

Mostly silent, but working. She hadn't slept much last night, thinking about Vi being pregnant and what her daughter and Foster wanted to do. She also thought about Jazzi's response to Vi's news. Daisy was surprised that Jazzi hadn't been more supportive of Violet. Did that have something to do with the fact that she'd felt abandoned when Violet had left for college? Her two girls had always been close, but Violet had started on her adult life and Jazzi hadn't.

"Daisy?"

Daisy heard Tessa call her name, and she glanced at her friend knowing she'd missed something.

"Where did you go? I asked you if you ate breakfast this morning."

"No, I didn't. I wasn't hungry."

Tessa narrowed her eyes and scanned Daisy up and down. "It's a slow morning again and we need to talk. We have plenty of help here today. Let's go up to my apartment and have a cup of tea."

Was she ready to do this? Did she really want to spill family problems to Tessa at this early stage before they figured anything out? Still . . . She and Tessa had been best friends since high school. She easily remembered how they'd helped each other with problems . . . from deciding on a prom dress to solving murder cases.

Daisy's hands went to her back waist and she untied her apron.

Tessa wore a colorful smock and she said, "I'm just going to leave this on. I haven't gotten it full of flour or cinnamon yet, but the day is young."

After telling Eva they'd be in Tessa's apartment, they went out the back door and over to the entrance to Tessa's place.

Tessa unlocked her door and turned off the alarm system. They climbed the interior stairway to the apartment on the second and third floor of the Victorian. As they reached the apartment, Daisy realized all over again how Bohemian Tessa's taste was, not only in dress but in her decorations and furnishings too. Her kidney-shaped sofa had a shawl stretched along its back in colors from red to blue to orange and wine. The fabric on the sofa was patterned with diamonds and chevrons in the same colors as the shawl. In front of the sofa, there was a little coffee table covered with a scarf in bright colors. A bunch of lavender stood in a vase on the table along with a wooden candlestick that held a candle. Tessa's platform rocker had wooden arms and a burnt orange fabric covering. Multicolored scarf valences in burnt orange, red, and yellow were draped over the rods in the front windows.

Tessa was a reader as well as an artist. The bookshelves along one wall proved it. An antique corner shelf held small knickknacks, and prints framed in walnut, pine, and distressed wood decorated her walls. Tessa had carried the colorful theme into her bedroom where a crazy quilt with patches from velvet to gingham to stripes acted as the main focal point of the room.

When Daisy and her aunt had redone this upstairs kitchen, they'd replaced the old cabinets with birch ones. Tessa had picked out the backsplash, which was a multicolored blue tile. Ceramic crocks in turquoise, yellow, and orange held flour, granulated white sugar, and brown sugar. One also held her utensils.

"I'll make the tea," Tessa offered.

"Do you want help?"

"Today I think it's safer if *I* make it."

Daisy knew where everything was in Tessa's apartment, and she often made tea. But today Tessa was probably right.

She crossed to the sofa and sat watching Tessa as she filled the teapot with water, set it on the front burner, and switched it on. Then she took a black polka-dot bone china teapot from a cupboard, spooned tea into the infuser, and crossed to the living room to wait for the water to heat. "I'm making green tea with chamomile. It will help settle you down."

"I don't think anything is going to do that this morning," Daisy responded with a catch in her voice.

"Do you want to wait until the tea is ready to start talking, or do you want to have a brownie first?"

"We haven't made brownies for the tea room for a while."

"That's why I made a batch. A brownie for breakfast?"

"That sounds good to me. Do you have nuts I could have with it so I get my protein?"

"Always the nutritionist at heart. Brownie and nuts coming up."

Being in Tessa's apartment, talking as if they were just two friends with nothing on their minds seemed unreal. Daisy felt as if she was living in more than one universe—one filled with the tea garden and friends and customers, tea and sweet goods. And the other with a family dilemma she didn't know how to handle.

The teapot whistled. While the tea steeped, Tessa brought into the living room a yellow ironstone plate with brownies and a bowl with almonds and walnuts. "Have a brownie first, then we can start talking."

"You sound like Detective Rappaport, except he doesn't offer brownies."

Tessa couldn't hide her smile. "If you can still joke, then the end of the world isn't coming yet."

"I don't know about that. It might be the end of the world as we know it."

"Daisy, why are you scaring me? Spill it."

"Violet is pregnant."

Tessa's brown eyes went wide, and her mouth rounded in an "O." Apparently, she was so surprised that she didn't speak until the timer went off for their steeped tea. "I'll pour the tea," she said in an amazed voice. "Maybe I should have made black tea. You might need to be braced, not calmed."

Once they were sipping and nibbling, Daisy said, "You haven't heard the best part."

"I'm afraid to ask."

"Vi and Foster want to get married immediately. She wants to quit school so she can get a job and help with their finances until the baby's born. Foster will keep working at the tea garden and try to pick up more computer work. He'll keep going to college unless he can't handle it all. If he can't, he'll quit college and return when life settles down." She couldn't keep her voice from becoming a bit sarcastic.

Daisy slid another brownie onto her plate. "They're making a mistake."

"Are they making a mistake if they're in love?" Tessa asked.

"They're blinded by feelings. They're naïve. Nothing about this is going to be easy. Both of them are coming to dinner tomorrow night, and the four of us are going to look at what they want to do and maybe formulate a plan. But I honestly don't know where to start."

"You said it yourself—they need to be practical. Give them a piece of paper and a pen and tell them to make a list of practical solutions to make their lives work if they *do* get married."

Daisy thought about it while she munched. After another sip of tea, she agreed. "If they look at their reality on paper, their plans might not seem so rosy. On my part, I think what I need to do is to make a list of possibilities and solutions to bring to the table. Maybe that list will keep me busy enough to keep me from brooding. Vi won't talk to me about the pregnancy without Foster being present. She doesn't want me to pressure her or convince her to do anything she doesn't want to do. I guess he will be her buffer."

"I suppose that works if Violet doesn't want to talk to you about it on her own. But I can't believe she won't want to eventually. A girl turns to her mom in times like this."

"In books and movies."

"Are you going to discuss this situation with Jonas?"

"Jonas is another matter entirely."

Tessa settled her teacup on her saucer with a little click. "What's *that* supposed to mean? I thought the two of you were dating and becoming more serious."

"I did too. Jonas and I were supposed to see friends of his in Philadelphia this weekend, but then Vi called and said she was coming Friday and she had to talk to me. I canceled those plans. Jonas wasn't happy."

"I don't get that. Jonas seems to be the kind of guy who would understand family commitments."

"Maybe so, but his friends were having a barbecue

and he wanted to introduce me to everyone. One of the couples was coming from out of town."

"I can see how that would be disappointing."

"I don't know, Tessa. He seemed to be upset that I couldn't put him first. Our relationship might have nowhere to go because with Violet's pregnancy I absolutely *can't* put him first. And I'm not sure where that leaves us."

After Daisy slipped into plaid pajama pants and a blue tank top that evening, she wished she could call Jonas. Jazzi was in bed and all was quiet.

Pepper lay on Daisy's Sunshine and Shadows quilt. The feline was stretched out, but her golden eyes followed Daisy everywhere she went. The soft white fur on Pepper's tummy invited a tummy rub. Marjoram was upstairs with Jazzi. It was unusual for the two cats to go their separate ways.

Pepper meowed at Daisy.

Daisy crossed to her bed and sat down beside the cat. "Do you want a belly rub?" she asked Pepper.

Pepper blinked at her, which was possibly a *yes*. Unlike other kittens who grabbed your arms with their front and back legs and might even bite when you touched their tummies, Marjoram and Pepper had never done that. So Daisy stroked Pepper's silky white fur, running her fingers through it. "Do you think I need company tonight?"

Pepper just laid her paw over Daisy's hand as if in a comforting gesture.

"I guess that's a *yes* too." Daisy felt a little misty that this cat could read her so well.

She was feeling a combination of so many things.

Of course, worry about Vi and Foster was at the top of her current list. Jazzi seeing a counselor was next. Daisy had made appointments for her for Monday and Thursday to start. Then, of course, there was Jonas. Somehow Derek's murder had slipped from first place. Maybe that's what she could concentrate on instead of strategies for Vi and Foster if they went ahead with their plans.

After she ran her fingers through Pepper's fur again, rubbed the spot between her eyes and down her nose, and heard her purr loudly, Daisy said, "I'll leave my door open if you want to go up to Jazzi's room."

But Pepper just curled up on her side and stretched out a paw as if she was deciding to stay for the night.

Daisy wandered over to her dresser. She opened the top drawer and removed a long navy box. Opening the spring lid, she studied the pearls Ryan had given her as a wedding present. She lifted them from the blue velvet lining and ran her fingers along each pearl. There was a knot between them. The gold clasp had a safety catch. It was silly, she knew, but she put them on. Her blond hair played down over them, and she fingered the pearls again. She hadn't worn these since Tessa's showing of her paintings at Revelations Art Gallery. Maybe that was because when she wore them, she remembered.

Although some memories were fading a bit, others were vivid. Suddenly, Daisy wanted to remember *everything*.

Crossing to her closet, she opened it and pulled out the white photo album on the top shelf. Taking it over to the bed, she sat propped by the pillows, her legs crossed under her. Slowly, she opened the album to the first page. It was a photo of her wedding party . . .

their wedding party. Ryan's mom had still been alive
then. Daisy's gown had been poufy—a Cinderella ball
gown. Tiny pearls decorated the tight-fitting sleeveless
bodice. Ryan, with his reddish blond hair and wide
smile, wore a black tuxedo, cummerbund, and black
tie. He looked so handsome and as happy as she appeared to be. Daisy had loved Ryan's mom. They'd
found an apartment nearby her house in Florida.
Nora had even flown to Pennsylvania for their wedding. It was the first time she'd flown, and she'd been
a good sport about everything.

Daisy's mom had been dressed in a long, pale
mauve gown. Nora's dress had been mid-length in the
palest gray. Since Daisy's aunt Iris had been her maid
of honor, she'd dressed in an aqua gown with ruching
across the waist.

Daisy ran her finger over a photo of Tessa, who had
been Daisy's bridesmaid. She'd worn the same aqua as
Iris. One of her dad's best friends was a groomsman
along with one of Ryan's friends that he'd gone to
college with. They were all so young.

Daisy and Ryan had met at Drexel University in
Philadelphia. She'd been a sophomore working
toward a bachelor of science degree in nutrition and
foods. Ryan had been a senior, earning a bachelor's
degree in business administration. He'd been offered
a job in Florida near his mom. But before he'd taken
the job, he'd proposed to her and asked her to go
with him. She'd hesitated and they'd spent a few
months apart. But then she'd decided to quit school
and go to Florida and marry him. She'd finished her
degree there.

Thinking about it now, Daisy knew that distance
hadn't been a good thing. Yes, you missed the person

you loved when they were far away, but distance also allowed doubts to creep in . . . it added uncertainty about the future and worries about day-to-day living arrangements.

After Daisy looked through the photos in that album, she put it away and lifted out another. These were the photos of their Florida home. Vi was three when they'd adopted Jazzi, moved out of a rental, and bought their own home. From the start, Violet had felt protective of her little sister. Ryan and Daisy had explained all about adoption and how Jazzi was a special child who they'd chosen. She was a child of their heart just as Violet was. There were so many photos of all of them at the beach, at Disney World, at Sea World, and at home in their own backyard. There was a photo of Jazzi when she was about ten with a little lizard on her arm. Vi had her hands in front of her face, screaming. She always ran from those lizards.

Suddenly, Daisy couldn't stand to look at any more photos. Those of Ryan stabbed her heart. Would that ever stop?

With Daisy sitting on her bed once more, Pepper stood, cat-stretched, then walked onto Daisy's lap, nestled in, and purred. Daisy petted her, knowing that her kitties could bring comfort. She needed that comfort tonight because . . . she felt alone.

Chapter Fourteen

On Sunday morning, Daisy and Jazzi attended church. It was a later service than usual. Vi was having morning sickness and not feeling well, so she didn't go along. Daisy hated to doubt her daughter, but did she really have morning sickness or did she just not want to talk to Daisy? Mothers' hearts were tender, but sometimes they couldn't let their children see that. Daisy knew she had to be careful with what steps she took with Vi and Foster. Hopefully, the church service would help a bit. Reverend Kemp was kind, thoughtful, and insightful. He could apply the concepts of the New Testament to everyday life. It was pretty much an interdenominational community. Daisy liked that fact most of all.

This church had been built about a hundred years ago. A historical plaque on the front brick wall proclaimed its established date. Simply fashioned, the church had been repainted inside about five years ago, according to Daisy's mom. That was when Reverend Kemp had taken the job as pastor. In his late forties, he was married with two children. He knew about family life.

The altar was simple with a cross hung from the ceiling above it. The podium was to the left. Reverend Kemp had ordered cushions for the pews after the church was painted. They were deep burgundy and made services more comfortable.

Today the pastor's message to his congregation was about spring and rebirth. Daisy tried to keep her mind on his sermon, but her thoughts kept wandering to Violet and Foster . . . to Harriet, June, and Derek Schumacher.

When the service was over, Daisy touched Jazzi's hand. "Let's just sit here a little longer. Today I don't feel like being stopped by a lot of people and have to carry on a conversation."

"Good idea," Jazzi agreed. "I know what you mean. I can't stop thinking about Vi's baby and what she's going to do."

Daisy squeezed Jazzi's hand. They waited until most of the pews had emptied, and then they went down the side aisle to one of the exits. But when they stepped outside, Daisy found a group gathered there. She recognized everyone immediately—Bradley Schumacher, his wife Lauren, and a little girl of about three who was absolutely adorable in a pink dress with ruffles decorating the skirt. The church secretary, Vanna Huffnagle, also stood there chatting along with Reverend Kemp.

Vanna was saying, "You give Harriet my regards. I think about her. I'm going to make time this week to visit. Should I call her first?"

"That would probably be best," Bradley acknowledged.

Reverend Kemp laid his hand on Bradley's shoulder.

"I want you to tell me if there's anything I can do to lessen your burden. I know grief comes and goes in waves. One day you're perfectly fine and the next day you're not. How is Harriet holding up?"

Lauren said, "Since her sister June came to stay with her, she seems better. But I'm sure she'd welcome a visit from you."

Reverend Kemp looked a bit embarrassed when he said, "I've been remiss in not visiting her more after her stroke. I did visit her about a month ago. I do have something to say, and I don't know if you or Harriet want to hear."

"We know you're honest with us," Bradley said.

The minister's hair was brown, laced with a bit of gray. He ran his fingers through it now as if he was thinking about exactly how to put what he had to say into words . . . and maybe be kind at the same time.

Daisy held her breath, wondering what was coming.

"I know Harriet went through rehab and had to work very hard while she was there. The physical therapists wouldn't have let her come home otherwise. But when she was in rehab, I spoke with her physical therapist. She was afraid that after Harriet returned home, she wouldn't try as hard to stay strong . . . to do her exercises every day so she didn't get muscle cramps. I really think if she pushed herself a little more, she could get around better than she does, maybe without that wheelchair."

"I'm hoping with June staying in Willow Creek for the time being," Bradley explained, "that will give Mom motivation to return to physical therapy. I'm going to talk to June about it tonight when we visit Mom. The one thing that does brighten her up is seeing Chrissy."

Chrissy, who had been quiet up until now, pulled on her mother's hand. "Can we go? I'm hun-gy."

She was an adorable little girl with brown ringlets surrounding her oval face. Daisy could see how this child would brighten Harriet's life. Would having a grandchild of her own brighten hers?

If she didn't alienate Vi and Foster. If they decided to keep the baby, would Foster really stay by Vi's side?

So many questions with no immediate answers.

The reverend was speaking again. "The physical therapy facility is only fifteen minutes from Harriet's home. Maybe you could make an appointment for her and just take her in to look around."

"If she's going to return to therapy," Lauren said, "we'd better let her make an appointment herself. If we don't, she'll be angry, and she doesn't get over anger easily."

"I'll pray that she's open to your suggestions, and also that she'll consider physical therapy as a real benefit to living a more fulfilling life."

One of the things Daisy liked about Reverend Kemp was that he was always positive. But convincing someone to change their behavior could be impossible. She wondered why the minister believed Harriet could do more than she does now. That was a question for another time. Both she and Jazzi wanted to get home. Maybe if they were around Vi enough, she would open up to them more.

Daisy could only hope.

Daisy thought about taking a cup of tea up to Violet who'd been in her room with the door closed most of the day. After church Daisy had made pancakes and offered a plate to her older daughter. When Daisy returned upstairs to check on her a half hour later, Vi had only eaten half of one pancake and wanted no part of conversation.

After Daisy had put a roast in the Crock-Pot for tonight—she knew Foster liked that—Daisy had checked on Vi again and she was napping. Daisy had just finished preparing a salad and set it in the refrigerator, when Jazzi came into the kitchen.

She put her elbows on the island counter, and her black hair swung forward as she leaned down. "Vi won't talk to me either."

Daisy gave her a look. "That's one of the most worrisome parts of this," she confessed. "Vi and I have always been able to talk."

"I've always been able to talk to her, too, but now I know why she hasn't called me. I have plenty of schoolwork to do along with practicing for the talent show, so I can keep my mind off of dinner tonight. What about you?"

"I'll just putter. Maybe peel the potatoes."

"You can peel those closer to dinner. I know you're anxious about her, Mom. Don't you have something you can investigate?"

When Daisy considered that, she thought about Miranda Senft and the way she'd come and gone from the funeral home. No expression. No condolences for the family. What was with that?

"Maybe I do have something to investigate."

Jazzi gave her a smile. "Good. What?"

Should she include Jazzi in this conversation? Wasn't it better if Jazzi was out of it altogether? Still, these days, any conversation created a bond with her daughter. So there was no harm in talking a little bit about the investigation.

"Derek Schumacher's co-host on his cable show worked with him for a long time and very successfully. Her name is Miranda Senft."

"You said she worked with him a long time. What happened?"

Her daughter had good deductive reasoning skills. "I don't know, and that's what I'd like to find out. It might not have anything at all to do with the murder, but it wouldn't hurt if I connected with Miranda Senft and asked a few questions."

"Do you know where to find her?"

"As you've taught me, I'll start with Google."

"Do you want me to look her up?"

Yes or no? Always decisions for a parent to ponder. But why not? This woman was a cook and nothing else, right? "Sure. Let me get my laptop. Is this going to interfere with your time for schoolwork?"

"I have all afternoon and later tonight. If I can help you, I'd like to."

Daisy went to her first-floor bedroom. On her way to the small secretary desk, she glanced at the Sunshine and Shadow quilt on her bed. She'd found it in Bird in Hand and couldn't resist. Her bedroom was almost like a walk into the past with antique pine furniture and a bowl sink in her bathroom that added another country touch. This room was a refuge. In a way her whole house was, and she wanted it to be that way for her girls too.

When she returned to the living room, she sat on the sofa and opened the laptop.

Jazzi took it from her, and with a speed Daisy still didn't understand, her daughter found Miranda Senft's website. Jazzi handed the computer back to her. "She's still a cook. She's teaching cooking classes at that gourmet kitchen shop in Park City Center. It's called Potz."

When Daisy looked at the site, she could see pots was spelled with a "z." There was a short bio on Miranda's website that listed her credentials—a culinary school and her years working on Derek's show. Daisy checked the hours for the shop easily because there was a link from Miranda's site to Potz. The store was open today.

"Do you mind if I go out for a little while?" she asked Jazzi.

"I don't care. I'll keep an eye on Vi if you're worried about her. I can always phone you if I need you."

That was certainly true. And she wouldn't be that far away. All in all, she could be back in an hour and a half.

"Okay, that sounds good. You do your schoolwork and I'll go to the shop. Maybe we can both keep our minds off tonight until tonight."

Jazzi gave her mom a hug, and Daisy held her tight.

Daisy arrived home in plenty of time to check the pot roast, peel potatoes, start them boiling, and mix up and bake biscuits for dinner. She'd called to Jazzi and Vi when she'd returned home so they'd know she was in the house. Vi had called back that she was working on a research paper. Jazzi had said she'd be down soon.

Soon turned into a half an hour, but that was fine. The only thing left to do was set the oak, distressed wood table for dinner. Daisy glanced at the chairs, which she'd found at a flea market. She'd refinished them herself. The act of rehabbing them had been therapeutic. Maybe she needed to do something like that again.

Daisy could hear Jazzi's footsteps as she came down the open stairway in the back of the living room, then into the kitchen. She'd changed into a pretty peach blouse and a pair of her good jeans.

Jazzi kept her voice low as she asked, "Did you find anything out?"

Daisy scooped biscuit dough into a muffin pan. "Not a lot, but some details that will help."

Jazzi opened the refrigerator door and plucked a carrot from the salad, popping it into her mouth. After she'd chewed and swallowed, she asked, "Like what details?"

After making sure she had approximately the same size scoop of biscuit dough in each muffin hole, Daisy clicked off what she'd learned. "There was a clerk working there who knows Miranda Senft. Her shift is the same time as Miranda's cooking lessons. She wouldn't give me Miranda's address—no surprise there—but she claimed I could find it in the white pages online. The most important clue was—the clerk told me that Miranda lives near Centerville. So when I get a chance, I'll do sleuthing online."

Jazzi checked the kitchen clock that looked like a copper teapot. "You probably won't have time before Foster gets here, and Vi doesn't seem to want to spend any time with us until he does. What can I do to help?"

"You can either set the table or mash the potatoes for me."

Jazzi made a face. "I'll set the table. Place mats or tablecloth?"

"Let's do place mats tonight. I'd need to iron a tablecloth."

"No point going to any trouble," Jazzi said.

"Jazzi . . ." Daisy warned.

Jazzi's nose wrinkled. "She's treating us like we're the enemy, and I don't like it."

"I know you don't. But just think what a shock it was when she found out she was pregnant."

"Do you think it really was a shock, or could it have been planned?"

"I certainly hope it wasn't planned," Daisy countered.

"In a way, wouldn't that be better? It would prove they weren't careless."

Daisy had always tried to talk to her daughters about their bodies. Over and over she'd told them making love was the most natural and beautiful thing in the world . . . with the right person. It was part of life. She hoped she'd given them the values they'd needed to make good choices.

So what exactly had happened with Violet? Maybe she'd find out tonight.

It wasn't long until Foster arrived, looking awkward and embarrassed. This time Daisy didn't even try to have a conversation. She welcomed him into their home and had Jazzi call Violet. Then she went to the kitchen to put dinner on the table. The sooner it was on the table . . . the sooner they would talk.

After they were all seated, had passed the platters around, and filled their plates with food, Daisy jumped right in. "Let's start at the beginning," Daisy said. "There's a question I have to ask."

Both Foster and Vi looked a bit panicked. Daisy didn't know how to make this any easier. "Was this pregnancy planned?" Her gaze found Violet's and held.

"No," blurted out of both Violet's and Foster's mouths at the same time. Then Violet, looking indignant, shook her head. "Why would you ever think that, Mom?"

"I was hoping it wasn't, but I had to ask. Sometimes when two people are in love, they'll do anything to be together. I thought that might be the case with you."

Foster and Violet exchanged a look, and Daisy didn't know what that meant.

They all spent a few minutes eating, though Daisy had no appetite at all. She saw that Jazzi was just picking at her food too. The tension around the table had cut all of their appetites, even Foster's. He usually ate like a football player. But not tonight.

Daisy knew she had to move forward with the questions and answers. "So tell Jazzi and me what your plans are."

Foster put his fork down and took Violet's hand. "We're in love, Mrs. Swanson. So getting married isn't a hardship for either of us. It's what we wanted for the future, but we realized our future just arrived early. We want to get married as soon as possible."

"I've been looking into apartments in Willow Creek and Lancaster," Violet assured Daisy. "I'm also putting a résumé together. We'll get married—nothing fancy. Maybe we'll just go to a justice of the peace."

Daisy's heart lurched. She didn't feel that was the way to start a marriage. If her daughter was going to get married, she'd like to see her married in a church. She'd keep silent about that for now. "So you're going to get married, find an apartment, and then jobs. Do I have that right?" she asked.

Both Violet and Foster nodded. The driving force here was that they were in love. They had a starry idea of what married life would be, let alone what life and the expenses included in having a baby would mean.

"What if you can't find jobs?" Jazzi asked.

"Of course, we'll find jobs," Violet shot back. "Why would you even say that?"

"Because maybe the only job you'll find will be a minimum wage one," Jazzi returned.

To Daisy's surprise, she realized Jazzi might have a grasp on what was involved in a marriage. Had she been observant of Daisy and Ryan's marriage? Had she listened when they talked about expenses and finances? Had she noticed the times in the lean years when Daisy had been out of work and the money for groceries at the end of the week could be tight?

It was hard to know. Maybe she and Jazzi would have that conversation sometime.

However, now Daisy wanted to make a suggestion to the couple that might help them face reality. "I'd like you to do me a favor."

"What?" Violet asked warily.

"First, are you going back to school tomorrow?"

"No," Violet answered quickly. "Foster and I have a lot of things to talk about yet. I'm going to leave Tuesday morning."

Daisy nodded as if that was a good idea. "All right. I'd like the two of you to prepare a budget for six months to cover everything you need for yourselves and a newborn."

"Mom, is that really necessary? Foster and I have other plans to make," Vi complained.

"Since you sprung this on me and Jazzi all of a sudden, I think it's the least you and Foster can do for me."

Foster gave Violet a reassuring smile. "We can do that, Vi. It will only take a couple of hours. What do you want us to do with it then?"

"I'd like the two of you to come for dinner again tomorrow night. Then we can talk about it."

"I don't see the point," Violet said stubbornly. "But we'll do it if it means you'll cooperate with us on the plans we want to make."

Daisy believed they had no idea how expensive those plans would be. She made eye contact with Foster. "Have you told your father yet?"

"No. After dinner tonight, we'll drive over and tell him."

Violet looked worried at the idea of telling Foster's dad. She turned to Daisy. "Will you stand by us through this?"

Daisy didn't hesitate to answer. "I'll always stand by you. But I want you to see the future realistically with a baby and without an education. Wouldn't it be better if you wait to get married until you're sure?"

Foster shook his head. "I want to give the baby my name and take responsibility."

Daisy didn't argue with him. She was hoping that if they made a budget and gained a practical view of what their life would be, they'd look for practical solutions.

Maybe since they were tabling the discussions until tomorrow night, they could enjoy the apple crisp she'd baked for dessert.

But she doubted it.

Chapter Fifteen

Business was so slow the next day that Daisy had too much time to think. The weather had turned gray and drizzly. Of course, Violet and Foster were first on her mind, but Daisy's Tea Garden was second. She was worried about the profit for the week since business was down. She suspected that the bus tours had taken Daisy's Tea Garden off their list. Who could blame them? No one wanted to eat food that might have killed somebody.

She spent time in her office doing everything that could possibly need doing. Finally, she gave up pretending she was busy and searched again for Miranda Senft's name on the computer. The clerk at the mall had told Daisy that Miranda lived in Centerville, which was even closer to Lancaster than Willow Creek. As soon as she plugged in Miranda's name and Centerville at one of the white pages sites, Daisy found the chef's address. It really was scary how much information could be found on anyone.

After telling her staff she was headed out for a while, she dashed through raindrops to the tea garden's parking lot and slid into her PT Cruiser. Her van was parked in the lot also, but they hadn't had to use it lately. It was for catering gigs, including parties. She'd had a couple of cancellations, and the calendar was empty for the next few weeks. She hoped that would change, but it might only change if she found out who had killed Derek.

Last evening when she couldn't sleep, Daisy had found reruns of Derek's cable show on one of the foodie networks. Miranda had been attractive, polished, and even funny at times. She'd acted as Derek's sous-chef, but it was easy for Daisy to see she executed excellent cooking skills. She might not be home when Daisy called. If she wasn't, Daisy would try again some other time. Nothing was going to deter her from her path to return her business to full throttle. Vi's pregnancy made that even more important.

After allowing a horse and buggy to rattle by, she followed the directions on her GPS. Eventually, she came to a farmhouse on Centerville Road. The exterior was white clapboard with a closed-in windowed porch on the front and side. It looked like a huge house for one. Did Miranda have a family?

Daisy checked the address again and saw that Miranda's address had a "B" after it. What did that mean?

Rain poured down and splattered her windshield as Daisy parked on the gravel driveway and walked to the front door. Running inside the glassed-in porch, she crossed to the front door and rang the doorbell. No one answered. Through the inside window, she could see that everything was dim. No sound or movement.

Putting up the hood on her lilac trench coat, Daisy returned outside and thought about that B after the number. There was a path from the front of the house

along the side, and she jogged around the corner. On
the back of the house, there seemed to be a small addition. As she approached, she saw the house number
with a B after it. Maybe this addition had been built as
a rental property.

Daisy went right up to the door and knocked, staying close to the building under a small overhang.

The door was answered immediately. Miranda Senft
stood there with a spatula in hand. The smell of tomato
sauce wafted out the door.

"Yes?" Miranda inquired with a smile that Daisy supposed was an invitation to introduce herself.

"Hi, Miss Senft. My name is Daisy Swanson, and I
own Daisy's Tea Garden. Could I ask you a few questions? I know you worked with Derek and I'm trying to
figure out who might have wanted to hurt him."

Miranda took hold of the doorjamb, ready to shut
the door.

Daisy quickly added, "I don't know what happened
with you and Derek. I don't know exactly why someone put something in my food that Derek ate, but my
business has been going downhill because the public
thinks I poisoned him. Will you please talk to me?"

Miranda took a huge deep breath, closed her eyes,
then opened them again. "You aren't the only one to
have found me, you know. I've had reporters here. Of
course, I sent them away too."

Daisy knew about reporters. A local reporter, Trevor
Lundquist, had contacted her. She'd put him off by
promising she'd give him an interview *after* the case
was solved.

"What about the police?" Daisy asked.

"Not yet. But I suppose they'll get around to me."
Miranda gave Daisy the once-over again, from her

trench coat to her white work clogs, to her purse decorated with cats.

"All right, come on in. But we have to talk while I cook. I'm trying a new recipe for pasta fagioli, and I'll be showing others how to cook it tomorrow. I have to perfect it today."

"I saw that you were giving cooking lessons at Potz."

Miranda made no comment.

Daisy unbuttoned her coat and let it slide over the back of the kitchen chair. This addition resembled a studio apartment. It was one big room, most of it kitchen. Daisy could see some expense had been put into the appliances and the granite countertop. On the other hand, the single bed at the back wall was covered with a light beige duvet. There was a door that Daisy suspected led to the bathroom. A corduroy love seat that looked as if it might have come from a thrift store sat near the bed.

"Before you ask, I don't have a TV. I stream on my laptop."

"So you do have Wi-Fi?"

"It's covered with my rent. I was lucky to find this place. The kitchen is all I care about."

This studio apartment gave Daisy an idea that might work for Vi and Foster. She might have to establish a line of credit or put a mortgage on her house . . . She roped her thoughts back where they belonged. "I saw you at the funeral home," Daisy admitted.

Again, Miranda remained silent.

"The way you approached the casket, not giving Derek's family any condolences, made me wonder about you."

Miranda stirred the sauce that was in a stainless-steel sauce pot. At the same time, she was browning ground beef in a frying pan on another burner. She gave it a stir too.

Finally, she asked, "So how did you find out who I was? Derek's mother?"

"No, a reporter named Clementine Hankey."

"Ugh," Miranda said with some vehemence. "She's such a bother. She lets me alone for a while but then comes back at me. I wish she'd just go away."

"So why was your behavior different than most at the funeral home?"

Miranda kept stirring the ground beef. After adding oregano, pepper, and thyme from the spice rack hanging above the stove, she turned slightly. "You really should leave."

"I imagine the police are going to ask you these same questions. You can use me as a practice run. I promise, I won't tell any reporter what you tell me."

"Why am I supposed to believe *you*?"

Miranda's question revealed that she felt hurt and angry.

"Because I'm giving you my word. If you'd like, I'll let you call and talk to any one of my staff. I keep my promises, Miranda."

Daisy could swear she saw Miranda's eyes glisten for a moment, but she turned back to the stove, switched the heat down on the ground beef, and sighed. "I was angry at Derek. He was dead in that casket, and I almost wished I had been the one who killed him."

"But you didn't?"

"No, I didn't. We'd had some good times. Derek and I had a great relationship on and off the show for years. Our ratings were high."

"What happened?"

"What usually happens to men?"

Daisy was puzzled at that remark, and Miranda must have seen it. "Are you married?"

"I was. I'm a widow now."

Miranda murmured, "I'm sorry."

"It's been about three years. I don't quite understand what you're getting at."

"Another woman. Derek went to a food festival show in Colorado. When he returned, he was different. His contract with the network was up, and almost overnight he brought in a chef he'd met at the festival. She'd won an award and was a hot commodity. She was also blond, pretty, and overtly sexy. Almost overnight I was out, and that was because of Derek. Loyalty and everything we'd shared meant nothing to him."

"Then why was Derek's show canceled?"

Miranda's smile was self-satisfied. She said with bitterness, "The blond bombshell bombed. She was an airhead. Oh, she looked good in front of a camera and could even perform now and then. But she had little common sense or instincts about food. The audience could see through her. Derek should have known that, but he must have been blinded by those dark brown eyes and that bleached blond hair. It was so over-highlighted. The ratings tanked and stayed tanked when Derek took over the show himself. Apparently, his bringing on the blond bombshell turned the audience against him. He just couldn't gain it back."

"Why didn't they invite you to return?"

"Oh, I had calls from the producer. But I never called him back. I could never work with Derek again, even if he'd asked me . . . even if he'd asked me to marry him."

The timer on Miranda's stove dinged.

"That's the focaccia bread. I have to take it from the

oven. That's pretty much it. I don't know if my info helps you at all."

Daisy knew she had to leave. Even though business was slow, she didn't want to be away from the tea garden for too long. Who knew what could crop up these days? And what if Jonas stopped in? Was he even back yet?

"And the name of Derek's new partner was Birgit Oppenheimer?"

"Oh yes. That was her."

Miranda took the bread from the oven and set it on the cooling rack on the counter. Daisy suspected she wouldn't get anything more out of Miranda today, even though she believed she knew more.

Miranda turned around to face her. "So you'll be leaving now?"

"If that's what you want."

"I have cooking to finish. Yes, that's what I want. Talking about any of this is such a downer. I don't need that in my life."

Daisy shrugged back into her coat and stood. "Thank you for talking to me."

"I doubt if it helped, but you're welcome. You can just let yourself out."

As Daisy opened the door and stepped outside again, she noticed the rain had stopped. Her gut feeling was that Miranda was a legitimate suspect. She'd been a woman scorned in more ways than one.

Daisy had a sense of déjà vu as she sat in the living room with Foster and Vi. This time Jazzi wasn't with them. This time she had to try to reason with them. This time could decide all of their futures.

Jonas hadn't called her after his weekend in Philadelphia. She hadn't called him. So her future was irrevocably intertwined with Vi and Foster's. She'd push any dreams she'd had about Jonas from her radar.

Foster had taken two folded sheets of paper from his jacket pocket. He opened them up and laid them on the coffee table. Daisy thought he and Violet both looked a little shell-shocked. From the budget they'd developed?

"Is that your six-month budget?" Daisy asked.

"It is," Foster said, meeting her gaze. His shoulders sagged. "We looked everything up online, from articles in baby magazines to parent magazines to income tax requirements."

"And what did you find out?"

"What you already knew," Violet admitted with defeat in her tone. "That we're going to have a hard time supporting ourselves and a baby. If Foster takes on extra work and I work as long as I can, and we find a really cheap place to live, we can do it if we can get a loan."

Foster cut her a quick glance. "The problem is—we don't have any collateral except for our cars."

Daisy nodded.

"Mom, you said you'd back us. Would you give us a loan?"

Thinking about the plans she'd considered all afternoon, she shook her head. "Loans are meant to be paid back within a certain amount of time. Also, they're given in hopes that your circumstances will change for the better."

"They will," Violet insisted. "After the baby's born, I'll get a full-time job."

Because it was necessary, Daisy played devil's advocate. "What will you do about day care?"

"We'll figure something out," Vi mumbled.

Looking from her daughter's face to Foster's, she asked the most important question. "Are you sure you want to get married? You could give up the baby for adoption." That idea tore at Daisy's heart. She didn't know if she could let it happen, but it *was* an option.

"No," came out of Foster's and Violet's mouths at the same time. "I won't consider that," Violet said. "Look at Jazzi. She searched for her birth parents, and they might not even accept her."

"But *you* would," Daisy said.

"I'm *not* going to put a child through that. Adoption means they'll always have a hole in their heart. I can't do that to a child."

After letting silence wash over the room, Daisy concluded, "All right. You've both made yourselves clear. I've been thinking about solutions, too, and I have a few ideas. But I want to talk to Foster's dad first."

Foster shifted uncomfortably. "I don't know if you should do that, Mrs. Swanson."

"Why not?"

"Because Dad's angry with me, and I'm staying with a friend. We told him about the baby, and he practically shouted the roof off the house."

"Hopefully, he's calmed down by now. Hopefully, he's thinking about solutions too."

"Oh yes, he has a solution. We should end the pregnancy now, and we should both go back to school."

"Foster, I'm sure you know that when people are upset they say things they don't mean. They also make decisions they shouldn't make. That's why I want the two of you to be absolutely sure what you want to do."

"When Foster came to Lehigh, we talked and talked and talked," Vi said. "We've talked every night since then too. We know what we want."

Being in the same room with the couple, listening to them, she felt that was true. "I'll call your dad and try to see him. Once we've talked, we'll let you know our suggestions and concerns. We'll figure out the best way to proceed. Okay?"

"You didn't say if you'd give us a loan," Vi protested. "We know Foster's dad won't."

"You don't know anything for sure right now except for the fact that you want to get married."

Foster bumped Violet's arm. "It's okay. Let your mom talk to my dad. She's done it before."

Violet studied Daisy for a few moments and then nodded. "We'll trust you, Mom."

Daisy just hoped she could live up to that trust.

Daisy was brewing herself a pot of white Himalayan tea when her cell phone that was charging on the counter played a tuba sound. After Foster and Vi had spent time alone outside, Foster had left. Vi had excused herself and gone upstairs. There was awkwardness between her and Daisy now that had never been there before. Jazzi had come home, and whenever Daisy passed the foot of the stairs, she could hear her daughters talking. That made her feel better.

Picking up her phone, she saw Jonas's face on the screen. How was his weekend in Philadelphia? What was he going to say to her? That they were finished? They might be.

She answered his call with, "Hi, Jonas."

"I just got home from Philadelphia a little while ago. I stayed an extra night. But I don't want the sun to go down on another night without us talking. Can I come over?"

It had been an ultra-emotional day today, but the sooner she talked to Jonas the better. She didn't want him finding out about Vi's pregnancy from someone else.

Fifteen minutes later, Jonas was at her front door. On her phone app she could see him from the video monitor. He was wearing an open-collar shirt under a green pullover, black jeans, and black shoe boots. She hated the idea of telling him what was going on with Vi and Foster, but she knew she had to.

Crossing to the front door, she opened it. He didn't give her a chance to say anything, but rather took her hands in his. "It's so good to see you. I missed you."

Her voice became a little shaky when she whispered, "I missed you too. But I was upset by what happened between us." She waited for him to become defensive.

He didn't. "I understand if you don't want me to stay long or to stay at all. Can we sit and talk?"

Daisy didn't know what had happened to her manners or her common sense. She felt as if she had been swept up into a swirling outer circle of a tornado and hadn't landed yet. She motioned to the sofa and the chairs.

Jonas looked as if he were going to take a separate chair, but with a serious expression, he sat down next to her on the sofa.

"No cats to greet me tonight," he said, maybe trying to lighten the atmosphere.

"They're both upstairs with Jazzi and Vi."

"Vi's still home?"

"Yes. We had a lot to talk about."

Jonas's gaze was questioning, but he didn't give her time to say more. Instead, he turned to face her. "I'm sorry for my attitude before I left. Of course, your girls have to come first. It took me about a day to get my head on straight. I thought about what we said to each other, and I'm so sorry about what I said to you."

"Jonas, me too."

His jaw tightened and his brow creased. "You spoke the truth. I've never had kids. More important, I never dated a woman with kids before. Your children might look grown, but as my friend in Philadelphia reminded me this weekend, when a woman has children they're forever attached by an invisible umbilical cord."

Jonas waited to see if Daisy would respond, but she couldn't. She felt as if she didn't have any air to breathe, let alone talk.

Jonas went on, "My attitude came from disappointment and not being able to spend the weekend with you. If I'd had any common sense, or had been thinking clearly, I would have stayed home and spent any time I could with you here."

Tears came fast and furious to Daisy's eyes, and a few leaked down her cheek.

Jonas took her hand. "What's wrong, Daisy? Can you forgive me for what I said, for causing a barrier instead of strengthening a bond?"

She studied their clasped hands and found her voice. "I can forgive you, Jonas. We're still feeling our way in our relationship. There are bound to be misunderstandings. But . . . Violet came home to tell me something that's going to change all of our lives. I have to be truthful with you. You're probably going to be even more disappointed and frustrated by any kind of future we'd have."

The lines around his mouth creased deeper, and his expression told her he had no idea where this conversation was going.

She blurted out, "I'm going to be a grandmother."

Jonas was looking at her as if she were speaking another language.

She hurried to explain. "Violet is pregnant. She wants to drop out of school and marry Foster as soon as she can. She's intent on what she wants to do, and Foster is too. They're determined to get married and have this baby. She doesn't want to give it up for adoption. She might quit college to get a full-time job. I can't imagine you're going to want to be involved with me with as complicated as everything is going to get."

Jonas cleared his throat, kept her hand in his, and looked straight into her eyes. "Do you *want* me to be involved?"

She shook her head. "I don't know because I don't have any idea what's going to happen next. I called Gavin, and we're going to meet tomorrow morning. I have some ideas on how we can help Vi and Foster. I'm hoping Gavin can see through his anger and frustration to help me convince the kids to make good decisions."

"I understand why you want Gavin to help you do that. As Foster's dad, he has a say in everything that happens. But I want you to know, I can support you, too, no matter what happens."

She thought about their argument before he left for Philadelphia. Just because she forgave him didn't mean she'd forgotten what had happened. "Jonas, you've said you don't know if you're ready for the responsibility of a family. This would be a lot more than taking on me and the girls."

"I know that." He studied her thoroughly. "You're afraid that, in the middle of everything that's happening, I'll walk away. The only way you're going to trust me is to start trusting me."

She took a very deep breath and wiped away any residue of tears. "I'm going to have to take one step at a time with Violet, with Jazzi, and with us. We're going to be in limbo for a while. Can you live with that?"

"All we can do, Daisy, is to be completely honest with each other about our feelings and our needs."

"After I talk with Gavin, I have a lot of calls to make for the plan I'm proposing. If Gavin goes along with it, and I can get the resources I need, then we'll have to convince Violet and Foster our plan is good for them."

"Are you going to tell me what the plan is?"

"I'll call you after I talk to Gavin. I promise. But even if we figure out a good way to handle this, I won't have much time for us, and I believe you'll get fed up with that and with me."

Jonas gently took her by the shoulders and turned her toward him. "I can't tell you I won't get fed up, but I can't tell you I will either. We'll just have to see what works. If we have to snatch fifteen minutes here or there, that's what we'll do."

In a low shaky voice, she asked, "Will that be enough for you?"

He countered with, "Will that be enough for *you*?"

She leaned forward and laid her head on his chest as he wrapped her in his arms. She wished she had a crystal ball to know if they were going to survive this or if their lives were going to fall apart.

Chapter Sixteen

The following morning, Daisy sat across her desk from Gavin Cranshaw at the tea garden, her office door securely closed.

Tessa and Iris were in the kitchen working on freshly baked goods and the soup of the day. Daisy had already baked cinnamon scones for the sales case. Last night on the phone, Gavin hadn't been very articulate, but she'd been able to hear the anger in his voice. Since Gavin was a contractor who started work early, they decided the best course was for him to come into the tea garden this morning. It was only six a.m., but they were both wide awake. She'd brewed a pot of black tea. Now it sat in mugs on her desk.

Gavin was about six feet tall and his hair was sandy brown. Like Foster, his square jaw and long nose brought interest to his face. He was wearing jeans, a white T-shirt, and a red flannel jacket. After he reached for his mug, he set it back down without taking a sip. "I know I didn't handle Foster and Violet's news well. I was so disappointed and frustrated that he's messing up his life."

Daisy wasn't sure how to bring calmness and reason to this discussion, but she knew she had to for all of their sakes. "I know Foster is a fine young man, and Vi is a fine young woman. I care about what happens to both of them. But I also believe we have to safeguard the baby."

Gavin waved his hand through the air as if all the pent-up energy inside of him had to go somewhere. "Vi should give up the baby for adoption, and they should forget about the marriage idea. Eighteen and nineteen. How do they ever think *that's* going to work?"

"I was eighteen when I married Ryan. How old were you when you got married?"

"Too young," Gavin snapped.

"Would you do it again?"

He gave her a cutting look that told her he knew what she was trying to do. "There's no comparison between then and now, and you know it. What happens if they can't make ends meet? They'll end up living with one of us . . . with a baby."

Taking a deep breath, she picked up her mug. "Gavin, I know we're both facing a challenge. But if we don't support our children emotionally as well as in other ways, what's going to happen? They'll run off and get married, they'll have the baby, and they'll end up living in a run-down apartment or in their car."

He scowled. "You sound as if you have an alternative."

"I do. At least an alternative as to where they can live. I thought about this long and hard."

"Go ahead." He took a swallow of tea.

"I don't know if Foster told you, but my house was an old barn with an outbuilding when I bought it. My husband's insurance money allowed me to start over here, not only with our home but with the business.

When I sold our house in Florida and moved here, I wanted something that would fit us and could grow with us."

"I don't understand." Gavin looked puzzled.

"We finished the house and it's exactly the way we wanted it. We turned the outbuilding into a two-car garage and the space above it is unfinished. My intention was to eventually turn it into an apartment for additional income. Or . . . if one of the girls wanted a place of her own as they got older and graduated, she'd have it. At the time, I'd decided I was tired of construction and didn't know exactly what I wanted to do with that second floor . . . or take out a loan to do it. So I waited."

"Go on," Gavin said.

"If Foster and maybe some of his friends are willing to volunteer sweat equity to do the finishing work, I would invest in the space for Vi and Foster. It will be a small apartment, but it could suit them until they can afford something else. While they live there, they'd have to pay utilities, but I'd forgo rent for the first year. This won't be a free ride. There are consequences to making mistakes or acting impulsively, whichever applies, but I'll keep the rent reasonable after the first year. What do you think?"

Gavin's face reddened. "You're not going to want me to kick in if it's an investment for you, right?"

"That would be best. But if you want to help them pay the utilities . . . or buy furniture, I have no problem with that."

"You're being too generous. They made a mistake, and this feels like a reward for that."

"Not a reward, but a way for them to start a life

together. If they want to get married, if they truly want to be parents, then I feel we need to help them."

"What would you do first?" he asked.

"First, I want to meet with the architect who helped me renovate the barn. He was easy to work with and did a wonderful job. The bones of the apartment are there. We just have to decide on the rest and what would be purely functional."

"They'd be on your property. Are you sure you want that? They could run to you for help anytime they needed it."

Daisy shrugged. "I think I'd rather have them in an apartment on my property than living in my house with Jazzi and me . . . or with you. Don't you think?"

Gavin shook his head and eyed her with a resigned small smile. "These kids don't know how lucky they are. If I had done something like this, my dad would have thrown me out."

Leaning forward, Daisy wanted to make one point perfectly clear. "I want to stay close to my children, Gavin. I want them around me for the rest of my life. Don't you?"

He grimaced. "I guess I do since I fought so hard to have Foster stay in the house. And if you'd like, I could be the contractor for the job."

"That would be wonderful! I'm sure Foster would really appreciate your help. And there is something to look forward to," Daisy added with a smile.

"What?"

"You're going to be a granddad and I'm going to be a grandmom. I like the idea of holding a baby in my arms again."

Gavin sighed and leaned back in his chair. "That

would sure bring back memories. You call the architect and check if all this is feasible. I'll try to put a crew together and see how soon we can get started."

"And think about being a granddad?" Daisy teased. They had to keep their sense of humor or they wouldn't survive.

He nodded. "I'll think about being a granddad."

"I have cinnamon scones ready to put in the case for today. Would you like one?"

"I would. Maybe a scone will help my disposition. Right now, Foster thinks I'm an ogre."

"He knows better than that."

Looking worried, Gavin expressed one of his concerns. "Somehow I have to figure out how to explain all this to my other two kids, as well as drum into their heads that Foster and Vi have made a monumental mistake."

Maybe it *was* a mistake. Maybe Vi's and Foster's lives would be harder because of bringing a baby into the world. But on the other hand, a baby could pull their families together. A baby could motivate Vi and Foster to achieve a better life than they might have had without one. She just hoped they truly loved each other, that they truly understood what vows would mean, that they would work to make a marriage a lasting one.

Wyatt Troyer, the architect who had helped Daisy design and renovate her barn home, met her in front of her garage when she returned home from the tea garden. She'd texted him when she'd left so he'd know what time to meet her. She'd picked up Jazzi at school so she could join them too. This was just an idea session. She'd have to clear everything with Foster and Vi if they wanted to do this. But first, she wanted to discover whether or not it was feasible. The space over the garage was about eight hundred square feet. Large enough for a couple and an infant?

Wyatt was probably looking at the other side of forty. He had a full head of blond hair that usually parted and fell to the side. He kept the back trimmed short above his collar. He'd once told her he wore contacts. She tried to imagine him with glasses and couldn't. Today he was dressed in his office attire since that's where he'd come from—dress slacks, a gray shirt with the sleeves rolled up, and black loafers. He was about five-foot-eleven with hazel eyes that had a tendency to twinkle. Since he had a good sense of humor, he often wore a grin. She liked him as a person and as an architect.

She raised the garage door from the remote in her car, drove her car inside, and climbed out with Jazzi. Jazzi hurried to the side door and opened it to let Wyatt inside.

"Hi there, Daisy," he said with his resident smile once they met at the staircase. "Jazzi, you're growing up too fast. In two years, you've gone from a child to a young woman."

Jazzi blushed.

Wyatt motioned toward the stairs. "I see you never really finished them. Those are still the construction stairs, correct?"

"Yes, they are because I wasn't sure what I wanted to do. We had talked about possibly creating a landing. I didn't want to decide on anything permanent until I knew how I was going to use the upper space."

"And now you do?"

She told herself there was no point being embarrassed about what she had to say. Life was life. When it threw rocks at you, you tried to catch them.

"My daughter Vi is eighteen and unmarried. She just found out she's pregnant. She and her boyfriend, who's twenty, intend to marry as soon as possible. If they stick by that, and it actually happens, they need a place to live."

Wyatt pointed up to the second floor. "That's not a huge space up there—maybe eight hundred square feet. But there are unique types of furniture and different things we can do with it to make an apartment work."

"I need ideas from you so I know what I want, or what Violet and Foster want. I just need to get an idea from you today if this is feasible."

Wyatt said, "You're using the extra space down here in the back for your garden tools and mower. What if you put a shed behind the garage for the tools. That would give you extra space down here that could easily be made into a small office."

She examined the area. "I like that idea. Foster does a lot of computer work. He wouldn't have to worry about space for that upstairs."

Always prepared, Wyatt took a tape measure from his pocket.

"An office is a great idea, Mom," Jazzi agreed. "It would be quieter to work down here if the baby is fussy."

"That's what I was thinking," Daisy said. "They could put a bookshelf in there and a desk. Maybe even two desks."

"It will be dark," Jazzi said. "Unless we put in a window or a door with glass at the top."

"That's not very secure," Daisy reminded her.

"But you have to get light in here somehow."

Overhearing their conversation, Wyatt responded to it. "First of all, you have enough space back here to put a small office. I know a craftsman who makes sheds. I can probably get you a discount. And as far as light in here . . . we could put a skylight on the roof to let more light into the apartment. I know you're going to be security conscious with your family living here, so I'm not going to suggest a window. But if I use Plexiglas under the skylight as flooring in the upstairs unit, say two-foot by four-foot, light would beam down into the office."

"That's a brilliant idea," Jazzi enthused.

Daisy smiled. It actually *was* pretty smart. "I didn't even know companies made such a thing."

"If you really want this to be economical, we can put solar panels on the roof. That would help keep heating bills down."

"That's something I hadn't thought of either. I suppose it depends on how much money I want to put into this. I'll get a break if Foster's dad, Gavin Cranshaw, does the construction. I'm thinking Foster and friends will help finishing projects to cut down costs."

"Sounds good to me. But you *will* need an expert for the solar panels. Why don't we go upstairs and look around?" Wyatt suggested. "You'll have to figure out if you want a baby section in addition to the couple's bedroom, or if you want a Murphy bed for them and go from there."

"What's a Murphy bed?" Jazzi asked.

"It's a bed that folds up into the wall. That way it saves space and you could put, for instance, a playpen in front of it during the day and fold up the playpen at night and put down the bed."

"Sweet," Jazzi said.

Once they'd climbed the stairs and took time tossing about ideas for a baby section and where they would put the bathroom, Jazzi announced, "You don't need me anymore. I'm going to the house and get started on homework."

"Turn the oven on to three-fifty, would you? I made a casserole last night."

"Do you want me to put it in?" Jazzi asked.

"No, I'll let the oven preheat. I'll put it in when I come in."

After Jazzi said good-bye to Wyatt, she took her time going down the steps, holding on to the rail.

As Wyatt retracted his tape measure, he looked away from Daisy. "I heard a rumor that something you made at the tea garden killed Derek Schumacher. Is that true? I don't want to know for gossip's sake, but if it's not true I want to know so I can tell people that it had nothing to do with you."

"It had nothing to do with me. The detective is checking out my staff, but I know they had nothing to do with it either. Derek took some of our sandwiches home, and my guess is somebody put the substances in there."

Wyatt eyed her curiously. "Substances?"

"The detective asked me not to talk about it."

Wyatt studied her. "I understand. I hope this doesn't hurt your business."

With another panicked pang, Daisy admitted, "It's hurting us already. For two years, we've built up a good reputation. I don't want it to be ruined."

"Derek wasn't an easy man to work with," Wyatt murmured, turning toward the stairs.

"He was your client?"

"He was. I designed and renovated his second floor for his mother."

"Why do you say he was hard to work with?"

Wyatt moved toward the stairs and so did Daisy. "Derek wanted the renovations done before Harriet came home from rehab and was very particular. At the same time, he counted every nickel. I understood why he decided to fix up the upstairs so Harriet would have privacy. I suggested he put an elevator in. Since his mom did so well in rehab, he decided to put the chair lift in instead because it was more economical, less than half the price."

"On Tourist Appreciation Weekend, I saw Harriet in her wheelchair. Bradley was pushing it. Does she ever go out without it?"

"Apparently, there was a reason for the chair lift rather than the elevator besides the cost. Harriet's doctor wanted her to be on her feet more. I'm not sure how much she's listening to that advice. On the other hand, Derek told me he once caught a glimpse of her walking around her apartment without her cane or her walker. I'm not sure what that meant. Derek seemed to believe she just wanted sympathy when she used her cane or walker or wheelchair, but that she was really strong enough to move around without it."

"What did *you* think?"

"Whenever I saw her, she was using one or another device."

Daisy couldn't imagine Harriet ever wanting to hurt her son. But if she could get around easier than everyone thought she could, she could have gone downstairs and put the heart medicine in Derek's cucumber sandwiches.

Wyatt continued, "You know, you mentioned some-one at the house might have put the substance in the sandwiches. Derek's brother and sister-in-law have keys, and Derek's first co-host, Miranda Senft, also still had a key. When we were renovating, Derek kept saying he had to ask for it back. But I don't know if he ever did."

So Miranda Senft, the woman scorned in more ways than one, could have let herself into the house, slipped the drugs into the sandwiches, and left them for Derek to consume.

Murder made easy.

Daisy sat at her computer mid-morning on Wednes-day, scrolling through the comments on her website. The rumors and gossip made her sick to her stomach. As Foster had suggested, she'd left replies as positively as she could. But with business so slow, she worried constantly. Especially with considering a construction project.

She left her website and put her computer to sleep. It was probably getting a lot more sleep than she was. Last night, for most of the night, she'd rolled around the idea of Miranda Senft putting drugs in Derek Schu-macher's sandwiches. It was certainly possible. It was also possible his mother could have done it. And what about Birgit Oppenheimer? Did she have a grudge against him too? No wonder Detective Rappaport was grumpy. So many suspects, so many interviews, so little time. The longer it took to figure out who the murderer was, the harder it would be to do it. There had to be clues somewhere. She just didn't know where to find them.

As she thought about what steps to take next, she considered meeting with Clementine Hankey. She could also visit Harriet and June again. She had the feeling that there was something in their background that they didn't want going public. The question was whether or not it had something to do with Derek. She'd really like to know what their thirty-five-year argument had been about. If she had that answer, would she find others?

She was contemplating what she knew so far when Tessa knocked on her office door. "There's someone here to see you at the sales counter."

"Thanks, I'm coming."

She'd slipped off her clogs under her desk and now she fitted her feet into them again and hurried out to the sales counter. There was a gentleman standing there. He looked very . . . proper. He was wearing a white dress shirt with a herringbone-pattern vest. His slacks were charcoal, and his tie was black-and-white-striped. His shiny shoes told her he'd polished them recently. He could easily be near her age or a little older. When he saw her coming, his light brown eyes lit up. His face had an orangey glow as if he used a tanning salon, or she supposed it could be one of those spray-on colors that was supposed to make you look tanned. One thing she was certain of was that she'd never met him before.

He held out his hand before she'd even stopped walking. "Mrs. Swanson?"

She took his hand. "Yes, and you are?"

He blushed a little. "Oh, I thought maybe you followed my blog. My name is Leonard Bach. I came here to meet you because I'd like to write a review about Daisy's Tea Garden."

Her immediate reaction was a profound "no." However, she tempered her reaction. "I don't know, Mr. Bach. I'm sure you're well aware of what happened to Derek Schumacher here. Our business has slowed considerably since then."

He frowned. "I'm so sorry to hear that. Then maybe my reviewing your establishment could help you. The truth is—I'm hoping to win over Derek's blog readers and build up my reputation, first in Pennsylvania, then up and down the East Coast."

There are two ways to play this, Daisy thought. She could tell him a straight out *no*; however, she did own a food establishment. She couldn't stop him from coming in and sampling her food. As far as a good or bad review? She didn't think either would make a difference right now. It wouldn't hurt her to be pleasant to him. After all, she was usually pleasant with everyone else. But food critics left a bad taste in her mouth these days. No pun intended.

"Were you and Derek friends?" she asked.

"You could say we were," he answered evasively. "We were colleagues who ran into each other quite often."

"How long have you been a food critic?"

"I've been a food critic all my life, but I just started my blog about two years ago, not long after Derek started his. Of course, his caught on because he was a celebrity."

It sounded to Daisy as if there had been a rivalry between the two men, at least on Leonard Bach's part. Did she want to aid and abet him?

Did she really have a choice?

Chapter Seventeen

As if she'd conjured her up, Daisy found Clementine Hankey in the main tea room when she'd finished baking brownies for the sales case. She probably needed the chocolate more than her customers. Motioning to Iris that she'd take care of Clementine, she went to the journalist's table.

Maybe Clementine had learned more about Derek's enemies . . . or maybe she'd unearthed some secret. She had another question she wanted to ask her too.

"It's good to see you again," Daisy said pleasantly. "You came back for the scones, right?"

Clementine nodded so quickly that her hair brushed across her cheek. "Actually, I did. And for some of your Daisy's Blend Tea. I wanted to take that along with me."

Daisy saw Clementine's cup was empty. "I'll be glad to bring you more."

"That sounds good," Clementine said. "And maybe you could bring me a serving of that grape and carrot salad? That's good for me, so it will make up for having two scones. Do you have a few minutes to talk?"

Right now, Clementine was one of two customers in the tea room. "As you can see, we haven't been busy."

"I wish I could help you fix that. Maybe if we put our heads together it will help."

"I'll be back with tea for two," Daisy assured her.

When she returned to Clementine's table, she was holding a teapot with a cozy around it on a tray with her own cup and a serving of the carrot and grape salad. After she arranged everything on the table, she sat across from Clementine. "Have you learned anything more?"

Clementine shook her head. "No. The police are tighter than clams. I can't get anything out of anyone down there. Usually there's a leak, but not this time. I've been checking Derek's blog regularly to see if anyone posts something unusual. Killers have been known to do that . . . even go to the funeral's guest page and pay their respects. It's sick, I know, but a killer has to be sick to murder."

"I'm not sure about that," Daisy protested, thinking about the last murder case she'd helped solve. "Sometimes it can be spur-of-the-moment anger."

"Or passion, I suppose," Clementine added.

Clementine's eyes targeted Daisy's. "Do you know what was in those sandwiches that killed Derek?"

"I do," Daisy said honestly after only a few moments' hesitation. "But I'm not supposed to say. All I can tell you about it is that someone had to know Derek to put in those sandwiches what they did."

Still studying Daisy carefully, Clementine surmised, "So what you're telling me is that it wasn't a usual poison like arsenic."

"I'm not telling you anything," Daisy said.

Clementine got that. There was an underlying message, but Daisy hadn't revealed specifics. "I talked to Miranda Senft since I last saw you. I didn't get much out of her. She told me that one day she was in and the next day she was out. Derek had met someone at a food and wine festival and decided he wanted her as his co-host."

"Birgit?"

Daisy refilled Clementine's cup, then filled her own too. "Yep. Miranda wasn't sure if there was a romantic relationship there or not, but she assumed there was, just as there had been with her."

Clementine gave a low whistle. "So Miranda's the main suspect?"

"She's on my list. I know nothing about Birgit or where to find her. I'm not sure she's in this mix, not if the show was canceled because of her or because of ratings."

"Still," Clementine said, musing, "if Derek dropped her because of it, she could be as angry as Miranda."

"That's possible. I did have an unusual visitor."

Clementine added a teaspoon of sugar to her cup. "Who was that?"

"Leonard Bach. Have you run into him when you were following Derek?"

"Oh yes," Clementine said. "Derek and Leonard Bach had an out-and-out scuffle in Baltimore when they both showed up to review the same restaurant. They acted as if they hated each other."

"Bach is coming to our full tea service next week after Easter. I'm trying to be prepared. He says he wanted to pick up Derek's fans from his blog."

"Leonard Bach doesn't have the following that

Derek had. Although Derek could be scathing, once upon a time he had a great sense of humor. Bach is very cut and dried in his reviews. He ate this. He thought that. Do you know what I mean?"

"Not much narrative."

"Right. So for that reason he'll never be the star Derek was."

Daisy supposed that if Leonard Bach knew that fact deep down in his soul, his rivalry with Derek might have led to murder.

Daisy felt at loose ends that evening. Jazzi had gone to Stacy's to practice for the talent show on Saturday evening. There had been discussion at the PTA meeting at the beginning of the year about concern having the talent show Saturday of Easter weekend. But the activities schedule hadn't permitted moving it to another weekend.

There were a hundred things Daisy could be doing. Instead of those, she sat on her bed with a legal pad on her lap. She wrote down the name of every suspect she could think of and what their motive might be. The last name she added to the list was Leonard Bach.

However, when she examined the list again, she circled June's and Harriet's names. She still believed that their secret, whatever it was, had to do with Derek's murder. It was a hunch, but it could be why June was evasive about their past.

She could be off base. If she was, she was hoping Detective Rappaport was covering all of the other bases.

The more she thought about the two hours she had

left before she picked up Jazzi, she knew what she wanted to do with the time.

Marjoram and Pepper had both jumped up onto the bed with her. She wasn't sure if they thought she was their surrogate mom, or Jazzi was. Thinking of Portia, she told the two felines, "I suppose it's all right to have two moms. We both care about you very much."

She could only hope that Portia cared enough to maintain a relationship with Jazzi.

She looked once more at her list and decided she wouldn't be able to rest until she talked to June and Harriet again. She didn't want to alert them by calling. They could just ignore her call. But if she showed up with a container of chicken soup she'd brought home . . . She didn't think Harriet would refuse the chicken soup.

Since daylight savings time had taken effect, she knew she had at least another hour of daylight.

Removing her lounge pants and T-shirt, she pulled on jeans and an oversized oxford shirt. Its yellow and blue pinstripes on a white background reminded her of spring. She didn't bother with a jacket because she wasn't going to be outside much. Enclosing her cell phone in her purse, she waved to Marjoram and Pepper who were napping. "I'll leave the kitchen light on for you two."

Marjoram opened her beautiful green eyes, raised her head, then closed her eyes and curled into a ball.

Daisy entered the side door of the garage and almost tripped over the head of the rake that she'd set just inside the door. There were other tools there too: a gardening spade, a hoe, and a Lesche shovel—a garden implement with a serrated blade. She was attempting to clean out the rear of the garage that would be the office for Vi and Foster . . . if they wanted it . . . if they liked her idea.

It took about ten minutes to reach the development where Derek's house was located. Daisy parked along the curb of the cul-de-sac and went to the door, carrying the container of soup.

To her surprise, Harriet didn't answer the buzzer from inside. Rather, June opened the door. "Hi there," Daisy said. "I brought you and Harriet some soup. Harriet said she liked the chicken noodle."

June smiled. "That's so nice of you. Why don't you come in? I'm afraid Harriet already went to her room for the evening. She's been doing that after supper. She's been sleeping a lot."

Daisy followed June inside. "She's probably depressed. I know any type of grief will do that."

June headed for the downstairs kitchen. "Even after my husband and I divorced, I went through a grief period. It was almost two years until I felt I was really living again."

Pleased that June was opening up about her personal life, Daisy went to the refrigerator. "Would you like this inside this refrigerator or in Harriet's refrigerator upstairs?"

"I've been enjoying cooking in this marvelous kitchen. I made Derek's recipe for shrimp scampi tonight. But Harriet hardly touched it."

"Is she losing weight?"

"I'm not sure about that. She has a doctor's appointment coming up. If she lets me, I'll go with her. Would you like coffee? I made a pot of decaf. Or I have wine, if you prefer that."

Daisy hadn't known what to expect, but she hadn't expected to be offered wine. Because June seemed more staid than that?

"A cup of coffee would be great. I have to pick up Jazzi, so I'd rather not drink wine right now."

"Those are the words of a true mom," June said. "You're setting a good example."

Daisy took a seat at the high island. Hopping up onto the stool, she put her feet on the bottom rung. When she thought about how Jazzi had gotten drunk, she wasn't sure about that good example.

Switching the conversation back to June, she asked, "How long were you married?"

After taking two cups and two saucers out of the cupboard, June poured coffee into them. "We were married for nine years. He was from Erie, and I moved my life there to be with him. The divorce had me spinning my wheels for a while, but I got back on my feet. Although Jimmy denied it, it was the fact that I couldn't have children that broke us up. Children can hold a marriage together. The lack of children can tear a marriage apart. All those expectations newly married couples have . . ."

Maybe if Daisy shared a little of her story—"I know what you mean. When Ryan and I tried to have another child after Violet, we couldn't. We had a bumpy time for a while. But then we decided to adopt."

June didn't say anything to that. She brought the cups of coffee to the island where a sugar bowl sat. After taking cream from the refrigerator, she offered it to Daisy.

Daisy added a little.

Apparently, the adoption idea had stopped June

cold. Time to change the subject. "Do you still live in Erie now?"

"Yes. I do. I have a tailoring shop."

"Were you and Harriet close when you were children?"

"Oh yes. Even though I was older, we still hung around together. We got into trouble wading in Willow Creek without permission, hiking through the cornrows, and playing hide-and-seek there. Those hot summer days were the best. We had each other, and nothing else mattered."

"I have a sister, but we aren't that close. Usually, I wish we were. But we're so different."

"Harriet and I were very much alike, except—" June stopped.

"Except . . ."

"It's not important. I suppose you know we didn't speak for thirty-five years. I think that changed both of us. We became more withdrawn, more introverted. But now everything is better again."

"Do you wish you had visited Harriet sooner?"

Without any hesitation, June shook her head. "No, I don't. There's a right time for everything. And this was the right time for us."

"My two girls are close. When Vi started college, Jazzi really missed her. She still does. Teens can get into a lot of trouble—with makeup, clothes, boys. Were you and Harriet like that?"

June took a few swallows of her coffee before she answered. "As teens, we weren't very wild. Driving to York on a Friday night to see a movie was our main escape. I guess you could say we were quite dull."

June changed the subject. "I'm hoping I can

convince Harriet to go back to Erie and live with me there. I think that would be the best for her."

"She might miss Bradley and Lauren and Chrissy."

"She might. But most of the time I think she feels like a burden to them. She knows she wouldn't be a burden with me." Suddenly, June hopped up from her seat, went to the cupboard, and produced a beautiful teapot. "I know you'll appreciate this. I bought it for Harriet this week . . . for when we have tea together."

Daisy recognized the pot right away—it was a Royal Albert Old Country Roses. It was a particularly fine six-cup teapot. "It's beautiful. I don't have one of those in my collection."

"It actually made Harriet smile. And now I know what I can buy her for Christmas . . . cups and saucers to go with it."

From then on, the conversation turned to teapots, bone China, and delicacies June had tried at other tea rooms. Daisy was listening, but she was thinking at the same time. June didn't hesitate to talk about her childhood with Harriet, but she always veered away from those teen years. She never went past the time when she moved to Erie as a newlywed. She'd told Daisy she'd been twenty-three. That meant Harriet had been twenty-one. It was easy to sense that June wasn't telling Daisy the whole story.

Just what could that story be?

In the kitchen on Saturday, Daisy was mixing ingredients for the potato salad dressing. Violet would be home any minute. She didn't want to miss Jazzi's talent show. And Vi, Foster, and Daisy had more to discuss. Daisy had taken off today, and tomorrow was

Easter Sunday. After lunch, Foster would be returning to the tea garden. Maybe then she and Vi could have a private conversation.

Foster had arrived a few minutes ago. He was in the living room talking with Jazzi. Any time Daisy had been around him at the tea garden this week had been awkward. Once they had this talk today, she hoped tension would ease. She had invited Gavin to lunch, but he'd refused. Even though he'd agreed to a few concessions for the couple, he insisted he still couldn't rationally discuss it. He needed to calm down and accept what was happening. When he reached acceptance, he said he'd let her know.

As Foster entered the kitchen, he asked, "Is there anything I can do to help?"

Her first instinct was to say *no*, but that wouldn't patch up their relationship. She pointed to the counter. "I bought a loaf of sourdough bread. Can you cut it in slices for sandwiches?"

"Sure," he said with a weak smile. After he opened the loaf of bread and placed it on the cutting board Daisy had set out, he took a bread knife from the drawer and began slicing. "Jazzi told me you went to visit Harriet and June on Wednesday evening. Did you make any progress with finding out their story?"

Foster had a stake in this, too, if he wanted business in the tea garden to pick up. Rappaport had cleared him as a suspect because of his alibi.

"I thought the evening would be a good time to visit Harriet, but apparently it wasn't."

"Wasn't Harriet there?"

"Although it was early evening, she'd gone to bed. I asked if she wasn't feeling well, but June said she seemed all right physically. She gets up late, naps every afternoon, and goes to bed early."

Foster said what Daisy was thinking. "She could be depressed. A year after my mom died, Dad slept more than usual. He closed himself up in the bedroom. Ben and I shot hoops to deal with our feelings."

"And your sister?"

"She had a friend who'd lost her dad, so they could talk about it together. That seemed to help her."

"Talking usually does help."

Foster took a sideways glance at Daisy over his shoulder. "Mrs. Swanson, I'm so sorry. I couldn't tell you what was happening because Vi made me promise not to. She wanted to tell you herself."

"Foster, you can call me Daisy. And I understand now. Of course, she wanted to tell me herself. But that put you in a very awkward position."

He shrugged. "I'll do whatever I have to for her . . . and our baby."

He cleared his throat, then changed the subject back to what they'd been conversing about. "Did you talk to Harriet's sister very long?"

Daisy smiled. "What you're asking is—did I learn anything else about Derek."

"I guess that's what I'm asking."

"June and I had coffee together. I got the feeling that June regretted not being there for her sister when Harriet's husband died. She reminisced about her own divorce and her childhood with Harriet."

"Any clues there?" Foster gathered the bread he'd sliced and piled it into a basket that Daisy had arranged with napkins for serving.

"She related stories about her growing-up years with

Harriet. But she stopped when she reached the time period when Harriet got pregnant."

"I wonder why."

Daisy wondered the same thing as she mixed the dressing with the boiled and diced potatoes. "After high school June had apprenticed with a seamstress who sewed slipcovers and draperies. She did custom work but then she moved to Erie. She asked Harriet to go along with her, knowing she could learn the most that way and maybe open her own shop someday if she went along. She did mention Harriet went to Erie to have Derek. She didn't say any more than that."

"Do you feel she was leaving something out?"

"I do. I don't think she was telling me the whole story."

Suddenly, there was a commotion in the living room. Daisy heard the excited high-pitched voices of both of her daughters. She set the potato salad in the refrigerator and went to join them. They all hugged, and tears came to Daisy's eyes.

Foster soon joined them. He hugged Violet, too, and gave her a kiss. After they'd all settled down, Daisy asked, "Do you want to talk first or eat first?"

Violet pushed her hair over her shoulder and exchanged a look with Foster. "Let's talk first. I won't be able to eat anything until I know what you're thinking."

When Pepper came over to Violet and rubbed against her ankles, Violet lifted the cat onto the sofa beside her. Maybe thinking she deserved the same amount of attention, Marjoram went to Jazzi. With a smile, Jazzi picked her up and sat her on her lap.

Daisy took a seat, too, and then told Foster, "I invited your dad to join us."

"He's so angry that he doesn't know what to say to me," Foster admitted, turning a bit red.

"I know, but he'll come around. Tell me what you're thinking about your future."

Vi and Foster were holding hands. Vi said, "We still want to get married as soon as possible. Somehow, we're going to do this, Mom."

"I kind of figured that. So I have an idea and I ran it by Gavin. I think it will help you make a budget and stick to it. I've always planned to finish the space above the garage. Now I have a good reason to do it. We can make it into an apartment. You can live there rent-free for the first year." Then Daisy addressed Foster. "Your dad might be angry, but he loves you. He's agreed to pay for furnishings if you and Vi can stick to thrift stores."

Violet was crying now. Pepper rubbed her head against Vi's arm. Vi released Foster's hand and came over to hug her mom. "I don't know what to say. I promise you that someday we'll pay you back."

"I want to know that this is what Foster wants too. He'll be living awfully close to his mother-in-law," Daisy said, half-joking and half-serious.

Violet turned to him. "How do you feel about that?"

"I'm okay with it," he said, a bit huskily.

"We can talk about the plans for the apartment later, but I want your input. You might start thinking about it."

Still crying, Violet returned to sit next to Foster. "I've already sent résumés to businesses in Willow Creek and Lancaster to get a job until the end of my pregnancy."

Foster added, "And Mrs. Wiseman has recommended me as a website designer to Arden Botterill.

I'll be handling her computer software setup as well as her social media. I opened a savings account for the baby."

Daisy was still worried about this young couple. She knew they were certainly going to have their ups and downs. But instincts had told her Foster was a responsible young man when she'd hired him. He was proving that. So no matter what her thoughts were about this marriage and what they wanted to do about schooling, she'd try to support their dreams.

Isn't that what parents should do?

Daisy sat in the school auditorium, so proud of her younger daughter that she had tears in her eyes. Jazzi had sung "Over the Rainbow," a tune she'd said meant a lot to her. After her dad had died, she'd seen a rainbow when they went to the cemetery. After that she looked for rainbows, considering them a sign that her dad was watching over her.

She looked spectacular tonight and older than her fifteen years. Daisy had helped her pick out a royal blue dress that had a sweetheart neckline, short sleeves, and sequins on the bodice. She'd worn heels, the gold locket necklace her dad had given her, and a pair of Daisy's drop gold earrings. Daisy had French braided small braids over both of Jazzi's temples and fastened them together in the back with a gold clip. Her long black hair was gleaming, and those high heels were what made her look older.

The high school's music teacher was about to announce the winners for the talent show. Daisy's mom and dad sat on one side of her and her aunt Iris, Vi, and

Foster on the other. Yesterday, Daisy had filled in her aunt on Vi's pregnancy and the couple's plans. It had just seemed right to confide in her aunt. Always supportive, Iris had added with fondness that she'd be glad to babysit.

Tessa was in the audience too. When Daisy glanced at her family and friends, they seemed to be holding their breaths as the music teacher took center stage to give out first-, second-, third-, fourth-, and fifth-place trophies.

Mrs. Portman announced the fifth- and fourth-place winners first. Neither of them was Jazzi. Jazzi's smile was wide as she realized she would be in the top three.

Mrs. Portman announced the third-place winner. That was Jazzi's friend Stacy. Daisy had given her okay for Jazzi to go to Stacy's house for a party after the talent show. Daisy was acquainted with Stacy's mom and knew that the girls would be safe without any liquor there.

After Mrs. Portman smiled at the audience, she looked at Jazzi and announced, "Our second-place winner is Jasmine Swanson. Congratulations, Jazzi."

The entire audience was clapping. Daisy was so pleased for her daughter that she didn't even hear Mrs. Portman announce the first-place winner. After the trophies were presented, the winners came down into the audience to find their parents.

Jazzi accepted congratulations and hugs from everyone who was there for her. After Daisy hugged her, Jazzi handed her her trophy. "Will you take it home, Mom?"

"Sure, I will."

"Did you know Jonas was in the audience?"

Daisy kept herself from turning around to see. "No, I didn't."

"He was with another man. I've never seen him before."

"Good to know," Daisy remarked, wondering who the other man was.

"You can probably catch him in the lobby."

"We'll see," Daisy said enigmatically. She gave Jazzi another hug. "You have fun at the party. I'll be waiting up to hear all about it."

"You can trust Stacy's mom and dad." Jazzi must have felt that Daisy needed to be reassured.

Jazzi waved at Stacy and her parents, then blew a kiss to Daisy, and ran off in their direction.

Daisy's family and Tessa were talking among themselves. Daisy told them, "I'm going to catch somebody in the lobby."

In the lobby, it didn't take long for Daisy to spot Jonas. There *was* another man with him. They were standing near the bulletin board, and Jonas was pointing out something. The guy looked to be around Jonas's age with blond hair and a lean physique. Daisy couldn't leave without speaking with Jonas. She cared about him deeply, and she couldn't ignore him.

She felt a bit awkward as she approached him. He was turning to say something to his friend when he saw her. He stopped mid-sentence.

"Hi, Daisy," he said casually. "This is Zeke Willet. He's a detective who's going to be working with Detective Rappaport in the Willow Creek Police Department."

Although they had once been friends, she knew that he and Zeke weren't friends now. It was a shame Jonas had lost his friendship as well as the woman he'd loved. She could see the pain of that now in Jonas's eyes as he looked at Zeke.

Zeke shook her hand. "So you're known as Daisy?"

Jonas blushed a little. "This is Daisy Swanson. She owns Daisy's Tea Garden. We'll have to stop in there some time. She makes the best scones."

Suddenly Vi and Foster were by her side, as if *she* was the one who needed moral support. They greeted each other and were introduced to Zeke. Jonas congratulated Vi on her pregnancy.

Vi put her finger to her lips in a *shhh* motion. "Not too loud. We're telling Gram and Gramps tomorrow at Easter dinner."

"We're engaged too," Foster added. "No ring yet. It might be a while until I can get her one. But we're going to get married soon."

Jonas clapped Foster's shoulder. "I wish you all the best."

Zeke explained, "I came to the talent show just to get a taste of the school, meet the principal, learn my way around a little bit. But I need to cut out now. I'm still unpacking."

He added, "It's good to meet you all." Although he addressed that to everyone, his blue eyes were targeting Daisy. She didn't know what to make of that.

Jonas took a step closer to Daisy. "How would you like to get a cup of coffee?"

"Oh, I don't know." She wanted to, but should she?

Violet nudged her elbow with her own. "Go ahead, Mom. Jazzi's going to that party, and Foster and I are going to go visit his dad. You came with Aunt Iris, so there's no problem with a car."

Daisy looked up into Jonas's very green eyes. "All

right, let's get a cup of coffee." She asked Vi, "Will you tell Gram and Gramps and Aunt Iris where I went?"

Once they were outside, Daisy touched the arm of Jonas's suit coat. "It's silly to go to a coffee shop. Why don't we just go to my place?"

His look was sober when he asked her, "Are you sure?"

"I'm sure."

On the drive to Daisy's house, they were quiet inside the vehicle until Daisy asked, "Are you sure you want to come in?"

Jonas cut her a quick glance, looking away for a moment from the rural road. "I'm sure. Are you sure you want to invite me in?"

Daisy closed her eyes and took a deep breath. "Everything's so complicated right now."

"And you're afraid I'll run at the least complication."

"You're the one who wanted to slow down after New Year's Eve. That's what you said."

"Yes, that is what I said, and it was a dumb thing to say. We never know how our circumstances are going to play out, and I was trying to shut the door before I made any mistakes. But I was wrong, and I told you that. And the weekend with my friends . . . I'd never asked a woman to come meet them and get to know them before."

"Not even Brenda?"

"No, not even Brenda. We kept our relationship a secret. With both of us on the job, that's the way we thought it had to be."

"Jonas, do you know what you're stepping into? I'm planning a wedding with Violet and renovating the top of the garage for an apartment for the two of them.

There will be a baby and diapers and crying, and I don't know how much I'm going to be involved in that."

"You worry about everything at once, don't you?" There was a bit of amusement in his tone that could have made her angry, but it didn't. He was right.

"I'm trying to see ahead for *you*," she said softly.

"No, you're trying to see ahead for *you*, so that you don't get hurt. Believe me, I understand that. But I'm going to prove to you that I'll stick around because you're worth it."

She was still emotional over Jazzi's performance, and she figured that's why tears came to her eyes again.

Once she and Jonas were in her house, Daisy brewed tea. Marjoram and Pepper trotted in, apparently eager to see Jonas. Marjoram sat on his foot while Pepper wound about his legs.

Daisy believed the cats were good judges of character. They'd liked Jonas from the first instant they'd met him. She knew he was a good man. But could she count on him?

She'd wait and see.

Jonas, familiar with her cupboards, pulled out mugs and plates. She took chocolate whoopee pies with peanut butter filling from the refrigerator. They were Vi's favorite, so she'd stocked up on them.

As she and Jonas sat at the island fixing their tea, a Silver Needle variety called Snowbud, Jonas asked, "Where are you concerning Derek's murder investigation?"

"There are more suspects than I know what to do with."

"The same is true for Rappaport. Maybe now that he has a partner, it will go faster," Jonas said without expression.

Daisy decided to let that subject go for right now. "A new suspect popped up—Leonard Bach. He's another food critic. Apparently, he and Derek were rivals. Clementine told me they even had a scuffle in public." She paused, then added, "But I still think the best clue lies in Derek's background. There's a secret between June and Harriet that kept them apart for thirty-five years."

"So where do you go next?"

"Taking a different course than Detective Rappaport probably is. I think I'm going to talk with Vanna Huffnagle, the church secretary. She's the same age as Harriet and a friend of hers, so she might know what happened way back then. If it's a dead end, it's a dead end. But I have to try."

Jonas took her hand. "I suspect you're a woman who doesn't give up."

His eyes were caring, and there was something else there, too, something else that made an electric charge zip through her. She hoped he was a man who didn't give up . . . because she might be placing their romantic future in his hands.

Chapter Eighteen

Daisy, Jazzi, Vi, and Foster had just entered the kitchen in her mom and dad's home on Easter Sunday, when her mother and Aunt Iris came rushing in from the living room. Rose gave Daisy, Jazzi, and Vi a hug and then stood in front of Foster. "Daisy told me you'd be coming along today. Your father didn't want you at home on the holiday?"

Daisy groaned inwardly and exchanged a look with her aunt. She could see how this day was going to go. Foster would wish he had gone to his dad's for dinner . . . *and* for supper.

"Vi and I will be going to my dad's for supper, Mrs. Gallagher. Instead of a big meal, he's going to barbecue outside. Ribs and burgers."

"A barbecue on Easter?" Rose asked with astonishment in her voice.

"That's the kind of cooking Dad does best. And since the weather is cooperating, he thought it would be a good idea. So do I."

"So do I," Violet repeated, looking at Foster with the

love in her heart. "We sure wouldn't want to have two ham dinners."

Rose laughed, then waved everyone into the living room. "Sean is already starting on the hors d'oeuvres. You'd better get some before he eats them all."

Daisy's dad called, "Breakfast was a long time ago."

Her parents had gone to an earlier church service than Daisy and her girls. Her mom wanted to take her time to make sure the table was set just so . . . and everything was cleaned to a sparkling finish. Daisy had often told her "perfect" simply didn't matter, but, as she'd learned years ago, her mother didn't listen to her.

When her dad had last phoned her, he'd told her he and her mom were having a date night every week. And every week he'd brought up a new aspect of what they should think about for the future. It was working to a certain extent, though her mother was fighting changes.

What would she think of Violet's big change?

Sidling up to Daisy, Vi said, "Should I tell her before dinner or after dinner? If I tell her before, then maybe we can all eat and enjoy dinner. If I tell her during dinner, we all could end up with upset stomachs."

Daisy couldn't help but smile. "You and Foster have to do what you think is best. Think about it while we nibble hors d'oeuvres."

They'd been seated about ten minutes, talking among themselves, nibbling on cheese spread and crackers, celery and carrot sticks.

Jazzi was having a conversation with her grandfather about the talent show, when Daisy noticed Vi glance at Foster. Foster nodded. The look they exchanged was obvious. Daisy almost felt that she needed a life vest for what was to come, though she could only imagine what Vi and Foster were feeling.

Rose and Sean were seated on the sofa with Jazzi next to them. Aunt Iris sat in a side chair and appeared as nervous as Vi. Daisy was seated in an arm chair. Violet had plopped into the recliner, and Foster leaned against the arm. When he hung his arm around Vi's shoulders, Daisy knew it was time.

Foster cleared his throat. "Can I have your attention? Vi and I would like to make an announcement."

Iris smiled with encouragement, but Rose was already looking disapproving. Daisy knew that wasn't a good sign. Her dad just looked curious.

"Mr. and Mrs. Gallagher, Vi has something she wants to tell you."

Daisy watched as Foster squeezed Vi's shoulder in a sign of encouragement.

Rose turned to look at Daisy and asked in a low voice, "Do you know what this is about?"

Respecting Vi's and Foster's wishes, Daisy simply said, "You'll know in about a minute."

With a resigned expression, Vi straightened her shoulders and sat up with the most correct posture Daisy had ever seen. Her daughter told her grandparents, "I'm pregnant. And Foster and I are getting married."

"That's ridiculous," Rose protested. "You shouldn't even *think* about marriage."

Daisy admired Foster as he kept his cool. "I intend to take responsibility for this baby. I love Vi."

"But how are you going to pay your bills?" Rose asked. "Where are you going to live?" She looked at Daisy. "Certainly not with you." She turned back to the couple. "Are you going to live with Foster's dad?"

Iris remained silent, probably so her sister wouldn't realize Daisy had confided their plans.

Daisy kept quiet, too, which seemed to aggravate her mother. "Seriously? Do either of you have a backup?"

Vi sat forward on the recliner and gazed at her grandfather rather than her grandmother. "Mom is going to fix up the second floor of the garage so we have a little apartment. She's going to let us live there rent-free for the first year."

Daisy's dad was pensive. "You said you wanted to finish that space into an apartment so the girls could use it someday . . . or you could rent it out. That's a fine idea. I suppose congratulations are in order."

"Thank you, Gramps," Vi said, her voice catching.

"How can you afford to pay for all of this?" Rose asked Daisy.

"I had a talk with the bank manager. My house is paid for and the tea garden brings in an income. He advised me to open a line of credit and told me I wouldn't have any problem securing it."

"Not that it's any of our business," Sean reminded his wife.

"You mean you did all of this without telling us first that Vi was pregnant? We could have advised you." Rose stared at the young couple with raised brows.

"Mrs. Swanson has been advising us," Foster responded. "And she did a good job of it, within the reality of what we are doing. And we're going ahead in the best way possible. We'll have a small wedding. And then we'll start getting ready for the baby."

Rose was shaking her head. "Are you going to quit school?" she asked Vi.

"For now," Vi said with a nod. "I'm going to work until the baby comes. We won't make any other decisions until then. If I could find bookkeeping work to do for small businesses, I could work at home. I've been doing Mom's books for years."

Daisy considered the fact that it was time she step in and put an end to her mother's disapproval. There was only one way to do that. "Mom, I understand how this news has rocked you. It rocked me. But they're in love and they're determined. So Gavin and I are going to support them in any way we can."

"Is he putting up half of what you're investing in the garage?"

"No. But he's going to buy the furnishings and, as contractor, he's going to wave his fees. I called Reverend Kemp yesterday. He's going to let us have an evening celebration in August."

Rose murmured, "This is all happening too fast."

"It is happening fast," Daisy agreed. "But there's one thing you have to remember—the baby's growing and you're going to be a great-grandma. If you want, I'm sure Vi and Foster will let you babysit."

For the first time since they'd started this discussion, Rose appeared to accept the news. "A baby. Our first great-grandchild." Then she stood and motioned to Vi. "Come here, honey, and let me give you a hug. When you need more advice, just come to me and we'll talk about weddings and babies. I'm still worried you're so young. But your grandfather and I will certainly welcome a little new life into this family."

Daisy's dad stood and extended his hand to Foster. "Welcome to the family."

Daisy and Vi exchanged small smiles. Maybe they wouldn't be getting indigestion at dinner after all.

* * *

Daisy had enjoyed the weekend with her daughters and Foster. She, Foster, and Jazzi were going to video conference with Vi this evening. Dinner with her parents hadn't been fun, but Daisy knew they'd love a great-grandchild as much as they loved Jazzi and Vi.

Mid-morning the Tuesday after Easter, Daisy called Vanna at the church's office. Vanna told her to come on over to the church. The minister was visiting members of the congregation, and she was caught up on her work.

Taking her lunch break early because they didn't have an overabundance of customers, Daisy parked in the church's back lot, then walked around to the side entrance. A member of the congregation must have planted snapdragons along the walk. There was a list where churchgoers could sign up for many of the things that needed to be done around a church.

Daisy rang the bell and, after a minute or so, Vanna opened the side door. The front door to the church was always open, but the back section with the minister's office and Vanna's as well as the Sunday school rooms were usually locked, unless some activity was planned there.

After exchanging greetings with the church secretary, Daisy climbed the three steps inside the door and walked down a hall, following Vanna. Vanna turned right. Her work area was located directly outside the minister's office. That door was closed now.

Vanna pointed to the ladder-back wooden chair in front of her desk while she sat on a rolling chair behind it. "I was curious why you wanted to talk to me."

Daisy hesitated a moment, then she said honestly, "The tea garden's business is suffering because of Derek's murder. I guess customers think we're going to poison them. Not only that, but my staff could be suspect because Derek's review was a bad one."

"I haven't seen it published on his blog."

So Vanna followed the blog too.

"No, it hasn't been, but Detective Rappaport told me some of what it said. A few of my staff have computer skills. He thinks they could have hacked into the blog and found the lineup of tea rooms. My review would have been in that lineup."

Vanna held on to the desk and brought her chair closer to it. "I can understand why you want the detective to hurry up and find out who killed Derek, but why have you come to *me*?"

"I need to know more about Harriet."

Vanna smiled. "There's really not much to tell. She was active before her stroke, a member of the Garden Club and the Art Guild. When her husband died, his insurance money and what they'd saved together had been enough to keep her comfortable."

Daisy already knew all of that.

"I'd like to go back further than the present day. Do you know who Derek's father was? No one has mentioned him."

"Mmm," Vanna intoned. "That was so long ago. Past history. Certainly, it can't have any bearing on Derek's murder."

"I'm not sure about that," Daisy countered. "I think there might be something in Harriet's past or Derek's past that could have led to his murder. Won't you tell me something about it?"

Looking troubled, Vanna stared past Daisy into the hall, but she wasn't really looking at that space. It was as if she was looking back in time. Finally, she told Daisy, "Derek's father isn't common knowledge, and that's the way Harriet wanted it. I need to keep her confidence."

Daisy picked up her purse that she'd set on the floor. She opened it and took out one of her business cards. "I respect that, Vanna, really I do. Harriet's sister won't talk about her past, either, and if this is a confidence and more people are keeping it for Harriet, then I have to wonder what the secret is. Secrets can get a person murdered."

She took hold of the pen that was lying on the desk. On the back of the business card she wrote her home landline and cell number. Then she slid the card over to Vanna. "If you change your mind, please call me, anytime, day or night. And just try to remember— where there are secrets, there can be motives and lies. Those are the basis for murder."

"Mom, I think the date we set up with Reverend Kemp will work. And . . . I still shouldn't have much of a baby bump."

Daisy sat in a folding chair in the second floor of the garage with an old table in front of her where she'd positioned her laptop. Vi's face stared back at her mother from her laptop screen.

Foster was standing beside Daisy on her left and Jazzi on her right.

Daisy turned to look at Foster. "Are you okay with the August date?"

Foster nodded as Vi spoke to her again from the screen. "Foster and I had a long talk about it last night. We know why you want us to wait at least until then."

"It will be easier to plan a wedding if we have some time," Daisy said, not for the first time.

"But you also want to know if the pregnancy is viable. You want me to get through my first trimester."

Daisy couldn't deny it. She hadn't asked a question that should be asked. "Tell me something. Would you and Foster still get married if you miscarry?"

"We would still get married," Foster insisted. "Either way. We do love each other, Mrs. Swanson."

He always reverted to Mrs. Swanson when he thought they were discussing something controversial.

Jazzi spoke to Violet now. "Four months would give you more time to plan a special wedding. Hopefully you'll only have one in your lifetime. You certainly don't want it to happen at the justice of the peace. We know Gram and Gramps, Aunt Iris, and Camellia will want to be there. As well as Jonas and other friends."

"I don't want a big wedding," Vi returned.

"I understand that," Daisy assured her. "It usually takes a year or more to find a reception place. And as far as that is concerned, Daisy's Tea Garden will be happy to host your reception."

"You're doing so much for us, Mom," Vi said as if she regretted it.

"You're my daughter, and soon I'll look on Foster as a son. I will always do anything I can to help you."

The side door to the garage opened and closed, and Daisy could hear someone coming up the steps. The stairs leading up to the second floor were definitely rustic. Soon Gavin would secure the treads and make them sturdy and more presentable. When she looked over her shoulder, she saw Jonas. She was inordinately happy that he'd stopped by, but she wondered why he had.

"I think we discussed everything I need for now," Daisy said. "Why don't you and Jazzi and Foster talk about color schemes for the wedding and where you want to look for your gown. You're going to be home again this weekend?"

"Yes. And I might make one trip home before finals to bring some of my stuff. I'm not sure I can pack it all in the car for one trip."

"Sounds good. I love you, Vi." Daisy threw her daughter a kiss. "I'll talk to you this weekend."

Daisy stood and let Foster take the seat in front of her laptop. She crossed over to Jonas who was standing at the top of the stairway.

"How are things going?"

"At the beginning of our video conference session, Vi and Foster went over with me what they think would be a good arrangement for this apartment."

Jonas scanned the space. "Where will the kitchen be?"

Daisy pulled a rough drawing from her sweater pocket. She pointed to the corner of the room where the kitchen would be located. "It's going to be small," she said. "Just like everything else. In some ways, it would be similar to a studio apartment. Vi and Foster are trying to decide if they want to wall off a separate space for the baby."

"I know Gavin will be overseeing construction," Jonas said. "But I'd be glad to make the cabinets for cost if you'd like that. If I start now, I should have them done by the time the other work is complete."

"I can't ask you to do that."

He placed both hands gently on her shoulders and drew her a little closer. "I told you, I will support you anyway I can, with anything you need. All we can do is look forward and try to make the right decisions."

When she gazed up into his green eyes, tears came to hers. Maybe, just maybe, she and Jonas could keep their bonds and deepen them. "All right," she said. "You can make the cabinets. I know they'll be solid and beautiful."

"Did you say Vi was coming home this weekend?"

"She is."

"I can find out then if she and Foster want a Shaker-style, or something a little more elaborate. Or should I be asking *you* that?"

"No, I'll discuss it with them. Whatever they choose is fine with me."

"You're a good mom."

"Am I? Or am I making this too easy for them?"

He shook his head. "If you weren't supportive, they'd run off and get married, and then who knows what they'd do next. This way you can make sure Violet's going to doctors' appointments and taking care of herself."

"What you're saying is that I'm a mom who wants control."

"Don't all moms?"

She laughed. "Maybe so. I guess you understand that making the cabinets for them will give you a lifetime membership for Daisy's Tea Garden for unlimited tea and scones."

This time he laughed. "I'm hoping for more than tea and scones. This will be a good first step."

Daisy hoped Jonas's words would come true.

On Wednesday, Daisy was at the sales counter ringing up a customer when she heard her aunt Iris say, "Hi there, Vanna. It's good to see you. You haven't been in for a while."

Daisy looked up to see Vanna just inside the door

with Iris ushering her toward a table. But Vanna was shaking her head.

Finished with her customer, Daisy came out from behind the sales counter and greeted Vanna too.

Taking a few steps closer to Daisy, Vanna said, "Can we talk somewhere?"

Vanna's skin wasn't as ruddy as it usually was. The lines under her eyes and on her forehead looked deep, signaling she was troubled.

Daisy asked her aunt, "Can you watch the sales counter while I help Vanna?"

Although Iris cast her a puzzled look, she nodded.

It was the middle of the afternoon, business was slow, and Daisy didn't think anyone was sitting at the tables outside. She said to Vanna, "If you want to sit outside, we'll have privacy and fresh air. I'll bring the teapot and strawberry tarts."

"I'm not really hungry," Vanna said with a shake of her head.

"That's okay. Maybe you'll be hungry once we talk." She suspected that was the reason why Vanna was here, perhaps to unload a secret. Daisy felt chills crawl up her back just thinking about it. Could this be the conversation that could help solve the case?

There wasn't anyone at the sales counter at the moment. Iris said, "I'll get Vanna set up outside while you brew the tea."

"What kind of tea would you like?"

"Green tea. No caffeine. Maybe it will help steady me since it has all those antioxidants and all."

Ten minutes later, Daisy was sitting with Vanna at one of the round tables, a yellow and white umbrella shading them. Vanna took off her sweater, letting it hang over her chair. It was white with pearl buttons. Her two-piece blouse and pant set was of the palest aqua.

Vanna turned her tea mug around and around. Then she added two teaspoons of sugar. Daisy gave her time to find her voice.

Finally, Vanna said, "I want to help you solve the murder. I don't think anything I can say had anything to do with it, but I realize one never knows. The thing is—you have to promise to keep this to yourself unless absolutely necessary."

"If there's any connection to Derek's murder," Daisy reminded her, "I'll have to share the information with Detective Rappaport."

"I understand," Vanna said with a sigh. After taking a swallow of tea, she set her mug down. "Working in the minister's office, I see and hear things that I probably shouldn't. If nothing else, what I have to tell you might explain Derek's behavior."

Daisy wondered what behavior Vanna was talking about, but she didn't want to sidetrack her.

Vanna looked around the back walkway to the tea garden, at the herbs that were planted in a row, and the pots with yellow and purple pansies. Finally, she said to Daisy, "Simply put, Harriet was a bookworm and she didn't date when she was young. At twenty-five no one had asked her out."

Daisy was surprised at that. Although Harriet wouldn't be considered pretty, her face had interesting bone structure and her hair was still thick and wavy. Daisy could imagine her much younger with an expressive smile.

Vanna continued. "Willow Creek was smaller thirty-six years ago than it is now. I have to admit, Harriet had a reputation for being bossy even back then. She also didn't pretty up much."

"You mean not much makeup?"

"Exactly. She always looked pale and didn't stand out."

Daisy couldn't imagine where this was going.

"I heard talk that her attitude and unfashionable wardrobe put men off. I got married and she seemed jealous of me. As a service project as a teenager, I had helped the minister at Willow Creek Community Church with paperwork. After I graduated from high school, he hired me and I've worked there ever since."

Daisy was practically at the edge of her seat, wondering what Vanna had seen or overheard, because she imagined that's where this conversation was going.

Vanna licked her lips as if her mouth was suddenly dry. She took a couple of swallows of her tea. "I was young then," she mused. "I didn't know much about confidentiality, not in a small town. I was working the evening that Harriet rushed in, her face tear-streaked, her clothes and her hair in disarray. She said she needed to talk to the minister. She'd gone to the house first, but no one answered the door and she seemed frantic. I told her the minister was in the church at the podium, practicing his sermon. Harriet disappeared into the church, and she hadn't come out when I left."

Daisy suspected what was coming, but she didn't want to derail Vanna's story. So she kept silent.

The sound of a horse and buggy clomping down the street took their attention for a moment. Vanna watched it, then looked around. She must have decided they were really alone because she went on, "The next morning the reverend's wife was in the office with him. I heard them talking. Harriet had gone out on a date with someone she'd met at the library. Apparently, he wasn't from Willow Creek. They went to dinner and afterward . . ." Vanna's cheeks pinkened. "The man raped her in his car. The minister's wife insisted Harriet should go to the police, but the minister said she wouldn't go because she believed they'd just blame her. After that day, Harriet met with the minister once a week, and I assumed it was for counseling."

Thank goodness Harriet had had someone she could talk to, Daisy thought.

Vanna shifted on her chair. "About seven or eight weeks later, a woman came to the minister's office who was a social worker. I saw the printout she gave the minister that listed homes for unwed mothers. Soon after, Harriet went to live with her sister June in Erie. At that time, June was married and trying to have a baby but having no luck. I took a phone call from Harriet and patched her through to the minister. But, God forgive me, I listened in."

Daisy could see that Vanna regretted it and considered it the worst wrongdoing. The church secretary closed her eyes as she said, "June wanted to adopt Harriet's baby, but there had always been a rivalry between June and Harriet. Harriet decided to keep Derek." She came back to Willow Creek with her baby, and no one dared ask her who the father was.

Vanna took her napkin and played with the edges. "Through the years, I could easily see the problem with her and Derek. Even though she never said it, and she never told me her story, I saw the way she looked at Derek. I imagine she could never forget the way he was conceived. I was seeing a lot of parishioners coming in and out of the minister's office with all types of emotions, and I swear that sometimes when Harriet looked at Derek, she hated him."

Vanna picked up her fork and poked at the strawberry tart. "She married two years after she returned. As Derek grew older, he didn't get along with his stepdad. One day when Derek was waiting to talk with the minister, he told me he had questions about his father but Harriet wouldn't give him answers. He was hoping the minister would. Although Derek was the older brother, he obviously became the black sheep. One of his problems was easy to see. He had poor self-esteem, and I think he tried to make up for that with his intelligence and acquired arrogance. When his stepdad died, he visited Harriet more and I think he was always trying to earn her approval. After he got his own TV show, I think he thought his mother would finally be proud of him. But then it was canceled. He became closer to his brother Bradley then. It was obvious when Lauren and Bradley stepped in to help after Harriet had her stroke. Derek was taking responsibility for her, but I'm not sure he was putting any emotion into it. After her stroke, Harriet confided in me that she believed he felt taking care of her was his duty, nothing more."

"It's such a sad story."

Vanna looked relieved now that the telling was done. "Yes, it is."

"Do you think Derek and his brother knew his mother's story?"

"There was never any sign of that," Vanna said.

"I think I need to talk to Bradley. When I do, do I have your permission to tell him what you've told me?"

"Harriet will find out!" Vanna exclaimed.

"Maybe. Maybe not. But I think Bradley's my next best lead."

Vanna looked dejected for a moment. "I think I knew this couldn't stay between me and you." She looked Daisy in the eye. "Do what you have to do. I just hope Harriet will forgive me some day for telling you."

"If I figure out who hurt her son, I think she will."

Daisy checked her watch. Maybe if she went to the high school, she could catch Bradley as he was leaving for the day. It was the best way she knew to find the next clue.

Chapter Nineteen

Only a few scattered cars remained in the high school's parking lot. Students who stayed after school participated in clubs. Almost everyone else would be gone. Daisy suspected Bradley, as high school principal, spent a lot of extra hours there. She was hoping she could catch him before he closed his office for the day.

Before Vanna had left the tea garden, Daisy again had asked her permission to tell Bradley the truth about his mother if he didn't know it.

Vanna had asked her if she considered him a suspect, and Daisy had admitted he could be on the list. So Vanna had agreed, hoping her relationship with Harriet wouldn't be damaged. Yet she knew if the police looked into Harriet's background, they could possibly find all of this information on their own.

Daisy felt a little nervous about confronting Bradley. Just *how* would he react?

As she approached his office, she noted that the secretary in the outer office was gone. Bradley sat at his desk sorting through papers.

She rapped on his office door. When he looked up,

he smiled. "Hi, Mrs. Swanson. Is there something I can help you with?"

"Please call me Daisy. And there is something you can help me with. Do you have a few minutes?"

He studied his desk, the manila folders, the loose papers, the red pens and highlighters. Then his gaze traveled to his computer. Finally, he determined, "The work will still be here a few minutes from now. Sure, I have a few minutes for one of the parents."

Daisy moved deeper into the office. "I'm not here in my parental capacity, though I do want to tell you the guidance counselor, Mrs. Cotton, really helped me with Jazzi. She's good, efficient, and more than competent."

"Good to know." Bradley's voice was even but he had questions in his eyes. "So what did you need to talk to me about?"

"Can we talk about Derek?"

"Derek," he exhaled with a resigned sigh. "I don't know what's left to talk about."

"I need to ask you a question."

"All right. Ask away."

"Did you know who Derek's father was? Did you know that your mother was raped and Derek was the result of that?"

Bradley's mouth opened, then closed, and opened again. It seemed he couldn't find any words. He turned pale and he looked shocked. Daisy didn't think he could be simulating those reactions.

Rubbing his hand across his forehead, he closed his eyes. His voice was low as he murmured, "That history would explain a lot."

"What do you mean?" Daisy asked gently.

"I never knew anything about what you say happened

to my mother. And my dad? He never acted as if he knew anything either. I always thought my dad and Derek didn't get along because Derek was a difficult child and an even more difficult teen. But maybe my dad did know what happened to Mom. From what I understand, my dad married my mom when Derek was two. I was born a year after they married. But I don't see how this has anything to do with Derek's death. Granted, my mother and Derek were never close, at least they didn't seem to be. It was as if there was no bond at all between them. I always wondered if that made Derek feel adrift. I can see it now. I could always see how Mom favored me, and I felt guilty about it. Again, I just thought that was a personality difference. I really don't understand how it has anything to do with Derek's death."

Daisy wasn't convinced. "What if Derek could somehow have known what had happened?"

"I don't know for sure, but I don't think so. Derek was outspoken. If he'd learned about the rape, I think he would have told me, especially when Mom had her stroke."

From Bradley's reaction, Daisy didn't believe he'd hurt his brother. But she still didn't know for certain. Just because Bradley hadn't known about his mother's history didn't mean that he and Derek couldn't have had an argument about something, an argument that had turned angry.

Keeping her thoughts on track, she asked Bradley, "Will you let your mother realize that you know?"

"I'm not sure what I'm going to do. I truly don't know if the police need to have this information or not. Why embarrass my mom? Why bring up a past she wants to forget?"

"Maybe the detective needs to know a significant piece of your mom's past."

Bradley sighed. "I'll think about it. Thank you for telling me. Now I understand my mother and my childhood much better. Her treatment of the two of us could have been the cause of Derek's anger when he acted out."

"Bradley, I'm so sorry about everything that has happened."

He shrugged. "The older I get, the more I realize that life is hard. Only the strong survive."

After Daisy ended the conversation with Bradley, bid him good-bye, and headed down the hall, she felt sorry for his whole family.

Daisy returned to the tea garden to help take inventory and close up for the day. To her surprise, Jonas and Detective Zeke Willet sat at a table in the main tea room. Jonas wore a chambray shirt with the sleeves rolled up and jeans. In contrast, Zeke was dressed professionally in a white oxford, button-down collar shirt and black dress slacks. A sports jacket was draped over one of the chairs. In front of each of the men were bowls of beef barley soup, brown sugar biscuits she'd baked earlier, and mugs of tea. Was Detective Willet a tea drinker, or had he given in to Jonas's encouragement to try it? The tea might have been brewed for them, but by their expressions and body language, she could tell tension brewed between them too.

Jonas immediately stood when she approached them. Zeke Willet did not. Jonas's smile was just for her when he said, "I wanted to introduce Zeke to the best gathering place in Willow Creek."

She motioned for Jonas to sit, and she took the chair at the round table between the two men. There were no other customers in the tea room.

Iris waved to her from the case that she was emptying of the day's selections.

"It's not much of a gathering place right now," she confessed. "Business has been terribly slow. I answered the comments on the blog as Foster suggested, but I don't think that did much good."

Zeke finished the last of the soup in his bowl and laid his spoon beside the dish. "Has business slacked off because of the murder?" he asked.

"It has. In small towns, news travels. Everyone knows Derek ate something from here that killed him. The fact that it wasn't poison isn't for public consumption. New customers and even old customers think it was our food that did it."

Zeke almost scowled, his eyebrows sneaking up. "You know what was in the food?"

She kept her voice low. "Yes, I know. Blood pressure medication. Detective Rappaport shared that with me."

Zeke looked her straight in the eye. "Why?"

"Zeke—" Jonas warned.

She didn't want to increase the tension between the two men, but just because Zeke was a detective didn't mean he could run roughshod over her either. She placed her hand on Jonas's, so he didn't try to defend her. "You could say I've helped Detective Rappaport with his last couple of cases. We've come to an understanding."

"And what kind of understanding is that?" Zeke asked tersely.

Already, Daisy could feel heat crawling up her neck

to her face. "The understanding that I'll be honest with him if he's honest with me. Are you on the case?"

Jonas moved his fingers under hers, maybe as a warning.

"I'm becoming acquainted with it."

"That's good," Daisy acknowledged. "There are so many suspects. If you help Detective Rappaport with interviews, that should help."

"You don't have to be concerned about our suspects and interviews."

His patronizing tone added fuel to her long fuse that was growing shorter by the second. "Oh, but I do. If this murder isn't solved soon, Daisy's Tea Garden is going to fail."

Zeke's eyes narrowed. "That won't be on us."

"I didn't say it would. It would be on the murderer. If I find out information here and there and it can help Detective Rappaport, I'll share it with him. I have a stake in this, Detective Willet."

"Just make sure your stake doesn't mess with our investigation or—"

Daisy held up her hand to stop him. "That's an old song Detective Rappaport has sung more than once. Believe me, I don't want to steal any of your glory. I just want to learn who killed Derek Schumacher."

Zeke looked as if he wanted to say more. Instead, he pushed back his chair and rose to his feet. "I'd better be going. I have reading to catch up on at the station or those interviews to schedule that you mentioned." He nodded to Jonas. "See you around." To Daisy he said, "Your food is good."

She knew there was a *but* there. Something like, *But your attitude needs an adjustment.* Still, she had to give him credit for not saying it.

When Zeke started to take his wallet from his pocket, Jonas said, "I've got this."

Zeke nodded, scooped up his sports jacket from the vacant chair, and left the tea garden.

"Don't say it," she said to Jonas after Zeke left.

"Say what?" Jonas asked ingenuously.

"That I should have kept my mouth shut."

His hand closed around hers. "Does that mean you've been sleuthing?"

"It means I might have told someone something I shouldn't have."

"I see. I stopped at the station to meet Zeke. The police grapevine says that they're bringing Harriet back in for questioning."

"So soon? I wonder if they discovered . . ." She stopped.

"Spill it, Daisy. What do you know?"

When she hesitated, she saw the troubled and disappointed look in Jonas's eyes. "Are we back to square one?" he asked gently.

Square one? No, they knew too much about each other now. Her feelings had grown past what was safe. "No, not square one."

He obviously knew what she meant, that the rocks in the road had tripped them up and they would be moving forward the best way they could.

He ran his thumb over the top of her hand. "You don't have to tell me."

Daisy released a sigh. "I told Bradley something about his mother that he didn't know. It was a secret. If Detective Rappaport found out about it, Harriet is going to be devastated that it's now revealed."

Jonas shook his head. When he did, a lock of his

hair fell over his brow and she had the urge to brush it away.

"You know that an investigation brings everything into the light," Jonas said. "Is it about Derek's parentage?"

Jonas was still a good detective whether he wanted to be or not. She nodded.

"Remember, the more that's added to this story, the easier it will be for Detective Rappaport to figure it out."

Daisy could only hope that was true.

A short while after Jonas left, Daisy spotted Russ Windom enter the tea garden and sit at a table over by the wall of shelves that housed teapots for sale. Iris went to his table, then to the kitchen to brew tea with her color high. Russ was grinning from ear to ear, and Daisy suspected why. Russ's grin could only mean one thing.

Daisy stopped by his table. "Afternoon snack?" she asked.

"Oh yes. And a chance to talk with Iris."

"She looked as though there was a spring in her step when she went back to the kitchen," Daisy prompted.

"There's going to be a spring in my step too. She's going out with me."

Daisy was happy for her aunt and for Russ. Even if they merely found companionship and became good friends, that was important. "Do you have a date planned?"

"I do. On Iris's next day off, we're going for a buggy ride. They've started again for the tourist season.

We're going to travel around the countryside and then have supper at Sarah Jane's. Do you think she'll like that?"

"I do. I bet she hasn't ridden in a buggy in years. We've had lovely weather lately, and I think you'll have a good time. I'm so glad you asked her."

"Sometimes I get the feeling she's as lonely as I am."

Daisy's aunt Iris had always been satisfied living her life on her own terms. She'd had a serious relationship years ago, but it had fallen apart, though Daisy didn't know why. When Iris and Daisy decided to become joint owners of the tea garden, her aunt seemed to be perfectly satisfied with her life and ecstatic about starting a new venture. But after her last brief romance had ended in tragedy, she had seemed to consider life differently. Maybe she wanted companionship for her golden years . . . or maybe she wanted more.

Iris was arranging a tray with two teacups and serving dishes when Daisy returned to the kitchen. She winked at her aunt, so Iris knew what she knew. Iris's smile grew even wider.

"Would you like me to take the tray to Russ's table?" Daisy suggested. "You can bring the pot after the tea steeps."

"Sounds good," Iris said with her eyes twinkling. "I'll bring the honey too. He likes that in his oolong."

Smiling because already Iris remembered a detail about Russ, Daisy carried the tray to his table and set it down. "Tea will be coming shortly."

Russ helped her remove the dishes and cups from the tray and set them on the table. "I visited June Seachrist this morning. Lauren had driven Harriet to an appointment at the medical center."

"You know June?"

"I knew her way back when. She was ahead of me in school, but my mother would take sewing projects to her and I often tagged along. She and I both had an interest in the classics, and we discussed them."

"Did Harriet have a regular checkup?"

"Apparently she is looking into more physical therapy. That will be good for her." He hesitated a moment, then went on. "When I was speaking to June, she seemed terribly distracted."

"Maybe she's thinking about returning home."

Russ shook his head. "No, I think she's planning on staying here at least another month, and there's a reason for that. She's helping Harriet go through Derek's things."

"Do you think that's what distracted her?"

"I do. There was a manila folder on the coffee table, and her eyes kept going to that. I didn't ask what it was because I didn't want to pry."

Could June have found something important? Something that might have gotten Derek killed? That could be a reach, but Daisy intended to find out just what it might be.

Chapter Twenty

Work on the garage had started when Violet came home from college on Friday. Daisy watched as Foster told her pregnant daughter not to lift anything more than five pounds. Daisy had to smile. He was going to be protective.

"I can't wait for you to see the garage," Daisy said as they all stopped in the living room to take a breath. Foster had been up and down the stairs twice with huge suitcases of Vi's. Vi carried a table light from her dorm room, ready for her second trip up the stairs.

"I can't wait to see what's going on," Vi said.

"The Sheetrock's going up," Daisy explained. "Next will be electrical work and plumbing. And Jonas is going to start building the cabinets. You'll have to decide if you want them stained or painted."

"Another decision," Vi mused as if she were already tired of making them.

"Get used to it," Daisy advised her. "Once you have a baby, you'll have to make ten decisions a day at least."

"My dad's finally talking to me without growling,"

Foster revealed as he pushed his glasses up to the bridge of his nose.

Daisy stooped and picked up one of the boxes that Foster had brought inside earlier. When she straightened again, she addressed Foster. "I'm glad. I'll have to invite him over to dinner, maybe when you're all free."

Jazzi came in the front door next, carrying Vi's laptop and headphones.

"Careful with that," Vi warned.

Jazzi just rolled her eyes. "As if I don't know how to be careful with a computer."

The two sisters studied each other for a moment, then Jazzi said, "In a week or so, I'll have to get used to you being home again."

"Same here," Vi agreed. "My roommate was out of the dorm room more than she was in."

"Boyfriend?" Jazzi guessed.

"Oh yeah," Vi confirmed.

Hiding her smile, Daisy suspected Vi and Jazzi wouldn't have a problem sharing the upstairs once more.

Upstairs, as Jazzi set the laptop on Vi's desk in her room, Daisy glanced over at Vi as Foster lifted a suitcase onto the bed. "We're all going to Gram and Gramp's house on Sunday. Aunt Camellia is driving down. I thought maybe you and I could make dessert."

"Sure," Vi agreed. "We could either do it Saturday night or Sunday after church."

Jazzi's cell phone played from her pocket. She plucked it out, glanced at the screen, then stared at her mom. "It's Portia."

"Go to your room and close the door if you'd like. Try to listen to her," Daisy said.

With a nod, Jazzi headed across the hall to her own

bedroom. Daisy heard her say, "Hi, Portia," as she closed her door.

Obviously perceptive about what was happening, Vi gave her closed suitcase a pat. "Foster and I will go downstairs. That way you can talk to Jazzi in private when she's finished."

Daisy gave Vi a hug. "If you want, I'll start unpacking your suitcase while I wait. It will give my hands something to do."

"Sure. Go ahead. I'll rearrange later." With a grin she followed Foster out of the room and down the stairs.

After Daisy unzipped the suitcase on the bed, she tried not to think about the conversation in Jazzi's bedroom. She didn't want her youngest daughter to be hurt. She also knew she couldn't protect her forever. It had been so much easier when Jazzi had been a baby and then in grade school. During these teenage years with Jazzi, Daisy knew worries would stack up one on the other as Jazzi learned to drive, as she dated, as she searched for the right college. But she'd never really imagined this situation with Portia, and she also wondered now if Jazzi would want to search for her birth *father*. They'd never really talked about that, and Jazzi had never said whether she and Portia had spoken about it. Finding one parent had taken all of Jazzi's emotional energy. What was happening now was continuing to do that unless the situation could be resolved. Maybe it never would be.

Remembering where Vi used to keep her T-shirts, her pajamas, her hair clips, and her socks, Daisy stowed them all away in the dresser. She kept busy and was hanging the last dress in the closet when Jazzi opened her bedroom door and came into Vi's bedroom.

The first thing Daisy looked for were tears on Jazzi's face. But she couldn't see any obvious ones. "How are you?"

Sitting on Vi's bed, Jazzi tossed her phone down in front of her. "I'm okay."

Giving Jazzi time to gather her thoughts, Daisy waited.

"I tried to do like you said and just listen. Portia seemed a little better. Colton moved back into the house, but there's a wall between them. Apparently, he doesn't want to talk about me."

"She told you that?"

"Not in so many words. I guess I'm not as important as their marriage. Portia's hoping she can convince Colton to talk to their minister."

"Counseling might be the best way forward for them."

"I know. Tara told me that counseling doesn't solve problems, but it helps the client get a handle on them."

If Jazzi was quoting her counselor, she was finding their sessions worthwhile. She'd had two so far and had mentioned to Daisy that having Lancelot, the counselor's yellow tabby, sitting in her lap while she talked to Tara kept her more relaxed.

"I don't want to talk about Portia anymore, Mom. Until she makes a decision one way or another, until her husband decides what he wants, there's simply no point. We have enough to deal with here with Vi's pregnancy. Do you think Gram will feel better about Vi and Foster on Sunday?"

"I hope so. She made a point of telling me Foster is included."

"Do you think he wants to go? Dinner on Easter was kind of tense."

"It's his choice. He insists that he'll be there right beside Vi."

"You don't want them to get married, do you?"

After a moment's hesitation, Daisy told Jazzi the truth. "I'm not sure. My initial reaction was that they should wait. But watching them together and hearing their plans, seeing that they're really ready to compromise and do what's best for the baby, marriage could make their bond even stronger. I was young when I married your dad."

"And you would have stayed married."

"I would have stayed married. Your dad and I might have been young, but we understood what vows meant. I did, thanks in large part to my mom and dad. Say what you want about Gram, but she loves your grandfather deeply."

"And he loves her," Jazzi said with a certainty that Daisy appreciated. Daisy held out her hand and Jazzi took it. She gave her daughter a slight tug up from the bed. "We have a few more trips up and down before Vi's car is empty."

Jazzi groaned. But then she followed her mom down the stairs, leaving her phone behind on the bed.

Afternoon tea service was sparse on Saturday. Iris had the day off. Daisy helped Cora Sue serve while Tessa and Eva handled the kitchen. They still had half a case of baked goods, so Tessa had let up on the baking. Eva had started another batch of chicken soup, but Daisy suspected that they would have plenty left over. Daisy had just finished serving a second round of tea at a table for four when her phone played its tuba sound. She motioned to Cora Sue that she was going to take a call as soon as she saw the name on the screen—June Seachrist.

Rounding the sales counter, Daisy answered while she made her way to her office. Once inside, she closed the door.

"Hello, June. How are you?"

"I'm not sure."

"Has something happened to Harriet?"

"No." June's voice was a bit wobbly. "I haven't told her about this." Harriet's sister kept her voice low, as if she didn't want Harriet to overhear. "Can we talk somewhere—somewhere private?"

Vi and Foster were going to his dad's for dinner, and Jazzi was staying overnight with Stacy.

"Why don't you come to my house? How does six thirty sound?"

"That's fine," June decided, her voice stronger now.

"Are you sure you don't want to tell me what this is about? You could go outside."

"No. Harriet would get suspicious, and I really don't want to talk about it over the phone."

"Do you know my address?"

"If you give it to me, I won't have to look it up."

Daisy rattled it off. "I'll see you at six thirty."

"Thank you, Daisy."

After Daisy said good-bye and ended the call, she wondered just what June was thanking her for.

The rest of the afternoon passed slowly. At four thirty, Daisy took an early inventory. No customers had entered the tea garden in the past half-hour. Tessa was counting the receipts and gathering the bills to put in the safe. Cora Sue was sweeping the floor. At exactly five, Daisy set the alarm and they all left. She didn't tell anyone about her meeting. What was the point?

As soon as Daisy stepped inside her house, Marjoram and Pepper met her. Pepper meowed.

"You missed me that much?" Daisy asked the two of them.

Pepper meowed again.

Daisy crossed to the deacon's bench and set her purse there. "I suppose you two would like supper?"

Both felines must have understood the word because they pattered toward the kitchen.

Daisy laughed and followed them. She took two of their dishes from the cupboard. She fed them wet food twice a day, and they nibbled on kibble in between. Taking down a can of grain-free certified chicken cat food, she popped open the can and split it between the two dishes. Then she set them on a mat on the floor. It was colorful and proclaimed, FEED ME OR PET ME around a huge cat face.

Deciding to change clothes, Daisy headed toward her bedroom. She exchanged her pale blue slacks and sweater for jeans and a T-shirt printed with the Lehigh University logo. Vi had bought it for her for Christmas. She also grabbed a flannel jacket. Before June arrived, she wanted to plant a forsythia bush her parents had given her for Easter.

Daisy didn't know how long her meeting with June would last, so she went to the kitchen and grabbed a container of peach yogurt from the refrigerator.

Pepper jumped up on a stool at the island beside her. Lifting a black paw, she washed her face, every once in a while eyeing Daisy.

As usual, Daisy told Pepper her plans. "I'm going

to plant a bush. Then we have a meeting. Maybe you and Marjoram can find toy mice to play with in the meantime."

Pepper paused . . . with her paw raised. She gave Daisy one of those maybe-it's-time-you-bought-me-a-new-toy looks.

"I'll try to find new mice next week. You've torn apart so many."

Pepper resumed washing as if what Daisy had said had no consequence.

Daisy tossed the yogurt container, washed her hands, and headed out the French door. The sky had already turned a darker gray. She realized that wasn't from dusk but rather rainy weather moving in. If she was lucky, she'd have the bush planted before a downpour and she wouldn't have to water the new planting.

Crossing to the garage, she grabbed a shovel from its temporary spot with other garden implements just inside the side door.

Twenty minutes later, she'd planted the forsythia under her kitchen window as a light drizzle began to spritz from the sky. She was taking off her gardening gloves, when her cell phone in her jeans pocket played its tuba sound. Maybe June had changed her mind about meeting.

However, Wyatt's number lit up on the phone screen.

"Hello, Wyatt. How can I help you?"

"I have a question about the size of the window over the sink."

"What about it?"

"Do you want a standard above-the-sink-size window, or would you prefer a garden window that opens?"

"I never thought about a garden window."

"I also need to know if you want a baby gate set in across the stairway at the top."

That gate would be a necessity as soon as the baby started crawling. "I'll go over to the garage and imagine it all. Then I'll talk to Vi and Foster about it."

"We have time. Think about the space, how much light you want in, and how practical you want to be."

"All right, I will. Thank you, Wyatt."

She would take a quick look around the garage's second floor before June arrived. The shovel she had used to plant the bush still had dirt caked on it. She set it outside the garage door, then went inside. Carefully she climbed the stairs . . . the new treads weren't attached yet. On the second floor, she studied the wall where the sink window would be. She also studied the top of the steps, thinking about a baby gate and what type would be best. Wood or aluminum? Just how high should it be? That might take online research. Plucking her phone from her pocket, she snapped photos of the entire second floor. They would help when envisioning the renovated space.

Afterward, she went downstairs, careful on the wobbly treads. She was scanning the rear of the garage and taking more photos, when she heard tires on the gravel lane. Setting her phone on her car's hood, she left the garage by the side door and spotted June's silver sedan coming up the lane.

In the rain that was now pouring down heavier than a drizzle, Daisy quickly waved her down.

June exited her car wearing jeans, sneakers, and a jacket with its hood over her hair as Daisy explained, "I'm just looking around and taking photos. We're going to make the second floor a small studio apartment for my daughter and her husband-to-be." If Daisy said it often enough, maybe she'd believe it.

"So you're going to be planning a wedding?" June asked.

"It looks like it."

Approaching Daisy quickly, June explained, "I know I'm early, but Lauren came to sit with Harriet, so I took advantage of the opportunity."

"I left my phone inside," Daisy explained. "Let's just go in the garage and get out of this rain."

Daisy led June inside the side door of the garage. At least they had shelter in here.

June looked around, scanning the empty bay and the space in the rear. "Your second floor should be big enough for a nice little apartment."

"I hope so. What can I help you with?"

"I don't know how to say this," June began, "so I'll just say it. Harriet asked me to clean out Derek's desk. She just didn't have the heart to do it. I was going through all the papers, and I found a letter."

Daisy's heart pounded faster. "A letter to Derek?"

"No, a letter from Derek to his daughter! Lauren's daughter Chrissy is *his*. I don't know if Bradley knows or not. I don't know whether to tell Harriet or to confront Lauren. What do you think—"

The downpour muffled any outside sounds as Daisy's mind raced. She hardly had time to formulate any thoughts, when Lauren burst through the door with the shovel Daisy had left outside. Before Daisy could blink, Lauren whacked June over the head with it!

Chapter Twenty-one

Daisy saw the glint of crazy in Lauren's eyes. Crazy from fear? Crazy from discovery? Crazy because she'd been out of her mind all along and no one had noticed? Rushing to June, Daisy took off her flannel jacket and held it to the wound on June's head. Had Lauren cracked June's skull? Would she live? How would Harriet be able to survive another loss?

Still concerned about June, Daisy almost missed Lauren's words when she mumbled, "I knew she'd find that letter. I knew Derek kept it, but I didn't know where. Then when I came in today to take care of Harriet, June acted really weird around me."

"Why did you come after her? Certainly, other people will know what she saw. All secrets come out." Daisy wasn't about to tell Lauren that June had already admitted what was in the letter . . . that Lauren's daughter was Derek's.

Lauren was mumbling again, looking down at June. "I followed her, hoping to run her off the road. But there was more traffic than I expected, and I couldn't find a good spot."

Daisy glanced at the car hood where she'd laid her phone.

Suddenly, Lauren stared at Daisy as if her eyes were piercing straight through her. "She told you, didn't she?"

"Told me what?" Daisy asked innocently, even though her hands were shaking, her heart was pounding, her ears were ringing. It was stress, and she had to make sure she didn't succumb to it . . . because Lauren was most probably Derek's killer.

"Told you that Derek is Chrissy's father."

Daisy kept all expression from her face. She wasn't going to confirm or deny. That wouldn't matter anyway since Lauren had just told her the secret. So if nothing else, maybe she could coax information from her. If Daisy survived this, she could tell the police.

Still stemming the blood oozing from June's head, Daisy asked Lauren, "Why did you kill Derek?"

"Because he was blackmailing me," Lauren shouted. "Originally, Harriet had in her will that her money should go to a home for unwed mothers. I'd almost convinced Harriet to change it so her estate went to Derek and Bradley. Why should that money go to a bunch of kids who didn't know better?"

Daisy was wondering why *Lauren* hadn't known better. "Was Derek blackmailing you for money?"

"No, not money. He told me if I didn't leave his mother's will alone, he'd reveal our secret, that we'd had an affair, that Chrissy is his daughter. And he wouldn't tell me why a home for unwed mothers was so important to his mother and obviously to him."

Although Daisy's thoughts were speeding so fast she could hardly catch any, one of them fell into place. Derek might not have known about Harriet's rape, but he did know that she was unwed when he was born. There wasn't any point in telling Lauren that. She obviously didn't have the compassion to understand. Apparently, Bradley hadn't told Lauren his mother's secret. Why not? Didn't he trust her? Did he suspect that Chrissy wasn't his?

Lauren came a few steps closer and suddenly raised the shovel. "Killing June will be easy. Another whack will crush her skull. But first I have to take care of *you*."

Violet and her pregnancy came to mind, the wedding Daisy didn't know if she approved of or not, Jazzi, Jonas, her aunt and Tessa . . . her parents and sister. She had too much to live for to be easy prey.

Lauren didn't expect Daisy's sudden movement. Lauren apparently thought she had time to bring that shovel down. Daisy scooted back away from her and ran up the stairs, feeling the new treads slip. Lauren rushed after her and brought the shovel down hard. Daisy evaded it. Almost mindlessly, she grabbed the loose stair tread above her and brought it down hard on Lauren.

In the next moment, Lauren lost her balance and fell backward down the stairs. As she groaned, Daisy ran down, fetched her phone, and got hold of the Lesche shovel that stood just inside the door.

Holding the implement to Lauren's chest, she speed-dialed 9-1-1. After she gave her address and explained what happened in a shaky voice, the dispatcher told her to stay on the line. But Daisy's mind cleared, and she told the dispatcher she couldn't stay on the line. She had other calls to attend to.

The next call she made was to Jonas.

Epilogue

From the space above the garage that was slowly turning into a studio apartment, Daisy heard the side door downstairs open. Jonas had left earlier to drive into town to buy paint to spray the cabinets. Violet and Foster had decided on white. After the cabinets were finished, Foster and his friends would come in to paint the walls the palest yellow.

With sunlight pouring in the plate glass window at one end of the garage, and more sunlight gleaming through the garden window over the sink, the space would be nice and bright. The shower and toilet had been set into the bathroom yesterday, and the counter and sink would arrive next week. Vi and Foster had decided to go with a double bed and an area for the baby that would be set off with a curtain. That didn't leave much of a sitting space in the middle, but they could fit in a small sofa.

Daisy had samples of fabrics laid out across a card table. Aunt Iris was going to make curtains for the big window, a valance for the garden window, and the separation curtain for the baby. Vi, Foster, and Jazzi had met Jonas at the home improvement store to choose hardware for the cabinets.

Jonas ascended the stairs that now had treads firmly attached as well as a sturdy railing along the side. He carried a bucket of paint in each hand. "Vi, Foster, and Jazzi shouldn't be too long. They were making their final decision on knobs and drawer pulls. I think they decided on a satin nickel finish."

"I can't believe in three months Vi and Foster will be married and living here." She thought about the cream lace dress with the empire waist that Vi had chosen for her wedding. Her baby bump probably wouldn't be showing yet, but she'd wanted to make sure she had enough room for her and the baby.

Jonas set down the paint cans and came toward Daisy with a gentle smile. "Are you nervous about the wedding?"

"Not nervous about the wedding per se. I really have no doubt that Foster and Vi are committed now. But bring a baby into the mix, and I don't know how they're going to handle it."

"How about if we take your mind off Vi and Foster for a few minutes. You told me you saw June and Harriet yesterday, and June is recovering with Harriet's help."

"Harriet has really stepped up. Yesterday she wasn't even using her cane. I think she and June are thinking about getting a place together, either here or in Erie."

"I ran into Detective Rappaport," Jonas mentioned nonchalantly.

"Ran into?" Daisy asked with a raised brow.

Jonas chuckled. "I stopped for a cup of coffee at his favorite doughnut shop. There he was."

"Pure coincidence," Daisy teased.

"I knew he'd be wrapping up details. I also knew you'd be curious. He said he was going to stop by the tea garden himself to tell you. Lauren confessed and told the whole story, how she and Derek had an affair, how he'd insisted on the DNA test, how he wanted to spend time with Chrissy but she wouldn't let him. I guess he'd had enough because when she tried to convince his mother to change her will, he blackmailed Lauren with their secret. And after Harriet's stroke, he also blackmailed her into spending time with his mother and helping with her care. Lauren was sick of the whole situation."

"Secrets always lead to destruction," Daisy murmured, still horrified by everything that had happened and still having nightmares about Lauren and that shovel.

"Lauren was the type of woman who couldn't see past her nose as far as resolving a problem. She wanted resolution. She stole some of Harriet's Cardizem and told Harriet's doctor that Harriet had misplaced the prescription. Then she stole some of Bradley's atenolol that was also prescribed for high blood pressure. It wasn't difficult to grind up all the pills and lace Derek's cucumber sandwiches with it when they were just stored in the refrigerator. Derek had stepped out for an errand and she had the opportunity. She's being charged with two counts of attempted murder and murder in the first degree."

"I feel so sorry for Harriet. She's still trying to accept everything about her family. She told me she wishes she could have been a better mother to Derek. Under the circumstances, that probably would have required counseling."

Suddenly, the chatter of voices came from downstairs. A minute later Violet, Foster, and Jazzi climbed the stairs and saw them.

Vi pulled out a knob and a drawer pull from the bag she was carrying to show to Jonas and Daisy. "Aren't they perfect?"

To Daisy they just looked like doorknobs and drawer pulls. But to Vi and Foster they meant the beginning of a new life.

Jazzi wandered over to the window. It overlooked Daisy's back garden and the house. Then she turned around and studied everything in the studio apartment, maybe imagining what it would look like when it was truly finished.

"This place is going to be so cool. I could even live here."

They all laughed as Vi, Foster, and Jazzi went to the card table to select the perfect material.

Jonas curved his arm around Daisy's shoulders. "You made the right decision in renovating this level of the garage for their apartment. Vi and Foster will have a good start thanks to you."

"I hope so."

When Daisy gazed into Jonas's green eyes, she realized that Jonas was beginning to see how her life was going to change with Vi and Foster living this close. Nevertheless, he seemed to accept that.

He squeezed her a little closer. "Remember, I'll be here to help you wrangle it all."

That was her greatest hope—that she and Jonas would come through this stronger than ever, closer than ever, maybe even more in love than ever.

ORIGINAL RECIPES

PIMENTO SPREAD

8 ounces cream cheese (softened about 20 minutes and chunked)
⅓ cup shredded cheddar cheese
1 ounce pimento, drained well (I buy a 2-ounce jar)
1 teaspoon onion flakes
1½ tablespoons mayonnaise
4 or 5 sun-dried tomato halves (sliced)
⅛ teaspoon garlic powder
Pinch of nutmeg

1. Add all ingredients to a two-cup food chopper and mix until smooth. Seasonings are suggestions. Adjust according to taste.

2. Serve as a spread or a dip.

EASY CAULIFLOWER CARROT CHEESE SOUP

1 quart chicken broth (I use Swanson with no MSG)
1 cup chopped or sliced onion
5 cups cauliflower florets
1 cup sliced carrots
¼ teaspoon salt
½ teaspoon white pepper

2½ tablespoons flour
1 cup milk
12 ounces CV Sharp Cheese, cubed

1. In soup pot, bring chicken broth with onion, cauliflower, carrots, salt, and pepper to a boil. Simmer for 15 minutes.

2. Whisk flour into milk. (I whisk it right in the measuring cup)

3. Pour whisked flour and milk mixture into the broth with the vegetables. Let mixture come to a soft boil for 2 minutes. Lower to simmer. Add cheese and stir until melted.

Serves six to eight.

RUM RAISIN RICE PUDDING

1½ cups cooked long-grain rice (I use Carolina's)
3 eggs
⅓ cup granulated sugar
1 teaspoon vanilla
1 teaspoon rum (or almond, if you prefer) flavoring
    (I use McCormick's)
¼ teaspoon salt
2½ cups milk, warmed, but not scalded
⅔ cup golden raisins (I use Sun-Maid)
¼ teaspoon cinnamon to sprinkle on top

1. Preheat the oven to 350ºF.

2. Slightly beat eggs with mixer. Add sugar, flavorings, and salt until well mixed. Slowly stir in milk, one-half cup at a time. Stir in rice and raisins.

3. Pour mixture into a 1½-quart casserole. Sprinkle the top with cinnamon. Ready a pan with hot water. I use a 9-inch by 13-inch cake pan. The casserole must fit into the pan comfortably. Hot water should be about an inch deep. Bake for 65 minutes or until knife inserted into the middle comes out clean. Remove the casserole from water. Can be served warm or cold.

4. Refrigerate leftovers.

Please turn the page for an exciting sneak peek of
KAREN ROSE SMITH's next Daisy Tea Garden mystery

Murder with Cherry Tarts

Coming soon wherever print and e-books are sold!

Chapter One

Daisy Swanson kept a keen eye on Karina Post as her server crossed to the sales counter at the end of their workday. Her twentysomething server with her purple hair and green neon clogs had given Daisy concern over the past couple of weeks. Daisy went by the philosophy that she should mind her own business . . . except when she shouldn't. The mother of two teenage daughters, she couldn't help but feel motherly toward her younger staff.

Karina smiled at Daisy as she approached the sales counter at Daisy's Tea Garden. She was usually a self-possessed young woman with plenty of confidence and sometimes even brashness.

Now, however, Karina kept her eyes lowered as she asked Daisy, "Is it okay if I take some of the baked goods still left in the case?"

Daisy noticed the bag Karina was carrying and recognized the size. In it there was probably a quart container of soup.

"Sure, you can," Daisy said. "I don't want them to go to waste. The cherry tarts are fine, but some of the white chocolate blondies have been in the case since morning. They might be a little stale. It seemed everyone wanted cherry tarts today."

"It's the special for the month, so that's probably why," Karina suggested, still not meeting Daisy's gaze.

"Has your mom been working extra hours at her shop?" Karina's mom owned a leather shop in town, Totes and Belts. In the summer, tourists provided most of the business for the shops in town. Busloads could arrive unexpectedly and wipe out a store's inventory.

"No, she has a good manager who's doing really well. I think she still wants me to come there and work full-time instead of working here. And I'm grateful to her. After all, she took us back in when Quinn was born. But we're around each other enough as it is. I can't imagine working for Mom too."

"Maybe you could move into that manager spot some day if you worked at Totes and Belts."

"That's possible, but I'd rather go to nursing school. I'm thinking about starting when Quinn is older, maybe after she goes into first or second grade."

Karina was a single mom. Daisy didn't know the whole story, but from rumors in Willow Creek's gossip mill, she'd gleaned that Karina had run away and lived on the streets before Quinn was born.

From things Karina had said, Daisy knew her mother Maris was a fine cook and she baked treats for Quinn. But for the past few weeks Karina had been asking for the day-old baked goods and buying quarts of soup if Daisy's kitchen manager Tessa didn't have any remaining in the pot at the end of the day.

"Will Iris be in tomorrow, or do you need me to cover her shift again?" Karina asked.

Daisy's aunt Iris, co-owner of the tea garden, had caught a summer cold. She knew better than to be around customers or their food.

"I spoke to her a little bit ago, and she feels she's ready to come in tomorrow. Her sniffles are gone and so is her cough. But—I told her to come in for a morning shift. Can you come in for the afternoon?"

"Sure. I always like picking up extra hours."

Karina *sounded* fine. She always acted as if nothing fazed her. But that didn't mean her bravado wasn't hiding something. Daisy took one more stab at coaxing information from her. "I hope you and Quinn and Maris enjoy the cherry tarts and soup."

Karina glanced away from Daisy and into the case. "Quinn tells me every day now that she's a big girl since she turned three and doesn't need her booster seat."

That was a non sequitur if Daisy ever heard one, and Karina had easily sidestepped her question. It was time to give up . . . for now. "They grow up too fast, that's for sure. I can't believe Violet's going to have a baby of her own come November." *And the wedding will be in a few weeks*, Daisy added to herself. The past few months had been a bit crazy.

After Daisy packed up the baked goods and Karina left, she began taking the rest of their inventory from the case. Cora Sue, another one of her servers who had been sweeping the floor while she and Karina were talking, asked Daisy, "Do you need help?"

Cora Sue worked full-time at Daisy's Tea Garden. Her bottle-red hair pulled high on her head in a topknot was as bouncy and bubbly as she was.

"Sure," Daisy answered, eager to drive home.

After the two of them finished emptying the case,

Cora Sue picked up the box and said, "I saw you talking to Karina."

"I was," Daisy responded.

"I heard her ask Tessa for the bottom of the soup pot again."

Daisy decided to be forthright with Cora Sue. "I'm a little worried about her. She's been taking second-day baked goods home for a while now, but she won't say why."

"That's not the only thing she's being secretive about," Cora Sue murmured.

Studying her server, Daisy wasn't sure whether she should become involved or not. A question or two wouldn't hurt. "Do you think she's in trouble of some kind?"

"I really don't know. My car was on the fritz last week, so I walked to work. It's good exercise, only about a half mile. The shorter route takes me up Sage Street, which I know isn't the best section of town. But I *have* taken kickboxing lessons, so I wasn't too concerned. The thing was—I spotted Karina twice last week at the lower end of Sage Street."

"Did she see you?"

"No, she didn't, but I casually brought it up."

Daisy was always interested in clues. After all, she'd helped solve three murders. Clues had led her to the killer in every instance. "What did she tell you?"

"She told me she enjoys looking around the antique shop in that neighborhood, Pirated Treasures. It should be called Pirated Junk."

A smile twitched up Daisy's lips. She removed the band from her ponytail and let her blond, shoulder-length hair free. "I've passed the shop, but I've never been inside. You know what they say—one person's junk is another person's treasure."

Cora Sue grimaced. "I saw a broken bust of Benjamin Franklin in there one time. They'd glued it back together. It wasn't pretty."

Daisy laughed. "So you shop in the store even if you don't like it?"

"No, a friend dragged me in there. She says she finds unusual things for her home décor. But mostly what she finds I wouldn't pick up at a yard sale."

Thinking of Karina again, Daisy sobered. "Do you think Karina really shops in there or she was using it as an excuse?"

"I don't know. If she has to lie about why she's on Sage Street, I have to wonder about her purpose for being there."

Realizing Cora Sue was right, Daisy told herself she should really mind her own business. But then again, what if Karina was in trouble?

That evening, Daisy backed her purple PT Cruiser out of her home garage, made a K-turn, then opened the driver's side door.

Her daughter Jazzi, sixteen now, had obtained her learner's permit. Daisy dreaded thinking about Jazzi on the roads with all the crazy drivers who passed through Lancaster County, especially in the summer. On top of that, her daughter would also have to learn how to handle driving on the roads with horses and buggies. Sometimes there was a separate lane for them, but most times there wasn't. In an accident between a car and a horse and buggy, the horse and buggy didn't have a chance.

Jazzi's long, straight black hair blew in the hot breeze as she asked Daisy, "When are you going to let me back it out of the garage?"

Daisy climbed out of the car, glanced at the garage, and then back at Jazzi. "I promise I'll let you. Maybe tonight we'll head over to Bird in Hand. The farmers market has a huge parking lot that will be closed. You can practice backing up there."

Daisy handed her car keys to Jazzi.

Jazzi winked at her. "I'm getting good, Mom, honest. You don't have to fear for your life when we go driving."

As Jazzi had probably intended, Daisy laughed. "You are *so* reassuring."

"What else are daughters for?"

As if that comment caused Jazzi to think about something more serious, once they were seated in the car, she was quiet.

Daisy guessed that meant Jazzi was thinking about her birth mother again. In the fall of last year, unbeknownst to Daisy, Jazzi had tried to search for her birth mother on the Internet. Daisy had known that time might be coming because she and her deceased husband Ryan had adopted Jazzi. Still, Jazzi's search had been a shock.

Knowing if she didn't support her daughter Jazzi might pull away, Daisy aided her in finding Portia Smith Harding. They'd enlisted the help of Jonas Groft, a former police detective who now owned Woods, a furniture store just down the street from Daisy's Tea Garden. At first Portia hadn't told her husband about Jazzi. It had been a long-kept secret. Once she *had* told him, he'd felt betrayed and had moved out of their house for a while. That event had made Jazzi feel guilty, so guilty it had affected her school-work and her friendships. Finally, however, in the spring Colton had moved back in with Portia and their children. But Jazzi's relationship with Portia now was tentative because of Colton's attitude.

"I wanted to ask you something, Mom."

Jazzi switched on her turn signal and made a right turn onto the rural road.

"Ask me anything." She hoped that was true. She hoped both of her daughters could trust her that much.

"It's only a few weeks until Vi and Foster's wedding."

"I'm well aware we still have a lot to do on our to-do list. Vi and Foster have to decide on a cake, and I'd like you and Vi to help me shop for a mother-of-the-bride dress."

"We might have to take Gran shopping too. She still doesn't approve of Vi and Foster getting married, does she?"

"I think she's accepted the fact that it's going to happen."

Daisy had had a problem accepting it too. But pregnant, Violet had insisted it was what she and Foster wanted. They'd been adamant. So Daisy had helped them figure out how they could make it work. Raising a baby and supporting themselves wasn't going to be easy. Since the floor above her garage hadn't been finished when her barn home was renovated, she'd decided to finish it into a small apartment for the couple. That had always been the plan for added income. Or for one of her girls if either decided to live in Willow Creek. She'd told Vi and Foster they could live there rent-free for the first year. Foster's dad, a contractor, had overseen the construction. It was finished now except for furniture.

"When Gran sees her great-grandchild, I think she'll be less disapproving," Daisy reassured Jazzi.

Jazzi still hadn't asked Daisy her question, and Daisy suspected that she was working up to it.

"I'm supposed to call Portia tonight."

"Okay," Daisy said slowly, almost afraid of what was coming.

"I'd like to ask her and her husband to the wedding. It would give me a chance to meet Colton and maybe spend a little time with them both."

Daisy had mixed feelings about the couple coming to the wedding, but this wasn't really her decision to make. "You know Vi wants to keep the wedding small."

"I know."

"Why don't you run the idea past Vi?" Daisy suggested.

"Portia might just come herself."

"That's true."

"If she and her husband both come," Jazzi added, "I suppose they could reserve a room at the Covered Bridge Inn, or Tumbling Blocks Bed and Breakfast. That could be expensive for them though."

Jazzi's comment was like a helium balloon that she wanted Daisy to bat back in some way. She thought about the situation. "Vi will be moving into the apartment as soon as she and Foster find time to go shopping with Gavin to buy the mattress."

"I like that headboard they found at the antique store in Smoketown."

"Apparently, Foster has good negotiating skills," Daisy said with a smile. She'd hired Foster Cranshaw as one of her servers back in the fall, never expecting him to become her son-in-law. He'd quickly become a valuable employee with his knowledge of tea and his social media skills that helped promote Daisy's Tea Garden.

After a pause, Jazzi glanced at her mom. "Are you saying Portia and Colton could have Vi's room?"

"Actually, they could have the whole upstairs if you slept on the pull-out couch in the living room."

A sly smile crept across Jazzi's lips. "That's a great idea, Mom. But I know you're going to be busy with the wedding and all and might not want to entertain guests."

"That could be your job." Daisy was half-teasing and half-serious.

"What if Colton doesn't like me?"

"What's not to like?" Daisy asked affectionately.

"Mom . . ." Jazzi drew out the word as she always did when she was frustrated with her mother.

"I'm serious, Jazzi. If Portia's husband comes, then he should at least keep a bit of an open mind, don't you think? Why else would he accept the invitation?"

Reassured, Jazzi nodded and concentrated on driving.

Daisy just hoped her logic was correct.

The following day, Daisy and her aunt Iris exchanged a look at the sales counter and high-fived each other with large grins. The last of the tour bus visitors had exited the tea garden to catch their ride home. The onslaught of sightseers was always good for business, but a tea blogger had once knocked the tea garden down a notch for service, writing that they needed more help. Since then, Foster had garnered more hours in preparation for his new job of husband and father, though he was still trying to keep up with his studies at Millersville University. Out of school, Jazzi and Vi were helping too.

Daisy glanced at the almost empty case. "I'll pull more cookies and apple bread from the walk-in."

"See if there are any more cherry tarts. We've been running out of them every day," her aunt reminded her.

"Will do. I suppose we'll have to keep making a double batch of them since they're so popular."

Violet, who had come up to the sales counter, heard them talking. Her daughter's medium brown hair had blond highlights, but she hadn't renewed the practice since she'd been pregnant. Her morning sickness, which had turned into all-day sickness at the beginning of her pregnancy, had gotten better. But today she looked tired. She had dark circles under her eyes, and Daisy suspected she wasn't sleeping because of this high-stress time. Last night she'd heard her daughter come downstairs in the middle of the night. The low whistle of the teapot had alerted her. The rooibos canister where Daisy kept the tea in her pantry was still on the counter this morning. She'd hoped the brew had helped Vi sleep.

Obviously overhearing Daisy's conversation with her aunt, Vi said, "I was hoping we could take cherry tarts home. I know Karina put three back for herself to take along tonight. Can we do that? Maybe four?"

Karina's food gathering in the evenings had continued. "Of course we can." After a pause, she asked Vi, "Has Karina told you why she takes along the baked goods?"

Vi shook her head and brushed her shoulder-length hair behind both ears. "No, she doesn't really talk to me like she used to. When she came in today I thought she looked upset, so I asked her if something was wrong. She insisted it wasn't."

Pushing thoughts of Karina aside for now, Daisy studied Vi more thoroughly. "Do you want to leave early? You look tired."

"No, I'm good. I'm putting the money that I earn together for a crib. Gavin wanted to find us a used one, but I'd like one new thing for the baby."

Daisy could understand that. "Standards on children's furniture change from year to year, too, so putting your money into the crib is wise. Maybe you can consider the kind that transforms into a day bed for when the baby is ready for his own bed."

"Or *her* own bed," Vi joked. "I know some moms want to be surprised, but Foster and I can't wait to learn the sex of the baby. At twenty weeks, we'll have the ultrasound and then we'll know."

Iris jumped into the conversation now. "Just remember, honey, I want to be your major babysitter."

"You might have to wrestle Gran for that job."

"Guess who would win?" Iris returned with a wink.

Daisy's aunt Iris and her mom didn't always see eye to eye. They had very different personalities. Where her aunt was a listener, accepting, and nonjudgmental, Daisy's mom was the opposite. Rose Gallagher liked to share her opinion before anyone asked for it. Daisy had lived under her mom's critical eye all her life, and her aunt Iris had always been her ally. Daisy and her own sister Camellia had very different personalities too. Their mother and Camellia usually stood firm together. As she was growing up, Daisy had often felt like the odd girl out. Thinking about that again, Daisy realized that conclusion wasn't completely true because her dad had always stood in her corner. At least it seemed that way.

Vi snapped her fingers. "Pregnancy hormones are affecting my memory. Tessa wants to know if she should put the rum raisin rice pudding on the menu for tomorrow. Something about needing more eggs from your supplier if you do."

"I'll talk to her. I can call Rachel Fisher and see if she has any extra eggs. I could stop on my way home and pick them up."

"Or I could stop for them," Iris said. "You have enough to do with getting the apartment ready for Vi and Foster along with wedding plans."

Her aunt was right about her to-do list. It seemed to grow longer instead of shorter each day. "I'd appreciate that," she said. "Let me talk to Tessa."

That afternoon on the way to the kitchen, Karina waylaid Daisy outside the office. "Can I speak to you for a minute?"

"Sure. Do you want to go into my office?"

"No, that's not necessary."

Daisy's gaze slid over Karina. Her hair was shorter, so she must have gotten it trimmed, and the purple was brighter. Her neon green clogs peeked out from the hem of the white slacks. Her yellow apron with the daisy logo seemed to complement Karina's personality. She looked like a colorful garden.

Daisy waited, knowing that if Karina didn't want to go into her office, then she didn't have anything serious to discuss.

"I need to leave around four instead of five. Is that okay?"

Even though the tourists from the tour bus had left,

the tea room was still filled with customers. However, when her employees needed time off, she usually complied, knowing they had responsibilities and errands outside the tea garden. "Do you need to pick up Quinn early from day care?"

Karina didn't answer right away. Finally, she responded, "No, but I have an errand to run before I pick her up. This is important, Daisy. Honest, it is."

There was vehemence in Karina's voice, and maybe something else.

"You can leave early today. We can cover for you. Will you be here for your regular shift tomorrow?"

"I'll be here on time and I'll stay for my whole shift," Karina promised.

"Sounds good. Some day when you're not working, you'll have to bring Quinn in for a visit."

"She talks a mile a minute," Karina said with a smile, and checked her watch. "I'd better get going. Thanks again, Daisy . . . for understanding."

Daisy watched her server as Karina left the tea garden. She had the sense that Karina was hiding something. Just what could it be?

Connect with Us

Visit us online at
KensingtonBooks.com
to read more from your favorite authors, see books
by series, view reading group guides, and more.

Join us on social media

for sneak peeks, chances to win books and prize packs,
and to share your thoughts with other readers.

facebook.com/kensingtonpublishing
twitter.com/kensingtonbooks

Tell us what you think!

To share your thoughts, submit a review,
or sign up for our eNewsletters, please visit:
KensingtonBooks.com/TellUs.